A KISS SO RIGHT

Sam's mouth hovered over hers. There was an invisible thread between them, pulling them toward each other. Billie was transfixed by his closeness, caught in his spell. Goosebumps ran up and down her arms. She could feel the layer of air between his face and her own, wanted to bridge the gap. The powerful feelings Sam's touch had unleashed would not be denied.

Slowly, Sam lowered his head until their mouths brushed. As their lips pressed together, Billie couldn't believe the thrill that raced through her. It felt right. Their lips molded to each other, deepened, and Billie's arms came up to clasp him around the neck, pulling him closer.

D1434619

SUPERSTITIONS

ANNIE McKNIGHT

LEISURE BOOKS   NEW YORK CITY

To Zeke, Puppy, and handsome, gallant Gray

and

to Billy, never far from my heart

A LEISURE BOOK®

July 1998

Published by

Dorchester Publishing Co., Inc.
276 Fifth Avenue
New York, NY 10001

ISBN 0-8439-4405-6

AUTHOR'S NOTE

Julia Thomas, Reiney Petrasch, Bert Mossman, and Jacob Walsh—the real "Lost Dutchman"—all existed. Everyone else is a product of my imagination, with no resemblance to any person living or dead. I would like to thank the usual suspects: Glenn McCreedy, Kim Lamb Gregory, Vicki Lewis Thompson, Rob Cohen, and my editor, Don D'Auria. Special thanks to Sinclair Browning, who generously offered me the use of her horse Gray and rode with me on the Coffee Flat Trail in the Superstition Mountains.

Prologue

October, 1891

Julia Thomas locked the soda shop with shaking fingers. Reiney Petrasch waited, his youthful impatience obvious in the way he paced back and forth along the corner.

"Are you sure?" Julia asked.

"I think so." The rumble of a passing wagon drowned out Reiney's words, but there was no mistaking the excitement in his tone.

As they hurried toward her house, Julia experienced a mixture of dread, relief and strangled hope. It was a mercy, she told herself. The old man had never been the same after the flood. This last bout of pneumonia was worse than any that had come before.

Reiney strode briskly, hands shoved into his

pockets. Julia's hobble skirt made her take three steps to his every one.

"I wonder if he's making it up." Reiney caught the look she gave him and blushed. "I just meant maybe he's delirious. You know he hasn't been right since he took sick."

Julia gripped her reticule with icy fingers. "You're forgetting how he helped me hold on to the ice-cream parlor last year. You saw the gold yourself."

"But that could be all he had. He's been talking about that mine for years, but I never—"

"Shut up!" Julia rounded on the youth. "The man's dying! I don't want to talk about it now."

As they reached the eastern outskirts of Phoenix, Julia glanced across a weedy field at the slump of adobe—all that was left of Jacob Waltz's house. It had caved in last spring, inundated with water when the Salt River flooded its banks. Jacob had spent the night in a nearby tree, shivering in his wet clothes. He never returned to his ruin of a house. Julia wondered if his cache was still there, buried somewhere in the mud, and immediately felt guilty. It had been hard and unpleasant work, caring for an invalid, but she never blamed the old man. *I like him,* she thought. *I wouldn't have stuck by him if I didn't. Certainly not for a gold mine that might not exist.* Still, she felt like a vulture waiting to pick the old man's bones clean.

It was not true. She wanted him to die because it would be a release. For him.

The little room was close and smelled of sickness. Jacob Waltz lay on the pallet, his breath rattling like a dry corn husk on a breezy day. His white beard, already brittle, lay on his chest. Still, he motioned to Julia and Reiney to come near. "I have to tell you," he mumbled. "Give me something to write with. I'll draw the map." He tried to sit up, but the effort was too great.

Julia placed a cool hand on his forehead. "I'll draw the map," she said gently. She gathered the writing materials and sat beside him. Reiney Petrasch leaned close, repeating Waltz's whispered directions in his strong young voice. Julia dutifully wrote everything down. She attempted a map, but when Waltz saw it he shook his head. "Try again," he said.

Hours passed. The old man grew querulous in his frustration. "You're not paying attention, Reiney. You can walk right over that mine and miss it."

"Yes, sir." Reiney Petrasch leaned closer. "You go over the mountain from the cow barn and then down to a spring."

The old German tried to sit up, his eyes bright and hard in the yellow light of the kerosene lamp. "No! That's not right! Listen. I'll tell you one more time."

Jacob died around six the next morning. After washing him and laying him out on the trestle table with two pesos to close his eyes, Julia Thomas went to sit outside on the bench by the door, holding the map she'd drawn last night. It was still dark, but a faint blush of apricot stained the horizon above the eastern mountains.

Reiney had gone to bed hours ago. He liked the old man, but didn't want to wait around for what they all knew to be inevitable. Julia had stayed up all night with Jacob. She was holding his hand when he passed on.

She had taken care of him in his declining years, and her reward was treasure—gold beyond counting. It was a fairy story come true.

Julia shivered, staring at the ragged line of mountains across the desert. It would be a dangerous trek for a woman. The Superstitions were treacherous, especially in hot weather. Some still thought they were an Apache stronghold. But as the sun peeked over the faraway peaks and spread its molten light across the desert, Julia felt only a stirring of excitement. Imagine, to be rich! All the folks who had dismissed her as a poor mulatto shopkeeper would change their tune then! The thought danced in her mind, a whirling, golden light, as golden as the nuggets Jacob Waltz had once shown her. She knew in her heart and soul that she would return a very rich woman.

From a Phoenix newspaper, September, 1892:

Miss Julia Thomas has traveled by wagon to the end of the Superstition Mountains in search of a gold mine and she has returned unsuccessfully.

The search for the Lost Dutchman Mine had begun.

Chapter One

The San Rafael Valley, Arizona territory
Ten years later

Her father was coming home today.

Billie Bahill drew rein on a rise of sunburned ground in the San Rafael Valley. Panic scrabbled just under the surface of her thoughts, waiting to claw its way into her conscious mind. She had to tend to business; it was the only way she knew to escape the terror that threatened to consume her.

Roland K. Bahill's vast La Zanja Ranch spanned the valley between two mountain ranges, extending all the way into Mexico. Billie had been born on the ranch and loved it deeply. Its familiar beauty resonated in her bones. But today her eyes hardly registered the masses of dusty green and brown leaves bending the oak boughs almost to the ground, barely saw their dark mantillas of shade spread out for the cattle to browse or lie under. She took no pleasure in the way the bright flaxen tops of the grama grass caught the sun, nodding gently in the breeze, or how blue the sky was overhead.

Billie's throat tightened. How could she face her father? She couldn't imagine telling him the truth. She had done the unspeakable.

Buttermilk tossed his head; the gelding was anxious to get down to business. Billie clutched numbly at the reins, her thoughts veering to this morning, the third morning in a row she had been sick. There was no doubt now, none at all.

Panic hit her afresh, careening blindly through the corridors of her mind, elbowing aside all reason. The act she could hardly remember had resulted in dire consequences. She was going to have a child. Soon everyone would know, even her father.

His face loomed in her mind's eye: his eyes burning into her like a brand, shock and revulsion in every line of his body. She knew what he would say. *I suspected as much. You let him use you, and now he's gone and left you to pay the piper.*

Her face flamed. She would have no retort, no retort at all. Because that was exactly how it looked.

Billie nudged Buttermilk into a trot, following a dry wash. Fear lodged in her throat, making it hard to breathe, hard to think. Although she quailed at the idea of facing her father, with a sinking feeling Billie realized she would have to stand her ground and face his wrath.

In a couple of months her pregnancy would be obvious. She could at least show him that she was still a Bahill. And Bahills didn't run from a fight.

"Billie!" Roy's voice jarred her back to the present. She waved to the cowboy riding along the ridge opposite. "I'll take this draw if you want to check the fence," he called. She nodded agreement and tried to marshal her fragmented thoughts.

The cattle she'd seen so far were healthy and fat; none of them needed doctoring. Next month they would be rounded up, the calves ear-marked, branded and castrated, then driven back out on the range to fatten up for the summer. She must check on the newest calves and see that none suffered from any of the myriad illnesses that could affect the young and the weak.

Billie was about to turn toward the river when the bellowing of a pain-maddened cow broke the stillness. Her practiced eye roved over the landscape, which looked flat but concealed several rounded hills and ravines. There it was, the rust red hide and white face of a Hereford cow in the ravine below her. The cow lay at the bottom of a rockfall, one of her front legs broken. Her day-old calf staggered around in the tall grass, butting vainly at her back, looking for the udder.

Billie took a deep breath. There was only one

thing to do, and it wasn't pleasant. She had done it countless times, but had never completely gotten used to it. The colonel's words echoed in her mind: *There's no room for sentimentality in this business, Billie*.

Steeling herself, Billie touched her horse's flanks and headed down the hill. Withdrawing her Colt, she dismounted and stepped through the high grass.

Her heart sank as she recognized the cow. It was old Rojo, one of their best producers. Rojo had lived on the ranch so long that she was a calming influence in any herd, and had led many drives to the cattle pens at Nogales. Now she lay in agony, eyes rolling with unreasoning fear.

"I'm sorry, old girl," Billie whispered. She felt tears well behind her eyes. Blinking rapidly, she set her jaw and cocked the gun's hammer. She'd been born and bred to run a ranch, and this was part of it. Her father didn't like her to cry. He considered tears a sign of weakness, in a man or a woman. Billie pressed the muzzle of the gun against the whorl of hair a couple of inches above the liquid brown eyes, eyes that seemed to plead for help. She squeezed the trigger and the explosion ricocheted through the oak trees. Rojo's head slumped, and her eyes didn't plead anymore.

Billie stood there for a moment, staring at the cow who had been one of her father's first purebreds to populate the San Rafael range, and felt a deep anger. Rojo was too smart to fall like that, and a Hereford cow's legs were much thicker

and stronger than any horse's. No, something—
or someone—had been running her.

And now she was dead, and her calf was too
young to survive on its own. Billie gathered the
calf into her arms, hoisted it over Buttermilk's
saddle, put her foot in the stirrup and swung up
behind.

As she rode toward the main ranch house, Billie glanced toward the south fence. One section
had been cut, and the ground between the posts
was pocked with hoofprints. Billie rode over and
saw that the trail was fresh. It all came together.
The same person who had run Rojo to her death
must have cut the fence. There were rustlers on
La Zanja.

As Sam Gray led his prisoner down the Harshaw road, he heard the bawling of an animal
in pain. He withdrew his Winchester and
spurred his horse up the hill in the direction of
the sound, his prisoner cursing as his own horse
lunged to keep up. Assessing the situation at a
glance, Sam started toward the Hereford cow
and her calf.

Suddenly a rider appeared from the stand of
black oak near the ravine where the cow lay. One
of the cowboys had heard the animal, too.

The figure stepped down from his horse.
Striding through the waist-high grass, the rider
withdrew his pistol with economical swiftness.
He put the barrel to the cow's forehead, to the
exact center of the invisible *X* that ran from each
ear to the opposite eye—the place that would kill

17

the animal instantly and humanely—and pulled the trigger.

The rider gathered the calf and hoisted it onto the buckskin's saddle. A breeze suddenly tugged the cowboy hat on his head. Hair tumbled down, a swatch of raven black silk. Shock ran through Sam's body. It was a woman!

"I'd like me some of that," Howard Daw said behind him.

"The way she handles a gun, you wouldn't get a chance," Sam said curtly.

Sam Gray had caught up with Daw at a bordello in Nogales. The prostitute with him had been beaten within an inch of her life. Too bad Sam couldn't add the beating to the charges against the killer; it was out of his jurisdiction. You could only hang a man once, anyway.

He stared at the retreating rider, wondering how he could ever mistake that tall, slender figure for that of a man, no matter how she was dressed. She was a good hand. The shot had been clean. And she was strong enough to lift the calf onto her saddle.

"Girl with those kind of looks is wasted in that getup," Daw mumbled. "I'd have her on her back, it was me."

"Shut up."

"Well, I'll be damned. The coolheaded ranger himself has a soft spot. Guess you like those Annie Oakley–type gals, huh?"

"Let's go," Sam said. "Wouldn't want you to miss your hanging."

He urged his horse forward, jerking the prisoner along behind him.

Billie saw to the calf, then went up to the house to check on preparations for the homecoming celebration. The main ranch house at La Zanja was set on a grassy bench of land overlooking the San Rafael Valley. A long, *L*-shaped structure, its limewashed adobe walls were two feet thick, topped by a cedar-shingled hip roof. The western face, which looked out on the valley, was shaded by a cottonwood tree whose green heart-shaped leaves sparkled in the sunlight. A wide hallway ran down the center of the ranch house, two sets of double doors opening to the outdoors on either end. La Zanja had many tall wood-framed windows, which, along with the white plastered walls, gave the rooms a light and airy feeling. Outbuildings, made of fieldstone and adobe, were scattered in a rough horseshoe shape nearby. The ranch was completely self-sufficient; all the food they needed was grown on La Zanja. Roland Bahill employed a small fiefdom of servants: housekeeper, laundress, gardeners, blacksmith, cowhands, foreman, haying crew, and the temperamental but brilliant Chinese cook, Ho Cheng.

As Billie walked through to the kitchen, she felt a tug of nostalgia for this house she loved so well. Now everything would change. She tried to suppress the heaviness in her heart, finding that it hurt even to smile. She must put on a brave face for Olivia, the housekeeper, whose nose for trouble was remarkably well developed. It was Olivia who had come upon her this morning, finding Billie vomiting into her basin.

The odors of cooking chiles and garlic filled Billie's nostrils. Ho Cheng bustled in and out the kitchen door, carrying large steaming kettles and pots. One of the Mexican boys had been put to work peeling potatoes.

Ho Cheng had everything well in hand. He made it clear, by virulent side glances and angry mutterings, that Billie's presence in his kitchen was unnecessary. Olivia was busy across the yard, in the cowboys' dining room, making sure the hands got their lunchtime meal. She didn't even notice Billie. Breathing a sigh of relief, Billie went to her room and changed into a crisply clean shirtwaist.

She walked out onto the veranda, trying to figure out how and when she would break the news to her father. Should she tell him at the train station in Nogales? Certainly not over dinner. She'd invited guests for dinner. There was no good time, she realized, and yet she would go mad if she didn't tell him soon. Delaying would only make things worse, and Billie couldn't imagine having to guard her every word and action to keep her deception alive.

Damn Elliot for leaving her like this! Maybe her father was right. Why else would he go away without a word to anybody?

No. She would not believe such a thing. If it were so, then she had been duped, and she would not believe it of the man she knew, the man she loved. There had to be some explanation. . . .

A breeze fluttered across the porch, cool and welcome on the warm day. Above the porch roof, the trailing branches of the cottonwood tree clattered softly. The veranda ran along two sides of the house, lined by white-painted wooden railings. Blowzy masses of yellow jasmine clambered up and over them in a tangled embrace. The shrubs were spangled with hundreds of yellow blooms, saturating the air with a honeyed scent that attracted swarms of bees.

Inhaling the heavy sweetness of the jasmine, Billie tried to think pleasant thoughts, but the balled fist of nervousness in her stomach clamored for attention.

She really had painted herself into a corner! Only twice had they committed "the act of love," as Elliot termed it. After that, she had refused him, saying that she could not reconcile their lovemaking with her beliefs. Apparently twice had been enough. Panic soared again, clutching at her throat. She swallowed back her fear.

Catching a movement out of the corner of her eye, Billie looked in the direction of the Harshaw road and spotted two dark specks—horsemen—against the tawny backdrop of the La Zanja range. For an instant, her heart leaped in her chest. Maybe it was Elliot, coming home. But even from here she could see that both riders had spent many hours in the saddle and were practiced horsemen.

The man in the lead was tall and broad shoul-

dered, following his animal's movement with accustomed grace. He wore a long-sleeved shirt,
shotgun chaps and a cowboy hat whose round,
flat brim was pulled low over his lean face. He
was unfashionably clean-shaven. The horse he
rode was the color their blacksmith, Tomás,
called dark bay: coal black except for its muzzle
and flanks, which gleamed like dark honey.

The other man was slight and wiry. His hands
were handcuffed at the wrists, and a chain ran
under his horse's belly, connecting leg irons. The
horse favored its near foreleg.

As they approached, the man riding the dark
bay removed his hat and nodded his head in
greeting. His hair, the same honey color as the
bay's muzzle, was caught in a short ponytail.
"Good day, ma'am."

Billie returned the greeting, lifting her skirts
as she hurried down the steps and stopped beside the prisoner's horse. "What happened?"

"He put a foot in a gopher hole. Lucky he
didn't break a leg. My prisoner tried to escape."

The prisoner leered at her, his eyes empty and
cold. His skin was raw where he must have hit
the ground, but Billie didn't feel sorry for him.
The way he looked at her made her skin crawl.
She turned to the blond man. "Are you the new
undersheriff?"

"No, ma'am. I'm an Arizona Ranger."

An Arizona Ranger. Billie knew the Arizona
Rangers were the scourge of rustlers. They were
tough and smart, and never gave up. This man
looked very serious—and strong-minded. Just

the kind of man who was needed on La Zanja right now. "What did he do?" Billie asked, motioning to the prisoner.

"Killed a man in Bisbee. I'm taking him back to stand trial." The ranger stepped down from his horse. "Could I trouble you for some water, ma'am? We came from Nogales this morning."

Billie called Olivia and sent for water. The ranger introduced himself as Sam Gray and the prisoner as Howard Daw. After they drank their fill, Ranger Sam Gray handed the enameled cup back to Billie. "Is there a pump where we could wash off? My prisoner got mighty scraped up."

"Around back." Billie nodded to the house. "You're welcome to stay the night."

"A washing-up will see us through to Patagonia. If you can sell us a horse we'll be on our way."

Billie motioned to the ketch pen. "All we have here are our night horses," she said, referring to their cowhands' favorite mounts that could be saddled and ridden at a moment's notice. "The rest are out on the range. We'd be happy to put you up for the night, and tomorrow I'll find you a good horse."

"That's mighty nice of you, miss, but—"

"You really have no choice in the matter. You can't possibly think of going on with a lame horse."

"Let me borrow one then. That buckskin looks good." He pointed at Billie's gelding. "I'll send him back in a week's time."

"That's my horse, Mr. Gray. Spring roundup's

coming up, and we just can't spare any of our good horses. If you're wondering what to do with the prisoner, we can put him up, too. The sheriff of Santa Cruz County comes through here all the time with prisoners. We're used to it." Except that none of them was as desperate-looking as this one. Mostly they were younger Mexicans who'd gotten into a fight after too much to drink—pretty harmless.

Billie caught the prisoner's eye and recoiled. He smiled suggestively at her, his gaze slithering over her like a dry, scaly lizard. She shivered, almost regretting her invitation. But the prisoner and the ranger came as a package. It would take time to reach the Arizona Ranger headquarters in Bisbee and request help against the rustlers, and here was one of them—one of the "Fearless Thirteen," right here on her doorstep. She couldn't let him go, not yet. Tonight over dinner he could learn about the situation, perhaps give them some advice, and carry their request for help with him to Bisbee. Billie knew that since there were so few rangers, they were assigned on a priority basis. Perhaps if Ranger Gray saw the situation firsthand, he would be able to influence the captain's decision.

A part of her realized that getting the rangers to help them would be another point in her favor, if she found the courage to tell her father her news.

Once again she pictured her father's face. His accusing eyes boring into her. Biting back her nervousness, Billie smiled wanly. "Why don't you stay?" she asked the ranger again.

The Arizona Ranger looked grim, but must have seen there was no polite way to refuse. "If you can't spare a horse today, I reckon we'll have to stay. I'm not going to make this animal walk any farther." He must have realized he didn't sound too gracious, because he gave her a quick, acknowledging nod. "Thank you for the hospitality."

Moments later Billie leaned against the fence to the ketch pen and watched the ranger's horse get acquainted with the others in the pen. She tried to concentrate on the present, on the scene in front of her rather than the growing dread in the pit of her stomach. Her gelding touched noses with the newcomer, then wandered back to his feed.

Beside her, Sam Gray was unsaddling his prisoner's mount in the shade of a tall cottonwood tree. Daw sat cross-legged at the big tree's base. He seemed content to watch as his captor dragged his saddle to the tightly knit mesquite log fence and hoisted it onto the top rail.

Now that the ranger had agreed to be her guest, Billie felt awkward in his presence. The colonel always said she bulled her way into every situation. "You know more about other people's business than they do. I'll never understand how I ever raised such a know-it-all." It was obvious that Mr. Gray wanted to get on with his business, and she had pressed her hospitality on him. Billie glanced at the lawman, feeling uncertain. She should try to make conversation, but he didn't look at all receptive. She settled on a compliment. "That's a nice horse you've got," she said, motioning to the coal black gelding, who was rolling in the dirt. Rocking onto his spine, the horse seemed momentarily suspended before, with a deft twist, he rolled over to his other side. Billie added, "He's a good one, all right."

Despite himself, the ranger grinned. "And how do you know that?"

"He rolled all the way over."

"That's an old wives' tale." But humor glinted in the ranger's eyes.

His smile was contagious. Billie smiled back. "Well, that's what I've been told, ever since I was little. I've had three horses, and they all rolled like that. Every one of them was good." She glanced at the prisoner's horse, and on impulse bent down and passed a hand over its foreleg. "There's heat, but I think it'll be all right," she said. "We can stand him in water, but you'll need another horse."

"Your skirt's getting dirty."

Her face felt suddenly hot. "I can change."

"You sure know your way around horses."

Billie straightened up. Was he being sarcastic? No, his expression showed only frank admiration. His eyes—a dark teal blue—were a startling contrast to his sun-bronzed skin. The ranger was a good-looking man, despite the grime of the trail and the day-old beard bristles that glinted copper, blond, and black in the bright sunlight. His gaze remained steady on her.

Her face grew hot. Why was he looking at her that way? Once, at a church social, she'd overheard the matrons talking about a young woman who was newly married. "She has that glow," one of the ladies had said, poking her friend in the ribs with her elbow. "I imagine there'll be a little stranger around here before too long." Could that be what Ranger Gray was seeing? Involuntarily Billie clasped her hands over her stomach, flat under the black gored skirt.

"Is something wrong?" He looked concerned.

"No," she said quickly. "Nothing. Let me show you where you'll stay." She turned toward the house.

He caught her arm. His strong fingers gripped her, warm against her flesh through the crisp material of her shirtwaist. "We can stay in the barn."

"Nonsense!"

His gaze held her steady. "With all respect, ma'am, Daw is a killer. I'd feel better if I kept him out of your house. I've slept in lots of barns." He grinned. "As a matter of fact, I kind of like it. I like the smell of horses."

Billie couldn't help but smile. She liked it, too.

As Billie led Sam Gray and his prisoner to the barn, she realized that the ranger was careful to keep his body between herself and Daw. The prisoner shuffled along in his leg chains. Billie could feel his desperation, like that of a trapped animal.

"You can sleep in the hayloft." She motioned to a platform high up in the cool adobe barn, with clean, sweet-smelling hay piled almost to the rafters. She tried not to think of what had happened there. Looking hastily away from the loft, she caught Daw watching her. His eyes were like two blank holes. She shuddered.

"Keep your eyes down in the presence of a lady," Sam Gray said. He spoke quietly, but there was steel in his tone that made Billie glance up. Daw stared impassively at his feet.

Flustered, Billie rushed to speak. "There's a ladder . . . I suppose your prisoner can't . . ."

"We'll manage." Sam Gray stood before her in the sunlight that filtered through the rafters of the barn, motes of dust dancing between them. He seemed completely relaxed, yet there was an awareness in his eyes that told her he was careful of his prisoner. It reminded her of the deceptive laziness of a mountain lion she'd seen once in the Patagonias. It had been stretched out on a rock, but its muscles were loosely coiled and powerful, ready to spring if necessary. Only its eyes betrayed its wildness. The ranger, too, was dangerous, but not to her. He stood before her, close enough to touch, and for a fleeting moment Billie felt the urge to place a hand on his arm, feel the hardness of lean muscle under his shirt, where it bunched under the garter that held the long sleeve up. At the core of her body, she experienced a sensual thrill, a sort of queer tickle. Then she thought of Elliot, of the hurried intimacy that had brought her to this impasse, and shame stung her. How could she be attracted to a perfect stranger, when it was Elliot who had—

Mortified, Billie looked away.

"Thank you again, ma'am, for your hospitality," the ranger said gently. Could he read her mind? At any rate, he was too polite to acknowledge the chain of emotions that had trooped so blatantly across her face. "You go on now, and don't worry about us."

She nodded, feeling as if the smile were pasted on her face. "I'll see you tonight at dinner." She lifted her skirt and walked briskly toward the barn's entrance, tripped on an uneven plank, and caught herself. She heard Daw laugh and her face suffused with heat. Without looking back, she continued through the door and out into the sunshine.

Chapter Two

Sam Gray wondered if every dinner at La Zanja was as tense as this one. Perhaps Miss Bahill was used to cheerless dinners, but he wasn't. He regretted letting her talk him into leaving Howard Daw under guard in the cowboys' dining room. Not that he was afraid Daw might escape—he was practically hog-tied—but even dinner with an accused murderer had to be a damn sight more congenial than this. The only good thing about this evening was Miss Bahill's presence.

He couldn't keep himself from looking at her. The proud tilt of her chin and the delicate black brows hinted at a serious side, but her sunny nature showed occasionally in the curve of her lips and in her eyes. Her eyes. They reminded Sam of aquamarines, startling against her golden skin. Her shining black hair was swept up into a smooth coil at the nape of her neck. The dress she wore matched her eyes. Its fabric was rich-looking, obviously expensive, and patterned with a floral design. Intricate ecru lace covered the bodice up to her neck. She was slender and almost as tall as a man, and yet she didn't slump as he had seen other tall women do. Billie Bahill looked every inch a lady.

It was hard to believe this was the same girl who could lift up a horse's fetlock as casually as another lady might lift a teacup, a young woman who could shoot a suffering animal without sentimentality. Entertaining obviously came second nature to Billie, but Sam could tell that something was bothering her. Every so often she glanced in her father's direction, as if she were monitoring his reaction. And once, when their guests, the minister and his wife and a neighboring rancher, were preoccupied with the serving dishes, an expression of such bleak desperation passed over her face that Sam felt cold to the core. Then she seemed to shake herself mentally, and her smile was warm and genuine again, making him wonder if he had imagined her unhappiness.

"Did you have a successful trip, Colonel?" Mrs. Auberge, the minister's wife, asked.

"Served its purpose." The colonel grunted and addressed Sam. "So you're an Arizona Ranger, eh? Heard some good things about you fellows. You have a ways to go, though, if you want to fill the Texas Rangers' shoes. Now they were something!"

"Daddy! I'm sure the Arizona Rangers are something."

"Now, Sweet Pea, a man's entitled to his opinion. Call me old-fashioned, but I'm not impressed with this younger generation. They've had it too soft. We're raising a whole passel of store clerks and nature artists."

Sam noticed Billie's sudden furious blush, even in the crimson glow of the satin-glass banquet lamp. Then she lifted her chin, her eyes sparkling dangerously. She opened her mouth to speak, thought better of it, and dabbed at her lips with her napkin.

Something was going on here. Uncomfortable in the extreme, Sam looked for a way to change the subject. He spotted an oval portrait on the small space of wall near the kitchen doorway. The woman in it looked a great deal like Billie, except more fragile. Her clothing was of a style that was popular twenty years ago. "Is that your mother, Miss Bahill?"

"Yes. She—"

"Billie's mother died when Billie was very young." Bahill dismissed the memory of his late wife with a wave of his fork. "How do you like our beef?"

Billie shot her father a punitive glance. "Perhaps Mr. Gray isn't interested in the beef." Her eyes sought Sam's and when she spoke again, her tone was defiant. "Mother was an artist."

"Billie loves to talk about her mother," the colonel said, "even though she can hardly remember her. Emily did love to paint. She was pretty good, too, I'll give her that, if you like flower gardens and sailboats. I don't hold much with that kind of fluff, but it's a good enough hobby for a woman."

Billie set her water glass down and stared at her father.

"See that painting over the mantel?" Bahill continued, motioning to a portrait of a Hereford bull above the ornately carved fireplace. "My prize bull, Albany. *There's* a painting!"

Sam looked at the portrait, which dominated the room. By contrast, Mrs. Bahill's photograph, relegated to the space near the kitchen, seemed an afterthought. At the window hung heavily swagged velvet drapes and lace curtains, but other than that, the large room was masculine. Amber light from the coal-oil lamps shimmered on white walls. Red leather chairs embossed along the arms and back with silver studs were grouped on an Oriental carpet. Cowhides draped the length of a matching red sofa. There was a chair with cowhorn legs and back, a leopardskin rug, the animal's mouth frozen in a perpetual snarl, and a Turkish floor lamp topped by a cricket-cage shade. Where was Billie's personality in this room? Unless she really was the tomboy he'd seen this morning. She sure didn't look it tonight.

"My mother's work was shown at a very fine gallery back East before she was married," Billie was saying.

Colonel Bahill set his fork down with a clatter and turned to Sam. "What do you think of this spread, Sam?"

"I like it," Sam said, feeling as though he were in an armed camp. Whatever was going on beneath the surface, he wanted no part of it.

"Progress," mumbled Bahill through his food. "Everything's big now. Scientific, efficient!" He leaned toward Sam, the light glancing off his wire-rimmed spectacles. "Has Billie told you about our breeding program? It's the most progressive of its kind in the territory. We raise only blooded stock—Herefords and Angus. Let me tell you, it's taken me almost twenty-five years to build this herd up to where it is now."

Sam could tell from the way the colonel was looking at him that a compliment was required. "I always did admire this country," he said. "This valley is part of a Spanish land grant, isn't it?"

Billie passed Sam the relish tray. "That's right. The San Rafael de la Zanja land grant."

"Saint Ralph of the Ditch," Joe McCarty, the rancher, said. "Although who Saint Ralph is, I don't rightly know. You have any idea, Reverend?"

Reverend Auberge shrugged. He seemed to be more interested in his port than in the conversation.

Sam speared a pickle. "Knew some folks out this way once. Ruiz."

"Hector Ruiz. Wasn't he the one who cut down our fences, Father?" Billie asked. Now that they were off the subject of artists, she seemed to have calmed down.

"I remember him now. Damn troublemaker. Here I let him graze his cattle on my land all these years, and what's he do? First chance he gets, cuts through my fences. He's in the hoosegow now. Had the nerve to tell me I was infringing on his rights to round up his cattle."

Billie explained to Sam. "A lot of the smaller ranches around here get together at roundup time and throw their cattle together. At the end of the day each outfit cuts out its own stock."

He nodded politely, although he knew all about cattle roundups. In his time he had been many things: a cowboy, a hunters' guide, a soldier, and more recently a lawyer. The West offered boundless opportunities to the energetic.

Billie's knife and fork were poised above her plate, her food forgotten. "Since the outfits come from all over, they drive any cattle they find before them. They expect to run their cattle through any boundary, even if they don't own the land. Everything was fine until last year, when we put up the fences. The squatters claimed that by stringing up fences we were putting an end to their roundups. But what they seem to have forgotten was all the years we let them through."

Had she learned this little speech by rote? Sam dabbed his lips with his napkin. "Well, if you'll excuse me for saying so, Miss Bahill, that's the way it's always been done out here. It's the neighborly way to do things, makes for good relations."

"Good relations!" Bahill exploded. "This is my land. I bought it with hard-earned money, the whole kit and caboodle. I have blooded cattle—bulls and fine cows that I can't afford to let mingle with those scrawny Mexican scrubs!"

"My father has been more than fair, Mr. Gray. He allowed most of those squatters to stay on our property for twenty years. But you must see why we can't let our good stock mingle with inferior animals."

"If the squatters were so bad, why did Colonel Bahill let them stay?" Sam asked her.

She looked puzzled. "What do you mean?"

"Isn't that obvious?" Bahill's face was red with anger. "I don't run roughshod over people, not if they meet me halfway!"

Sam leaned back, feeling his own anger. The "squatters" were mostly Mexicans who had lived on the land for years, fighting off the Apaches and holding on to land that everyone else had given up on. A number of them were descendants of the original land-grant holders. But now the Indian wars were over, and the eastern interests had moved in. As a ranger, Sam had been sworn to protect the landowner, but there were times when he hated his job. And he'd seen this particular trick a few times before. He leveled his gaze at Miss Bahill. "I'll tell you what I think. The colonel let them stay because as long as there were a few small outfits on the outer edges of La Zanja, none of the big spreads could horn in. I imagine even those scrub cattle came in pretty handy, holding the land until you could put your own stock on it."

"That's ridiculous! Where did you find this man, Billie?"

"I told you, Father. He's a guest."

"Well, he's damn well forgotten his manners!" the colonel bellowed.

"I'm sorry if I offended you," Sam said. "But I believe in plain speaking."

To his surprise, the colonel laughed. "I'll be damned. A man who speaks his mind! It's refreshing to hear it."

"There are rustlers on La Zanja," Billie broke in. "I was hoping Mr. Gray might be able to help us."

"Rustlers? Where?"

"The fence is down in the south pasture. Some of our cattle are missing."

"Probably those squatters your friend here likes so much," the colonel said.

Billie ignored her father and looked at Sam. "Could you help us?"

"I have to take my prisoner back to Bisbee. But I can ask Captain Mossman to send out somebody when I get back."

Billie smiled, and Sam felt his bad temper evaporate.

"Why don't *you* come back," Bahill said imperiously. "I'm sure Billie would be happy to see you again, wouldn't you, Billie?"

Mortified, Billie looked away.

Bahill leaned forward, the light catching his

wire rims. "What do you earn as a ranger?"

"Enough to live on."

"Not as much as a cattle rancher with a spread like this, I'll wager."

"You're right, there."

"This is a real moneymaker. A man could be set for life." Colonel Bahill's eyes narrowed. "You in the war?"

Sam thought that Bahill could have been more subtle. Would he like a look at the Gray family tree next? "First Voluntary Cavalry," he said reluctantly.

"Teddy's Rough Riders. Good for you! Not like that gutless wonder—" One glance at the warning in Billie's eyes, and Bahill decided not to pursue it. "Have some more wine, Sam," he added, pouring from the decanter into Sam's glass. "You know, Elizabeth here is quite an authority on wine—she does all the buying. Would you get that good cabernet from the cellar?"

Sam knew that Billie was seething, but she rose without a word and headed for the kitchen.

"She's amazing, that girl. She can do anything. You know she hosted a sit-down dinner for twenty people when she was barely out of her teens?" Bahill swallowed some more wine and looked at Sam. "She's a good hand on a horse, too. Can do anything my men can do. A real help on a spread like this."

"I've heard she has a lovely singing voice," Reverend Auberge said. "Perhaps she should come to church and join our choir—"

"She's too busy for that. Mr. Gray, you have folks in the area?"

"Prescott."

"That's damn fine country. Ranch stock, are they?"

Mrs. Auberge said tentatively, "You know, Harshaw isn't that far. Elizabeth really should develop her spiritual inclinations. Perhaps if she paid attention to the more feminine pursuits . . ."

"Nonsense," Bahill said, dismissing her. "This is the new West. A man needs someone as strong as he is, someone he can depend on. Billie—Elizabeth—she's got everything to make a man happy. Beautiful, strong, capable. Don't you agree, Mr. Gray?"

Before Sam could answer, Billie spoke from the doorway. "I'm sound of limb and have all my teeth." She held a wine bottle by its neck, and Sam thought she was contemplating using it as a weapon.

"What are you doing, sneaking up on us like an Indian?" sputtered the colonel.

Billie sat down and spread the linen napkin on her lap. "What do you want me to do? Go back and wait in my room until you've shaken on the deal?"

"Missy, you are forgetting yourself!"

"I'm not going to sit here and listen to you parade me around in front of this man like a—" She glanced at the portrait of Albany. "Like your prize bull!"

"Oh, goodness," Mrs. Auberge said, fluttering

a napkin at her throat. Reverend Auberge shot a glance at Billie before reaching for the decanter.

Bahill's eyes narrowed. "Apologize to these people, Elizabeth. You've been trying my patience ever since—"

"Elliot left me in the lurch? Go ahead and say it, Colonel. Everyone here knows the story—"

"Billie!"

"Mr. Gray," she said sweetly, "you should know that should you decide to take me for your bride, yours will not be the first these lips have touched—"

Colonel Bahill slammed his fist down on the table. "I won't have this!"

Mrs. Auberge fanned herself furiously.

"Damaged goods, Mr. Gray. But I would be most humbly grateful if—"

"That's enough! You're making a damn fool of yourself. Just like you did over that nature artist—"

"That's not true."

"Then where is he?"

Billie said nothing.

"Elliot Stevenson is gone; can't you get it through your thick head? He took off, and you're a damn sight better off without him!"

The air seemed to hum with shocked silence. Mrs. Auberge was trying without success to stab a beet with her fork. The good reverend checked his pocket watch. If Joe McCarty had been standing he would be shuffling his feet. As it was, he stared at the tablecloth with deep concentration.

"I'm sure you will all excuse me," Billie said quietly, as she set down her napkin and stood up from the table.

"Young lady, you will not leave this table!" Colonel Bahill roared.

Billie's only answer was the whisper of her skirt as she walked out of the room, her head erect.

Embarrassed murmurings followed.

Finally the colonel said, "I don't know what's gotten into that girl. She defies me at every turn."

Sam suddenly found the colonel's good beef tasteless. He would wait a polite interval, and excuse himself as well.

A dinner at La Zanja was as likely to give a man indigestion as a whole plate of jalapeño peppers.

Billie lifted her skirts and hurried down the steps and into the yard, her face burning with mortification. What had made her bait her father like that in front of company? Her plan had been to humor him, ignore his barbs. Rise above it all, as a lady should.

She'd hoped that during his trip back East, the colonel would have had time to mellow. But her father had a memory like an elephant. He never let go of his prejudices, especially when he thought he was right. She should have known he would look for every opportunity to drive his point home.

She had taken the bait, and now she would

pay for it. How could she tell him about Elliot's child now?

It was warm for a spring night, and very bright. The wide swath of grassland, bleached of color, stretched out blue-gray in all directions under a full moon. Black oak—what the Mexicans called *bellotas*—huddled on the hill like a herd of shaggy buffalo. Gray clouds, limned with silver, dappled the indigo sky like the spine of a herring. With a pang, Billie remembered a night similar to this just two weeks ago, when she and Elliot had walked among the oaks, discussing their future. He had promised to talk to her father that very night about their engagement. Although she didn't know it then, that was the last time she would see him.

Over in the bunkhouse, one of the hands played a mournful song on a guitar. His voice was sweet and sad as he sang the Mexican ballad.

Billie whistled to Buttermilk, who was standing at the far end of the corral. He pricked his ears and ambled over, nickering when he saw the carrots in her hand.

She fed him his carrots and clasped her arms around his neck, pressing her hot face against the tangle of his mane. Tears stung her eyes as it all came down on her at once: the anguish, the fear, the humiliation that had been her constant companions for two weeks. She sniffled, trying to keep from crying. The colonel's voice rang in her ears: *Crying is a sign of weakness*.

"To hell with what you think," she said, and clutched the patient horse's neck tighter.

But realistically she knew her entire future depended on what Colonel Bahill thought.

Sam excused himself soon after Billie left, saying he needed to go collect his prisoner.

As he walked out onto the veranda, he tried to remember where he'd heard of Elliot Stevenson. It had been recently, sometime in the last couple of weeks, and the name held an unpleasant association for him.

He'd just about got it when he saw the slender shape of a woman leaning against the corral fence. Billie.

After that scene inside, he doubted she'd want to talk to him. He walked toward the cowboys' dining room, a long fieldstone building with a few small windows. Oil lamps lit them from within, giving off a welcoming apricot glow.

The heavy scent of jasmine filled his nostrils. A distant guitarist sang of love and loss. It was a beautiful night. A night for lovers, he thought wryly. The bright moon was occasionally snared by the dark clouds, but shone through and around them. The oaks near the corral threw pools of black shadow on the hills. A cricket chirped. The trimmed lawn that aproned the house was springy under his feet.

He was almost to the dining room when he glanced at the still figure again. She had her arms around the buckskin's neck, holding on for dear life. She looked forlorn, vulnerable.

Colonel Bahill had humiliated her. It was obvious she loved this Elliot Stevenson, even though he'd left her. Sam knew what that was like. For the colonel to twist the knife—

He clenched his jaw. No doubt Billie thought he'd been laughing at her, enjoying the joke. He couldn't let her think that he had had any part of it. He changed directions.

At the sound of his footfall, Billie drew away from her horse. Her eyes widened slightly as she saw him. An unspilled tear resided in the corner of one.

"I'm sorry—" they both said at once.

"I shouldn't have embarrassed you like that," Billie rushed on before he could say anything else. "It wasn't your fault that my father saw you as a prospective husband."

"That didn't bother me. He shouldn't have treated you that way, especially in company."

She laughed shortly. "He doesn't care what they think."

"They?"

"The Auberges, McCarty. They're just window dressing. He likes to have a few people in to celebrate his homecomings. The colonel doesn't entertain. He holds court." She parted the mane along her buckskin's neck. Sam watched the graceful movement of her tapered fingers, the little half-moon nails glimmering softly. "Everyone's caught on by now, except for McCarty, and he's new to the territory. The reverend doesn't care as long as there's a good supply of port, and his wife hasn't given up on turning me into a lady."

He took her in: the aqua dress fitted to her wand slim figure, the curve and swell of her bosom under the lace and seed pearls, her full lips and dark-lashed eyes, and the delicate, aristocratic planes of her face. "You look like a lady to me."

She tilted her chin up to him, her eyes luminous with irony. "I can pass for one in polite company. But Mrs. Auberge despairs of getting me out of the saddle and into a pew."

Sam laughed, remembering Mrs. Auberge's attempt to convince Colonel Bahill to attend church. "She doesn't look like she's winning."

"We live on a working ranch, and traveling all the way to Harshaw and back for a two-hour service is . . . capricious."

"Are you quoting your father?"

"It's hard to know. When you live with someone all your life, it's easy to assimilate his opinions."

"Maybe so, but it looks to me like you just reached a fork in the trail."

She laughed. Her laugh was light, more carefree than he would have given her credit for, given the circumstances. It fluttered in the air like confetti. "We did, at that."

They stood in companionable silence, drinking in the night. The tension seemed to have left her, or she was a better actress than he'd thought. Perhaps her years of playing the hostess made her able to cover her emotions. "Do you always fight like that?" he asked at last.

"We lock horns every now and then."

"I'll bet you win more than you lose."

"Sometimes. But he hardly ever admits it, even when he's wrong." She stared into the middle distance, her expression sad. "Maybe this time I'm the one who's wrong. . . ."

"Hmm?"

She shook her head. "Nothing."

He wanted to say something, to tell her he understood what it was like to lose a loved one, but it was not his place. Billie was a strong woman; she would come out on the other side of this pain. He would guarantee it.

"You must think I'm an awful fool," she said softly.

"Why? Because you dared to love someone?"

"The colonel's right. Elliot did leave." She looked straight ahead. A few wisps of hair had escaped the pins, framing her profile in soft tendrils. The tear spilled from her dark lash onto her cheek, and she wiped it away.

"Then he was the fool."

She turned to face him. "You don't know me."

"I know enough."

Behind her eyes, which had struck him as forthright and honest, he saw a glimmer of something else. Anguish? She turned away. "I've got to go," she said abruptly, and hurried to the house.

Billie couldn't sleep. Her mind lingered on the ranger. He had been kind, and she appreciated it. But there was something about his proximity that disturbed her, made her heart beat faster.

He was a handsome man, but she had long since gone beyond schoolgirl crushes.

She was no longer a child. She had loved Elliot in the way a woman loves a man, and now she would suffer the consequences. So why, when the ranger accidentally brushed her arm earlier today, did her head whirl? Why did she keep darting furtive glances at him when she didn't think he was looking? Why had she been utterly humiliated when her father pushed her at him tonight?

I love Elliot, she told herself firmly. *He's the father of my child. And he will come back. There's been some sort of misunderstanding.*

But that explanation sounded hollow in her ears.

Trembling shadows from the cottonwood tree outside her window played on the sprigged wallpaper of the room, and moonlight gilded the music box on the marble-topped dressing table. The music box had belonged to her mother; Olivia had found it in a trunk in the attic. The housekeeper had also salvaged one of Emily's oil paintings, a barn cat sitting among sunflowers, and a few sable brushes, which Billie kept in a place of honor in a jar on the mantel. Billie's father had packed up everything else and given it away, as if by doing so he could obliterate the painful memory of his wife's death. Although Billie used her mother's china and crystal to entertain, the rest of the house was the way the colonel liked it: a man's domain. All except this room. Olivia had helped her decorate it, had argued with the colonel when he balked at the idea of buying flowered wallpaper and lace curtains for the windows. *You'll ruin her, giving her those kinds of notions. She'll grow up weak, like her mother.* But Olivia had stood her ground, and Billie's room was a girl's room.

Billie had ambivalent feelings about it. Sometimes she felt as if she were a rope in a tug-of-war between the colonel and Olivia. In truth, Billie didn't know who she was. She could dress like a lady, and entertain like one, but she lived most of her life as a man. She loved horses and fresh air, and the freedom her father had given her.

Maybe Mrs. Auberge was right. Maybe her tomboyishness had scared Elliot off.

Billie rolled onto her back and stared at the ceiling. If Elliot didn't mean to come back, what would her life be like from now on? How would she be able to live with her father, when each day started with a deception? And when she dredged up the courage to tell him . . . she didn't dare think about that.

If only she could go back to that night, the night before Elliot left. If she'd done something different, if Elliot hadn't gone in to talk to the colonel . . . What had really gone on that night? Not her father's story, but the truth. What had the colonel said to make Elliot leave? She tried to remember that night, the ardor of Elliot's kisses, but her mind pressed inexorably on to the conclusion, to the following morning.

*　　*　　*

She had awakened early and, feeling excited, had gone out to check the south pasture. Elliot wouldn't be up for hours. The early sun gilded the leaves of the cottonwoods along the Santa Cruz River and picked out the blue-green arrowhead shapes of pine trees on the distant Huachuca Mountains. Billie could barely contain her joy. She knew her father didn't like Elliot, but she was already twenty-three years old, and offers of marriage didn't come every day. Surely her father would realize that.

At last she could stand it no more and turned back for the ranch. But as she rode, instinct told Billie something was not quite right. Perhaps the colonel had refused to give them his blessing—she wouldn't put it past him.

Even if the colonel didn't approve, it wouldn't stop them. She would marry the man she loved. So why was she so nervous?

Billie felt as though she were at the edge of a great chasm; one she could not see, but one no less frightening for that. The closer she came to the ranch, the more urgency she felt. There was no logic to her nervousness, but she was suddenly filled with a slow, agonizing dread. Her heart hammered, and she barely saw the country unrolling before her.

She couldn't wait any longer. She had to know. By next week she might very well be Mrs. Elliot Stevenson, which would be a relief indeed, because already she suspected that she might be in the family way.

But when Billie reached the ranch house, Elliot didn't answer her knock. Her father, however, was sitting at the table, finishing his breakfast.

Billie swallowed, her mouth dry. How would he react? Was he mad at her? She cleared her throat. The colonel looked up, his face grim.

"I checked the fence," she said as cheerfully as she could. Why was he looking at her like that? His face was drawn, his eyes bloodshot. She knew he had trouble sleeping, but he looked even worse today.

"Is it down anywhere else?"

She helped herself to a biscuit, and sat opposite him. "Not as far as I could see. I rode about two miles each way." She glanced at the clock. It was almost ten. Surely Elliot would be up by now. Again the feeling of dread pricked her. "Where's Elliot this morning?"

The colonel cleared his throat. "He's gone."

"Gone? You mean sketching?"

"No." Her father held her gaze, and suddenly she knew what he was going to say next. "He's gone for good."

His words hit her like a punch to the stomach. She stared at him, feeling her tongue work in her mouth but unable to say a word.

Her father's face swam before her. "I told him he would never see one penny from La Zanja. He decided to try his luck elsewhere."

"I don't believe it," she said. But the nausea in the pit of her stomach told her he was speaking the truth.

The colonel placed his balled-up napkin on his

plate. "I'm sorry," he said heavily. "I never approved of that scoundrel, but I don't want to see you hurt."

Her ears were ringing.

"I know how you must feel. But in time you'll see this is for the best."

"For the best?" She stared at him incredulously. *For the best?* Fear, icy cold, snagged at her heart like a rusty wire. She might be pregnant. Elliot was gone. How could that be for the best?

"That fellow only wanted your money. It's a good thing we found that out before you made the mistake of marrying him. I had to know what his intentions were, and I found out." The colonel leaned back in his chair, looking proud of himself. "I offered him money to leave, and he took it."

Billie couldn't believe her ears. How could he have done such a thing? How could he, when she might be carrying Elliot's child—

She should have told Elliot of her suspicion. If he'd known, surely he wouldn't have left her alone to face a hostile world carrying his child . . . but why did he leave? Did he really just want her money? Was he paid off so easily? The thoughts clamored for attention. She bowed her head and clapped her hands to her ears. She couldn't believe it. Her father had to be twisting the truth. "He wouldn't do that!"

"He did do it." The colonel leaned forward. "He is the most vile, disgusting, low-life scum it's ever been my misfortune to come across. When

it was clear you would not inherit La Zanja—
that I would cut you off without a cent if you
married him—he showed his stripes soon
enough."

"How could you?" Her voice shook. "How
could you do this to me?"

"I saved you, missy, from a life of misery and
uncertainty! I did you a service!"

She felt sick. What would he say if she told
him the truth? What would he do if he knew that
he might have spoiled her one chance to legiti-
mize the child in her belly? Would he be so
proud then? For an instant she wanted to tell
him the truth. That would wipe that self-
satisfied expression off his face! Anger boiled up
in her, flowered in her heart like some deadly
flame-red plant. "You've ruined everything," she
said in a hiss.

"Ruined? I saved you! It was obvious to me
what was going on. I had to stop it!"

She saw the glitter of triumph in his eyes. And
then she pictured Elliot leaning down to kiss
her, admiration shining in his gaze. *I love you.*
How many times had he told her that? How
could she doubt him now, at the first sign of
trouble? There had to be an explanation. "He
loves me. He would never do such a thing. I
know it!"

"Are you calling me a liar?"

"You don't know him; you don't understand—"

"You're the one who doesn't understand!"

"He loves me! I don't know what you did to

make him leave, but Elliot would never hurt me like this!" Impotent rage blurred her vision with tears. "What did you do? How did you get him to leave me?"

Colonel Bahill turned brick red. His fist hit the table. "Don't you take that tone with me! Do you really want to know what he thinks of you? Do you? He thinks you're more man than woman. He called you an old maid. He said no other man would want you!"

Billie felt as if all the air had left her body. The words cut across her brain like whiplashes. Stunned, she could only stare at her father.

He leaned heavily on the table, and sighed. "I was hoping I could spare you some of this, but you have to know. It's like a gangrened leg. Got to be severed before the poison destroys the rest of the body." Awkwardly, he moved around the table and stood over her. "There, there," he told her gruffly, patting her shoulder. "I didn't want to tell you, but it's the only way for you to cut him out of your life."

She flinched away from him. "I don't believe you."

Her father's voice turned cold. "Believe it or not, he's gone. And he won't be coming back." He walked over to the peg holding his coat near the door. "I'm going to ride out to the line camp near Canelo. Want to come along? No? Then stay here and mope." He banged out of the room.

Billie sat at the table, absolutely numb. Fear had left her. If Elliot really felt that way about her, then nothing was important anymore. Not even the child—if there was one.

She supposed there would be hell to pay when her father found out that she was no longer a virgin, but now she didn't care. Nothing else could hurt her as much as the words he'd spoken this morning.

Slowly, achingly, she stood up and walked to her room. Lying on the bed, Billie stared unseeingly at the golden land of La Zanja.

The next day the colonel departed on his cattle-buying trip back East, and Billie was left to face her fears alone.

Chapter Three

Sam was ready to leave. Early that morning, one of the La Zanja hands had taken him out to the remuda, and he had picked out a likely-looking horse for his prisoner. Daw was still asleep; Sam would rouse him soon. But first he thought he'd say good-bye to Billie and thank her for her hospitality.

He found her sitting on a stump under the oak trees lining the dry wash behind the corrals. She wore a simple white shirtwaist and dark plaid skirt, her hair bound in a long raven braid down her back. A bridle and a can of saddle soap sat at her feet on a bed of dry, brittle oak leaves that made him think of a mass of jigsaw pieces. Her head was bent forward and she stared at something in her hand.

As he approached, a twig cracked under his

55

boot. Startled from her reverie, Billie stood abruptly, and the object slid off her lap and onto the ground. She and Sam both bent down to retrieve it at the same time, nearly colliding.

His hand closed on the heavy silver frame. He handed it to her. The oval portrait showed Billie standing behind a seated young man, one hand on his shoulder, before a potted palm and a swag of velvet. Slender and girlishly handsome, the man looked like a good wind would blow him over. A fine mop of black hair fell down to his shoulders and framed his pale face, which sported a neatly trimmed mustache and goatee.

When Sam saw the portrait, all the pieces came together. He knew where he'd seen Elliot Stevenson before. "Now I remember," he muttered, unaware he'd spoken aloud.

Billie looked at him quizzically. "You know Elliot?"

He wished he hadn't said anything. Even though Sam had only met him once, his opinion of the man had been formed with swift finality. Elliot Stevenson was a cheat, a fool and a coward. A cheat because he tried to cheat at cards; a fool because he tried that trick with a professional gambler; and a coward because when the trick was discovered he begged for mercy, crying like a baby.

Sam saw the hope shining in Billie's eyes, and he wished he could take the words back. At last he said neutrally, "I've met him."

The question trembled on her lips. "When?"

Sam thought about telling a lie, but didn't. "A

little over a week and a half ago. In Nogales. We were in a card game."

Billie absorbed this, her eyes on some inner landscape he was not privy to. When she spoke, her voice was small, tentative. "A week and a half ago? Are you sure?"

What else could he do but confirm it?

Billie sat back down again. Her skirt stirred the dust. A teal-colored piñon jay flashed from the adobe barn to an oak a few feet away. "Did he—did he say where he was going?"

Safe ground. "No," Sam replied.

He recognized the urgency in her body. He knew what it was like: the pounding heart, the dry mouth, innards turned to jelly. The straightness of her spine, as if every sense were straining to know, to understand. He knew it well. When she looked up at him, he saw hope and fear at war in her clear eyes. "Please tell me everything," she said.

"We played a card game in Nogales. He . . . quit early. I didn't see him again."

"That's all?"

No, he thought, *that's not all. Should I tell you about the two-dollar whore hanging on his neck? Should I tell you that he was boasting about his recent windfall? That he didn't look like a man who had just been forced to leave his true love, not that cocky son of a bitch, talking up his winning streak and his grand plans and dealing from the bottom of the deck?*

He debated telling her the truth. If she knew what a wastrel he was, she might be able to shake his influence. Go on without him. In time, she'd meet another man. But when he saw the look in her eyes, he couldn't do it. Elliot Stevenson was gone. From what Sam had seen, he wouldn't be coming back. Sooner or later Billie would accept it. What was the point of hurting her again? That was her father's bailiwick. "That's it," he said.

Billie looked as though she dearly wanted to ask more questions, but to her credit she didn't. Instead she asked, "Will you reach Bisbee today?"

"I hope to. I'll send the horse back as soon as I can."

"You'll talk to your commandant about the rustlers?"

"I will."

She stood, pushing the framed portrait into the pocket of her skirt. Again he thought how beautiful she was. He doubted she would remain bereft for long. "I guess I'd better get going," he said, feeling suddenly stiff and formal.

"You're always welcome at La Zanja."

Sam swore he heard a hint of shyness in her tone. Abruptly, he felt the urge to lean down and kiss those petal soft lips and make her forget all about Elliot Stevenson. He stifled it, turned awkwardly on his heel and walked toward the barn.

Later, as he rode out, he looked in the direction of the corrals and the oak-lined wash beyond. Billie Bahill was gone.

Chapter Four

Billie stood on the boardwalk of the weathered frame building that housed the Harshaw Dry Goods and Mercantile, clutching the folded notepaper against her breast.

The bell above the door jangled. Hastily Billie stuffed the letter into the pocket of her skirt and pretended to look at the advertisement cards tucked into the windowsill. A man emerged from the store and brushed past her. Her father must still be inside. Luckily he'd asked her to go to the post office for the mail while he picked up the butcher scale he'd ordered.

Another customer emerged from the store. Billie stared straight ahead, trying to concentrate on the colorful cards in the dusty window. One, an ad for Ayers Sarsaparilla, was a colored lithograph of a beautiful young mother and a sweet-faced little girl. The caption said, "Gives Health and Sunny Hours."

Yearning filled her. If her father hadn't forced Elliot's hand, if Elliot had known about the baby, then maybe she could have been like the woman in that picture. She could almost see the three of them, a happy little family, their daughter sturdy and apple cheeked, with a tumble of raven curls.

Now that hope had been revived in the letter in her pocket, whose words she had nearly committed to memory.

My Dearest Elizabeth,

By now you must be frantic over my absence. Your father has probably told you many vile things. They are not true. Yes, he offered me money to leave you. Think of it! He tried to bribe me because he wanted to deny you the happiness of marriage and children! But you must believe me when I tell you I did not take it, no matter what he says. A father who would do such a thing has no right to expect your trust.

When it became obvious to me the lengths your father would go to keep us apart, I decided that I must leave. If money is the only thing he prizes in a potential husband, I have no choice but to find a way to make a fortune. I have decided to look for the Lost Dutchman Mine. If I should find it, I will be able to return to you as an equal. I know, dearest, that you would run away with me tomorrow, but I cannot in all conscience marry you until I can support you. If we started out our lives in poverty, you would grow to hate me, and I could not bear that. Please have faith, and wait for me. I am, as ever, your faithful servant and loving fiancé,

Elliot

Billie closed her eyes and let relief wash over her. At last she knew the truth. Elliot knew how much she loved her father, knew how she loved the ranch. He had left her because he didn't want her to lose her inheritance. He didn't want to destroy her life. If he'd known about the child, he would have realized that they had to be together at any cost. He had overestimated the colonel's hold on her, and underestimated how much she loved him.

And now he was heading into the most dangerous country in Arizona to find that mine so they could be happy.

He was risking his life for her.

Well, she wouldn't let her father get away with this. Elliot would know about his child. She would tell him herself.

Resolve flowed back into her body, filling her with strength. She would choose poverty with the man she loved rather than live the empty life the colonel had planned for her.

Suddenly pain at what her father had done took her breath away. If she had betrayed him with Elliot, hadn't he betrayed her a thousand times over when he offered to pay the man she loved to leave her?

How could her own father make such vile accusations? How could he say those things to her? *He called you an old maid.*

Anger, hard and brilliant, filled her heart.

The door chime banged and Colonel Bahill emerged from the mercantile. "There you are. Any mail?"

She shook her head. "No."

He stopped, his eyes searching. "You're not ill again, are you? You look pale."

"No, I'm fine."

"That's good. You should be over that flu by now."

She lifted her chin. "I *am* over it."

His eyes widened. "Well, a little spirit. For a while there you had me wondering just what kind of ninny I'd been raising. You know how I feel about vaporish women."

"I'm stronger than you think," Billie replied. Lifting her skirts, she picked her way across the boardwalk and walked toward their wagon, her back straight and her head held high.

One of Billie's earliest memories was of sitting before her father on his big gelding, Ringer. At four years old, she was given a horse of her own. That year she rode drag on her first cattle drive. The colonel took her on business trips to the stockyards in Kansas City and Chicago. He called her his good-luck charm and let her sit in during the deals. She remembered a series of dark wainscoted hotel lobbies, and her father's associates, big but unthreatening, who chucked her chin and offered her gumdrops. They turned the air blue with cigar smoke, and she was lulled to sleep often by the murmur of masculine voices.

As she grew to adulthood, Billie learned every job on La Zanja, from branding and castrating calves to tallying the herds, blacksmithing, haying and keeping the books. She would always be Daddy's girl. Billie's recollections of her mother were fragmented, more dream than reality. Elusive memories of a beautiful woman drifting like a shade through the rooms of the house intrigued Billie to this day. But Emily Devereaux Bahill wasn't real to Billie. She wasn't made of solid flesh and blood, as Billie's father was. She was a dream.

Billie's mother hadn't been on the ranch very long. When Billie was five, Emily Bahill had to "go away."

They went to see her every month at St. Mary's Hospital in Tucson. The ghostly bulk of the hospital with its wide veranda and cactus garden scared Billie. Children weren't allowed in the tuberculosis ward, so she spent a great deal of time outside in the company of one of the nuns.

But one memory stood out more than all the others. It was dusk, and she and her father stood hand in hand by the statue of the Virgin Mary in the center of the cactus garden, and she remembered her father crouching down, his beard like sandpaper against her face. Her own stubby arms were clasped around his neck, and she tasted his tears, salty on her tongue. He started to cry, big wrenching sobs that shook him.

"You must be very brave," he'd told her.

"When's Mother coming back?" she had wailed, frightened by the fact that this big strong bull of a man was crying.

"Your mother won't be coming back. She's gone to live with the angels."

"Like Peaches?" Peaches was her old gelding who had died the year before of colic. She'd come across him herself, lying horribly still in the corral among blowflies, as stiff and unyielding as a chunk of wood.

"Like Peaches."

Billie became hysterical. She was six years old and had met death many times on the ranch, but this was different. This was the first time she'd seen her father cry.

Shortly after, the nightmares began. Billie never remembered them, but her screams woke the household. Her father always came up to hold her, but eventually she could tell that he was losing patience. She sensed his disgust. That was not the way big girls acted.

A few months after her mother's death, Colonel Bahill took Billie with him to doctor some calves. Billie loved to ride alone with him; they had not gone out together since her mother died.

They found a couple of calves that had been infected with screwworms. Billie was sickened by the terrible wounds on their bellies and sides.

Her father poured creosote into the wounds, then motioned to Billie. "Come here," he called. "Your fingers are tiny. Clean out these wounds."

She slid from her horse, her legs trembling. "But there are worms in there."

"If you don't get them out, these calves will die." Her father's voice cut like a whip. "You don't want that, do you?"

"No." She felt the tears start behind her eyes, and wiped her nose with her hand to stop them. She approached one of the calves, saw the white maggots crawling in the blackened, open wound. Her stomach gurgled, and bile rose up into her throat.

"Do you want to be a rancher's daughter?" her father demanded.

"Yes, sir." She felt faint.

"Then don't let me down."

She closed her eyes and wriggled her fingers up into the wound, sure she would vomit. Crooking her fingers, she pushed the worms out and nearly gagged.

"Now that's my cowgirl!" her father boomed.

She had passed the test.

From that time on, Billie wasn't bothered by nightmares.

As Billie settled her saddle onto Buttermilk's back, she reflected that her father might regret the toughness he'd drummed into her. A "vapor-ish miss" would probably accept her fate, and wander around the ranch house wailing and fainting and crying over her lost love. But Billie

65

had a choice. She knew what it was like to camp in the open under the night sky, knew how to track, knew how to handle travel situations on her own—taking a train, checking into a hotel room. Billie wasn't sheltered and she wasn't timid.

The rest of the day went by in a blur. With each hour her determination grew. The helplessness, the near-panic she had felt when she first learned of her pregnancy had vanished, replaced with determination. Billie was never comfortable unless she was able to take action, and now, at last, this was something she could control. Elliot would know about their child. He would abandon this ridiculous quest of his, and they would marry. They would scrape by somehow. All they needed was love for the three of them to be together.

But first she had to find him.

It was late afternoon. Billie had begged off working cattle today, and now she was glad. Her father, cheered by the change in her demeanor, had ridden out this afternoon to check on some cattle up in the Patagonias, leaving her a clear field.

Billie went to look at Freddy, the calf she'd rescued the day the ranger came to La Zanja. Freddy would soon be strong enough to be turned loose on the range. Giving him his bottle for the last time, she stroked him gently. She had already left a note for Tomás, asking him to take care of Freddy.

After securing the yellow Fishskin slicker on

top of the bedroll, Billie tightened Buttermilk's cinch. Balancing her valise against the gelding's neck, she swung astride. Buttermilk humped his back. He always bucked a little when she rode him for the first time each day, letting her know he was not to be taken for granted. "Act like a gentleman," she said sternly, neck-reining the buckskin into a tight circle and giving him a taste of her heels. After one halfhearted crow-hop, Buttermilk decided to take her advice, although a suspicious ear remained cocked back at the bulky valise bumping against his shoulder. He wore a halter under his bridle; he would be shipped as he stood, and she didn't want him breaking his good bridle. She would carry that.

Billie planned to change into traveling clothes at the station after seeing Buttermilk into the boxcar. She'd debated taking him at all, but there was the trip to the train station, and she didn't want to leave him with anyone. Besides, if Elliot had already struck out for the Superstitions, Billie wanted a horse she could depend on. She could buy supplies in Phoenix, and a mule, if necessary.

Once again she thanked Heaven that her father—who had little patience with numbers—had let her take care of the ranch's finances. She had plenty of money, and could draw on her own account in Phoenix.

She turned Buttermilk's head toward the railroad station, the first stop on her way to Elliot.

Chapter Five

The widow snored. She lay on her back in her beaded jet peignoir, her flesh puffing out like an undercooked pastry. The morning sun etched a myriad of lines into her face. Her painted mouth hung open. It was a wonder the flies buzzing at the window screen didn't fly right in.

Elliot shifted his weight with care, sliding out from under her flabby arm. He was terrified of waking her. She would want him again, and he just didn't think he could do it. It was amazing that he'd managed as well as he had the past week, since the sight and smell of her cooked his noodle.

Cooked his noodle. That was an expression he'd learned from the hands on the Bahill ranch.

At the thought of the ranch, his stomach clenched. La Zanja should have been his. Ever since Buffalo Bill Cody's Wild West Show had visited his hometown, bringing with it the only bright spot in a violent and miserable childhood, he had dreamed of becoming a cattle king. La Zanja had been more perfect than any world he could have conjured in his imagination. He could have had it all: a beautiful wife, money, power, and a big cattle spread of mythic proportions. All gone because of his temper! It was the only thing he'd inherited from his brute of a father, who had died drunk in a Philadelphia gutter when Elliot was ten.

Elliot's mind swerved away from the scene in Bahill's library, the moment that had put an end with surgical accuracy to his aspirations to be baron of La Zanja. As he looked down at Dorothea Blodgett, he felt deep anguish. What a comedown from Billie! And Billie had been young enough, naive enough, that she was still malleable. If there had been time, he was certain he could have shaped her into a woman to be envied in any social circle. He could have made her his willing slave.

Instead, *he* was the slave, to this coarse, fat sow. *Darling, do be a good boy and bring me my snuff. It's hot in here, will you fan me? I want some mineral water. Just a touch of bitters. Not in that glass. The green one. Do be a dear and fetch me that pillow? No, no, not under my back, behind my head! Fluff it up first!* All of it couched in sugary endearments, but he never missed the smug gleam in her eyes, telling him, If you want my money, then you'd better do my bidding.

Tomorrow she planned to marry him, and then he'd be her servant for the rest of her life! There must be easier ways to earn his fortune.

He dressed quietly, at any moment expecting one evil eye to slit open and pin him to the wall like a butterfly to a display board. Stealthily, he rifled through the things on the dressing table. He knew he wouldn't find much; the cunning old whore banked most of her money and hid the rest. She'd made it clear she didn't trust him. Oh, she trusted him enough to make him run his feet off for her, but that was all. He'd been the perfect beau for two weeks, and all he had to show for it were a few steak dinners, a new suit and sore feet.

His fingers found the black-beaded chatelaine bag she wore around her waist for evenings. There was a small bill in it and a few coins. Tightfisted hag! Well, he had bigger fish to fry.

A loud snort froze him in his tracks. Dorothea heeled over in the sheets like a lazily frolicking whale, but didn't awaken. Elliot started breathing again. He gathered his things quickly, making sure that the map was safely tucked in the inner pocket of his vest, then shut the door behind him.

He followed the broad dirt avenue a block before turning south on Washington. Redbrick two-story buildings lined the street. Signs advertising every possible commodity—hardware, toiletries, clothing, the names of businesses—were painted on the brick in bright colors. Telegraph and telephone lines snared the sky, and streetcars clanged and rumbled their way down the middle of the avenue. Elliot stood in the shadow of the cupola belonging to the National Bank of Arizona building and watched the bustle for a while. The air shivered with dust and noise—horses and wagons and people of every description. Elliot's exhilaration mounted. There was an excitement to this city, a feeling that anything could happen. It already had. It had happened at the precise moment he'd met the mulatto woman yesterday, on the western edge of town.

Dorothea had retired for her afternoon nap. Elliot had gone for a walk, trying to reconcile himself to marrying her. He wasn't looking where he was going, and nearly ran over the mulatto woman hawking maps on the street corner. The mulatto turned out to be Julia Thomas, the last person to see old Jacob Waltz alive. She had sold him the map for ten dollars, a copy of the one she had drawn at the old German's bedside all those years ago. "Anyone who buys this map has a chance to find it," she had told him. "If they can just read it right, this is the key to the Lost Dutchman Mine." She'd turned away, already intent on her next sale. And then, stiffening, she turned back to face him. Her sharp eyes studied his face, as if looking for something.

"What are you looking at?" he'd asked, unnerved.

"Come inside for a moment." She led him into her adobe shack. The interior of the shack was dark; the windows were covered with sheets. Julia Thomas built a fire in the room's small fireplace. Already stiflingly hot, the room became an oven as the fire flickered to life. Taking down three small bottles of colored powders from the pantry shelf, Julia Thomas poured them onto the flames and recited incantations.

Her face, the color of creamed coffee, glistened with sweat in the firelight, and her eyes looked like black currants. "Yes," she said softly as the last bit of color was devoured by the flames. "You will find gold. But be careful. You will find more than you bargained for."

He would find the gold!

"You are destined to be a wealthy man. But you will turn away the treasure that awaits you."

Elliot grinned. He would never turn his back on wealth.

She caught his grin; her eyes were pitying.

He met her pity with indignation. What right did some scrawny dirt-poor half-breed have to pity *him?*

Her face closed up. "Don't believe me, then. I see gold. That's all."

That was enough.

She'd spoken with such conviction that even now, Elliot shivered at the thought of it.

You will find gold. The Lost Dutchman Mine would be his! With the bankroll from Colonel Bahill, he had enough money to outfit himself for the trip into the Superstition Mountains with some left over.

Everywhere he went in this town, Elliot had heard stories about the Lost Dutchman Mine. It was one of the few remaining chances for a man to make his fortune. The gold was just lying around out there, and the man persistent enough, well equipped enough, would have only to find it, scoop it up and bring it back. And he was the one who would find it. He would have enough money to buy six ranches as big as La Zanja!

Suddenly a new fantasy sparkled in his mind's eye. He pictured himself driving up to La Zanja in a fine coach and shoving a fistful of currency in old Bahill's face. He would buy La Zanja, and everything on it. Including Bahill's charming daughter, Elizabeth.

That would show the world once and for all that he belonged, that he was born to be a land-owner and a gentleman.

Looking back on it, Elliot was glad he'd sent the letter to Billie. At the time, he'd had no plans to look for the Lost Dutchman, although the thought of such a romantic adventure did appeal to him. He'd just hooked up with the widow, and although a trifle dull, marriage seemed preferable to risking his life in the desert. He had written Billie purely on instinct. It never paid to burn bridges. The reference to the Lost Dutchman Mine had added a certain dashing flavor to the letter, in addition to making him sound more sincere. But now . . . he had a chance to redeem everything he'd lost. If Julia Thomas was correct—and why shouldn't she be?—one day very soon he would return to the ranch in triumph, and take what was his.

He breakfasted at the Garden City Restaurant, compliments of the widow Blodgett. The restaurant also provided swimming and bathing facilities. After a long soak and a shave, he headed toward the livery stable on Center. He needed a horse and a mule. He'd left the horse from La Zanja at the depot at Nogales.

The proprietor of the livery stable tried to steer him to an average-looking brown horse, but Elliot would not be tricked. A white beauty in the far corral caught his eye. The animal was massive, with a snowy mane and tail, pink eyes, and hooves that made him think of polished mother-of-pearl. "What about him?"

"The albino?" The stable owner rubbed his chin thoughtfully. "You got a good eye for horseflesh, mister. That's my personal riding horse. He's mighty fine, all right, but probably more than you can afford."

Elliot stifled his annoyance. "Is he for sale or isn't he?"

"He'll cost you dear."

Elliot raised his chin and sighted down his nose. "Let me worry about that."

He wasn't disappointed. The horse, whom he'd already christened Pegasus, arched his neck and tail and pranced like the old time chargers of Gaul. Elliot purchased a mule, a saddle trimmed with big silver conchos, and a packsaddle. The stable owner sent him to a friend of his to buy the rest of his supplies. "Tell him Jed said to do real well by you."

When the man at the Red Indian Mercantile

heard that Jed had sent him, Elliot was treated like visiting royalty. "That's a fine horse you got there. How much did you pay for him?"

"Two hundred dollars."

The man grinned. "How much money you got to spend?"

The clerk, whose name was Ollie, heaved sacks of beans and flour, coffee and canned goods onto the counter, then looked thoughtfully up at the floor-to-ceiling shelves lining the store. He pulled down folded blankets, a bedroll, a yellow slicker, a white duster and a felt-covered canteen and piled them next to the provisions. "You'll need stuff for camping and, let me see . . . what kind of mining you figuring on doing? Panning or hard rock?"

"I don't know."

"Better have both, then, just to be on the safe side."

Elliot watched in amazement as the treasure trove grew. A shiny new pick, ax, and shovel, a gold pan, a Winchester repeating rifle and a hunting knife with a gleaming wooden handle. Pots, pans and kettles of every description. "You'll need something to cook with." Out came the Mighty Mite camp stove, "the very latest thing," and the Sears and Roebuck Kamp Kook's Kit, camp chairs, a camp cot—

"Why do I need a cot? You've given me a bedroll."

Ollie looked at him as if he were crazy. "To keep the rattlesnakes from gittin' you."

Elliot didn't argue the point.

"You gonna wear them duds?"

"Of course not—"

"Good. Got some real authentic stuff back here. It's what the cowboys wear on the range."

As Elliot tried on clothing, the clerk kept pushing things through the door at him. At last he had the money to dress like the cowboy he'd always dreamed of being. He chose only the most expensive weaves, admiring himself in the three-sided mirror. He bought a white cowboy sombrero with a peaked crown, red angora chaps, a leather vest, three linen shirts, two silk neckerchiefs, boots and Texas spurs. Twin ivory-gripped Smith and Wesson revolvers rested in leather holsters slung low on his hip.

When he was finished, he had three dollars left.

"How do I look?" he asked Ollie, glancing over his shoulder to catch the right angle.

"Like one of them legends of the West."

There was something in Ollie's smile that made Elliot doubt the man's sincerity. For the briefest instant he wondered if he was being taken. The cowboys at La Zanja didn't dress like this.

And then he realized that the cowboys at La Zanja were mostly Mexicans. That would explain it. He dismissed the doubt from his mind, smoothing the large silk neckerchief into a triangle on his breast before securing the ends at the nape of his neck.

Ollie was kind enough to help Elliot pack his

supplies onto the mule, patiently showing him how to do it for himself.

"Here's your water," Ollie said, loading two large canvas bags on the mule. He brought out two more, but Elliot refused them. He'd kept a running tally of the bill in his head. He couldn't afford much more if he wanted to spend the night in town.

"Are you sure? It's fierce country."

"I'm no fool," Elliot said. "I've talked to prospectors who've been in those mountains. There are plenty of canyons with lots of running water. I heard a lot of that country is oak and pine."

Ollie shrugged. "Suit yourself."

Elliot led his purchases back to the livery stable.

That night he spent his last three dollars on a steak dinner and a room at a good hotel. He would be getting up early to start his adventure.

On the brilliant April morning Elliot started on his quest for the Lost Dutchman Mine, Billie Bahill had already spent a night at the Adams Hotel not a block away. And Sam Gray had just boarded the train for the copper mining city of Globe.

Sam dismounted and strode quickly across the boardwalk to the door marked SHERIFF, barely glancing at the mine gouged into the bare, rusty mountain above the town. He had spent all night riding the Gila Valley Globe and Northern train from Bowie, unloading his horse and riding up Broad Street just before dawn. He was dog-tired and still haunted by the hanging he'd witnessed in Tombstone.

After leaving La Zanja a little over a week and a half ago, he'd taken Howard Daw to Bisbee, then accompanied the killer to the county seat, Tombstone, where after a fair trial the man was hanged. Feeling somewhat responsible, Sam had stayed for the hanging. He always believed that a man should face the consequences of his actions, and refused to run from unpleasantness. Daw had died cursing Sam's name.

Yesterday morning word had come for him to get to Globe as soon as possible. Two men had tried to rob the Old Dominion Copper Company payroll.

Sam introduced himself to the sheriff and listened grimly to the particulars. Apparently the payroll was being transferred from the train to a waiting wagon when the robbers appeared, wearing gunnysacks over their heads. Although the eyeholes were large, it was impossible to see who the highwaymen were. They tried to blow the safe, but the dynamite misfired. Angry and nervous, the highwaymen shot two guards and rode hell-for-leather out of Globe, killing any bystanders that got in their way. One of the casualties was a pregnant woman, and the town was up in arms.

The sheriff shook his head. "It was a massacre. Four people dead, and the bastards didn't even get the money. Utterly senseless. We sent out a posse, but they lost us. I think they went into the Superstitions."

Sam passed a hand over his eyes, his head throbbing. "They have water?"

"They stole a mule and water at gunpoint in Silver King. I guess they thought if they holed up in the Superstitions, no one would bother going in after them. Could be they're right, too. I don't have a man to spare right now, what with the union unrest at the mine and all. Lucky we've got you fellows to help us out."

Sam nodded absently, thinking about the maze of forbidding canyons. It was an easy place to lose pursuers, but the Superstitions could also be a death trap. If they had water they would make it to a spring. If not . . .

Glancing at the sheriff's desk, he saw a reward poster on top of a stack an inch thick. The lithograph showed the head and shoulders of a young woman.

His stomach lurched. It was Billie Bahill. "What's this?"

"That? Oh, just got it in yesterday. The young lady's missing. They think it might be foul play. I don't imagine she'd be up in this neck of the woods, but why don't you keep an eye out for her?" The sheriff handed Sam the lithograph. She was as pretty as he remembered. White blouse. Black hair tied with a wide dark bow.

"Go on. Take some. You never know."

Sam took a few of the reward posters and slipped them into his saddlebags. "What do you mean by foul play?"

"The sheriff down there thinks her boyfriend might have kidnapped her."

Sam doubted that. He had a feeling that Billie Bahill could outshoot and outride Elliot Stevenson. He wondered what had really happened. Had Stevenson gone back to La Zanja? Maybe he'd gotten her to go away with him.

"My deputy survived," the sheriff told him. "Thought he recognized one of the thieves' voices."

"Who does he think it was?"

"A couple of brothers. Real bad news. I heard tell they watched their brother hang last week and they're madder than hornets."

Involuntarily, Sam's thoughts returned to the hanging he himself had just witnessed.

"Say, you look like something the cat drug in. You all right?"

Sam caught himself and grinned. "Nothing a pot of coffee won't fix. You say they might be brothers?"

"There's a whole nest of 'em near Blue River." The sheriff sat back on his swivel chair and lit a cigar, then mumbled around it. "Bad bunch. Go by the name of Daw."

Chapter Six

Forty miles east of Phoenix, Arizona, a shelf of volcanic rock towered three thousand feet above the desert floor. Sphinxlike, it guarded the canyons and mountains beyond, ever silent, ever watchful. Sheer walls of tuff and dacite thrust upward, scored by deep fissures and planed by sun, rain and wind into a thousand rough facets. The rock face itself seemed to shift and crawl in the dancing heat waves of summer like chandelier crystals, lavender-blue in the dry air. Jagged rock fangs snapped at the sky. At the base of the cliffs, alluvial fans spread like unevenly poured cake batter onto the desert surface, pinned in place by saguaro cactus and choked by desert brush. It was a hellish country, baking under temperatures reaching, in summer, 125 degrees.

The southern escarpment was called the Superstition Mountains, a suitable name for a place that had always been shrouded in mystery. It was a place of silence and lengthening shadows, of unseen tension that seemed to hover in the air. The mountains lured the unwary with the siren call of easy riches, but served up only poverty, dementia and death. There were many legends in this country, but the most famous legend of all was that of Jacob Waltz and his fabulous lost mine.

The winter of 1900 and early spring of 1901 were warmer than usual. There had been only two minor snowstorms in the high country above the Mogollon Rim, and as a result, the melted snowpack that usually fed the Tonto Basin, Salt River and the draws and washes of the Superstitions was nonexistent. Most of the canyons were bone-dry, except for a few isolated springs and pools that held water year-round. The mountains and desert already shimmered in the heat haze of early summer, and soon it would be too hot to travel in the middle of the day.

After camping near the Bark Ranch at the foot of the Superstitions, Billie and the guide she'd hired in Phoenix headed into the heart of the mountains.

She had stayed only one night at the Adams Hotel, long enough to withdraw some money from the bank and find a less visible boardinghouse on the outskirts of Phoenix. Although she'd used a false name on her railroad ticket,

Billie knew her trail would be easy to follow. Her father would know that she had withdrawn money in Phoenix.

Billie had no doubt whatsoever that he would come after her. He was rich and powerful and used to having his own way, and no wayward daughter would make a fool out of him.

Many times that week she had had the creeping feeling that someone was watching her. She hated looking over her shoulder all the time, wondering when her father's men would show up. Keeping a low profile, she wore hats with veils to obscure her features in case the colonel had circulated her picture. The best thing to do was to get out of Phoenix as soon as possible and cover her trail. But first she had to find Elliot.

Her inquiries eventually led her to Julia Thomas. Miss Thomas studied the portrait the professional photographer had taken of Billie and Elliot.

"How long have you been married?"

Flustered, Billie replied, "We aren't married."

Shock darkened Julia Thomas's eyes. "When was this picture taken?"

"About a month ago."

Julia Thomas gripped Billie's left wrist, stared at her engagement ring. "You're betrothed?"

"Of course we are."

The mulatto dropped Billie's hand. "Bad luck."

"I don't understand you."

"A betrothed couple should never have their

picture taken together. It means . . . it means you won't stay together."

"I've never heard of that particular superstition," Billie replied stiffly.

"Believe it or not. It doesn't matter. No good will come of this. He has a dark aura."

Puzzled, Billie started to ask what Julia meant, but the mulatto's tone became businesslike. "I sold him this map. I sell lots of them, but only one person will find Jacob's gold. If you can decipher it, you will be the one. That's what I told him. He will find gold, although I can't say if it is Jacob's. It might be a lot, or it might be a little. I know the map's right," she added with sudden agitation. "Reiney and Hermann blamed me because we couldn't find it, but it was them who couldn't read it properly. Well, the curse will get them, too. It already has."

Billie realized that Julia was talking about her foster son and his older brother. They had gone on the search with her. But what was this about a curse?

"Those mountains are evil," Julia continued. "Look at what happened to me and Reiney. We were happy until we started looking for that mine! Now Reiney and his own brother have fallen out over it and both of them will be wandering those hills until the day they die! Reiney's still young; he's got his whole life before him, but he's throwing it away for nothing! He'll never find that mine." She squeezed her eyes shut and her face became a rictus of pain. "I had a vision the other night—I saw him as a broken old man, a hermit. He shot himself. That's all he'll get out of the Lost Dutchman Mine!"

Suddenly she clutched at Billie's arm. "I'd like to go again," she said in a low, urgent voice. "Would you take me? Maybe we could find it first."

Billie shivered. She could feel Julia Thomas's desperation like an electric current between them.

"Please," the woman cried. Her fingers dug into Billie's arm. "I know I can trust you. I've waited ten years to find someone I can trust. You won't double-cross me, I can tell. It's your aura."

"What's an aura?"

Julia Thomas waved a hand dismissively. "It's just a word. Take me with you. I know those mountains. I can help you find the gold."

"If you think it's such folly for Reiney to search for the mine, then why should it be any different for you? Aren't you afraid of the curse?"

"I've already been cursed! I lost my life savings looking for Jacob's mine. Look around you. Would you want to live like this? Let me go with you!"

Gently Billie disengaged the woman's hand from her arm. "I'm looking for the man, Elliot. Not treasure."

Julia Thomas seemed to shrink before Billie's eyes. "I couldn't go anyway. I'm not feeling so well these days." Turning away, the mulatto held up the sheaf of crudely drawn maps. "This is Jacob Waltz's map," she shouted. "Only ten dollars, the key to a fortune in gold!"

85

She took no notice as Billie, stunned into silence, walked away.

The experience was unsettling. Had Julia really seen Elliot? It was hard to tell. Obviously, Miss Thomas's disappointment at not finding the mine had affected her sanity.

As Billie walked through town, the memory of that poor desperate woman stayed with her. The Lost Dutchman Mine might or might not be cursed, but certainly it had wreaked havoc on Julia Thomas's life.

Billie had followed Elliot's trail to the Red Indian Mercantile. The proprietor told her he had outfitted a man matching the picture she showed him.

"You can't miss him. He's riding a white horse and wearing red chaps."

From his place by the pickle barrel, a swarthy little man with a scruffy beard barked like a hyena. "What a tenderfoot! I sold him the horse. An albino—blind as a bat in the sun!"

Horrified, Billie rounded on him. "You sent him into those mountains on a blind horse?"

The man backed up, palms thrust out to ward off her rage, which he seemed to find amusing. "Now don't get riled. I tried to sell him a good animal. Besides, the horse ain't blind, exactly, he just can't see as well as a brown-eyed horse, not in the sun. He just stumbles a little."

The proprietor shook his head. "Seems to me anyone who had sense to get out of the rain would refuse an albino horse in this kind of country. Their hooves are pink, see, so they're softer. They ain't meant for tough going over rocks. He'll go lame in no time."

"I know that." Billie glared at the bearded man. "You could have told him, though." She turned to the store clerk. "Do you know which way he went into the mountains?"

"Ain't that many easy ways in. My guess is he went in at Jim Bark's ranch or over by First Water. Take your pick."

Jed's eyes sharpened. "What's a pretty thing like you doin' chasing that dude for?"

"That's my business," she snapped.

He eyed her speculatively. She didn't like the nasty glint in his eyes, as if he could see right through her to her chemise and drawers. He spat a stream of tobacco juice into the cuspidor at his feet. "Like that, is it? Seems to me you could do a lot better than a dude like him. I could show you a real good time."

Billie lifted her chin. "I'm afraid you'll have to save your show for someone else." She swept out of the store as regally as she could.

Her skin crawled at the thought of the way that man had looked at her. There was no doubt what he was implying.

It had decided her on something right then and there. A woman alone in those mountains would be fair game for lechers. She had always felt at home at La Zanja, respected as "one of the boys." But she wasn't on La Zanja now; she wasn't the boss's daughter.

Billie went to another store and bought bandages, men's clothing, and a packet of strong hairpins. Back at the boardinghouse, she wound the bandages around her chest as tightly as possible, dressed in the men's clothes and tucked her hair up under her hat with the pins. Close up, she looked like a woman, but she'd fool most men from a distance. She would just have to avoid meeting anyone on the trail.

Billie had outfitted herself for the trip and secured a guide recommended by the outfitter. She didn't like him. He wasn't openly lecherous like the bearded man, but refused to look at her when she spoke to him, and wanted his money in advance. She had no choice. He was the only man she could find on such short notice who didn't object to taking a woman into the Superstition wilderness.

He certainly was an incurious sort. He didn't even mention her strange mode of dress. Billie hoped his lack of interest in her affairs would ensure her anonymity.

Now, one week to the day after she'd arrived in Phoenix, here she was. Her first night in the Superstitions had been uneventful.

Billie looked at Julia's map frequently, although the childish drawing bore little resemblance to the area. They headed toward a peak that resembled a gigantic Mexican sombrero. Weaver's Needle, which looked as if it had been sawed off at a sixty-degree angle, was the only thing really identifiable on the map. Since the Bark Ranch looked closer to Weaver's Needle than the First Water trail, Billie decided to go in that way. The country was very rough on the horses; rocky, steep and dangerous. They camped within sight of the Needle, at a spring that was almost dry.

Elliot was nowhere to be seen. She decided to explore the canyons to the south of the Needle.

At ten o'clock in the morning, the merciless sun reflecting off the surfaces of the rocks made it uncomfortably hot. The heat radiated upward, baking her like an oven. But at least she didn't feel sick, and the ever-changing scenery fascinated her. Here and there a few wilted wildflowers stood out like tiny flags in the snarled tapestry of desert shrubs. They looked as if they would shrivel up and blow away like the dust devils that periodically touched down on the path. Billie stared at the clumps of brittlebush, burrobrush and prickly pear cactus jostling for room along the trail. From a distance they softened the contours of the hills, like a velvet glove hiding a fist that ended in broken, skeletal knuckles. The brooding tension of the mountains rode on the air, as thick as the dust that rose in puffs from the horses' feet. Hooves clopping on rock and crunching in sand, and the dry scuttle of an occasional lizard were the only sounds to break the stillness. The shadows of the pocked, salmon-pink cliffs stretched in inky slabs across the trail. Their darkness was almost palpable. The sky stretched above, a throbbing, aching blue. Billie stared at the high ridge above and experienced a vague uneasiness. She was aware that anyone on the ridge could watch their progress.

Billie had heard a host of stories about wild-eyed prospectors shooting at interlopers. For all she knew, crazed, gold-hungry Reiney Petrasch was watching her right now. If he was half as crazy as that poor woman, Julia Thomas . . . Billie suppressed a shiver.

Around midday, a rifle report ricocheted off the canyons, echoing several times. Buttermilk shuddered underneath her, although he was no stranger to gunfire. Even before the echo died away, the guide wheeled his horse and high-tailed it back down the trail.

"Come back here!" she yelled.

He didn't bother to look back. After all, he'd already been paid.

For a moment panic flew into her throat, beating like the wings of a frightened bird against a cage. She should turn back. There was the child to think of. This whole idea had been an exercise in madness.

Billie actually turned Buttermilk's head the way they had come. She could go home, away from this alien landscape, where it was safe and she wasn't alone and—

And then she thought of her father, telling her that Elliot had taken money to leave her. Lying just to keep his hold on her. Knowing full well how much pain that lie inflicted. She had no home. Not now. Grimly Billie swung Buttermilk around again. The mules—one snubbed to her saddlehorn and the other tied nose-to-tail to the first one—wheeled around to follow. The Super-stitions weren't that big. She'd find Elliot in a matter of days, tell him her news, and they would be back in Phoenix within the week. She'd made it this far, hadn't she? Love would carry her the rest of the way.

Elliot Stevenson had his own troubles. Two days before Billie's guide was frightened off by gunshots, he'd lost his horse and mule.

It had been a stupid, unforgivable error. When he cinched his saddle on Pegasus, the wretched beast had puffed out its belly, making it appear that the cinch was tight. As Elliot mounted, the saddle shifted sideways, pitching him onto the rocks. Pegasus started bucking, kicking the saddle to pieces and stampeding the mule.

Elliot brushed a cholla plant on his way down, and a segment of the cactus clung to his upper arm like a limpet. When he hit the ground, the impact drove the fishbone-fine spines into his skin.

Some of those spines were still embedded in his flesh, causing an excruciating bristle of pain when anything brushed against them. He'd had to tear the sleeve of his good shirt off, because the material rubbing against the needles had almost driven him crazy. It made him shiver to think about it.

After pulling out most of the cactus spines with his fingers—and jabbing himself bloody in the process!—he had limped up the canyon on a turned ankle, looking for his horse and mule. The sun was fierce, burning his face—the damn horse had trampled his hat into the dust—and searing his bare arm. His ankle throbbed, and the rocky ground caused him to stumble often.

Everything in this cursed country looked the same. Crenelated ridges, cactus and dry gullies running like ragged seams through this hellish, sand-colored mountain range.

Tears pricked his swollen eyelids. He would die here. All his dreams had come to this.

Why couldn't Billie's father have accepted him? Then none of this would have happened. *If I ever get out of here alive, I'll kill the bastard.*

Or destroy Billie. That would be better. The old turkey buzzard would die a slow death if his daughter were ruined. Elliot permitted himself a grin, although it hurt his cracked lips. He'd show them both. He'd seduce her again, and this time he'd make sure she was carrying his bastard before he left her. That would give the old man a heart attack.

But first he had to get out of here. The only things he had left were the clothes he stood in and Julia Thomas's map.

The damn map was useless. Oh, Julia had marked Weaver's Needle, all right, but trying to find that one spot where the mine was supposed to be was impossible. He had spent almost five days following the canyons and trails radiating from the peak's base. The country around here seemed flatter than the old-timers had described—a shallow basin choked with cholla. The landmarks and offshoot canyons didn't seem to match up. Had he gone too far east?

Elliot sat down in the shade of an acacia tree.

What was he going to do? He hadn't seen a soul out here.

He would sell his soul for a drink of water. He kept thinking about those canvas water bags that had gone with the mule, couldn't help but fantasize about the warm, tasty water that he had splashed into his mouth with careless abandon. He tried to suppress the panic that constricted his throat and screamed in his ears. But fear threatened to overwhelm him. He realized for the first time that he just might not get out of the mountains alive.

I'll have to walk out. Elliot shielded his eyes against the glare and looked up the offshoot canyon he'd taken earlier in the day. Was that the way back? He was so turned around he couldn't tell. Heaving himself to his feet, he started trudging along the gully. He didn't notice the bits of red angora from his chaps that snagged on every prickly mesquite limb, marking his trail. If he had, he could have backtracked quite easily.

Two hours later the canyon turned into a dead end. He retraced his steps, coming to the mouth of a bigger canyon on the left. Could this be the way he'd come in?

Elliot stumbled, almost fell. He was so damned thirsty. *Thirsty.* The word ran around his brain like a rat in a maze, clawing and shrieking until he thought he'd go insane. Maybe there was water in this canyon. If there wasn't, he'd die here in this godforsaken wilderness. And he would die a poor man.

* * *

Roland K. Bahill had traced Billie as far as the Adams Hotel. He set up headquarters there, calling in the sheriff of Maricopa County and asking him to look into the matter of his missing daughter personally. Two of Bahill's best men scoured the city. They found Julia Thomas, and the man who outfitted a woman who was headed into the Superstition Mountains.

"She's goin' after some tenderfoot, a real city fella," Ollie Hodge of the Red Indian Mercantile told a grim-faced Colonel Bahill. "Reckon she fancies him."

Roland K. Bahill stifled his anger. So the girl was making a fool of herself over Stevenson again. He'd take care of that soon enough. "Do you rent horses?" he asked.

"No, but I know someone who does."

Shaken by the gunshots and her guide's desertion, Billie made camp early. After hobbling the horse and mules, she built a fire and made dinner. Her appetite had returned the moment she'd left on this trip. Maybe her nausea was a thing of the past.

After eating, she sat before the fire, feeling terribly alone. A coyote howled and yipped close by. The flickering fire normally would have kept her fears at bay, but this was the Superstitions. Pulling her serape more tightly around her shoulders, she jumped like a cat at every sound.

Before spreading out her bedroll, Billie pounded the ground with a stick to scare away anything that might want to crawl in with her.

She wrapped herself tightly in the blankets, and soon dozed off.

It was still dark when she awoke. A dry cucumber smell tainted her nostrils. Suddenly she realized she wasn't alone. Something solid and bulky was snuggled up against her calf.

Like a many-tined fork, fear pierced her heart. A snake. That was the cucumber smell; someone had once told her that snakes—rattlesnakes—had that smell. She froze, her paralysis due more to abject terror than to any act of self-preservation. She'd heard about this before, but it had never happened to her. The cowhands had told her that snakes liked warmth as much as anybody, and often crawled into bedrolls with humans.

She looked down at the mound wedged into the blankets near her leg, and her worst fears were confirmed. It was big. Rattlesnakes were big.

The fork jabbed again at her heart. Heat suffused her skin; perspiration trickled down her armpits. Her face burned. She lay there, legs as stiff as boards, adrenaline pumping through her veins like a roaring river, demanding action. The roaring was in her ears, too. She rummaged through her memory for the hypothetical knowledge she had learned, but came away with a fistful of emptiness and panic that filled her brain with tortured screams.

Logic told her the snake could be one of the harmless varieties, but in her heart she knew it was a rattlesnake. She saw in her mind's eye its broad, flat, triangular head, the beady eyes.

Think! There's a way out of this.

She pictured its fangs sinking in, injecting its poison.

And then it came to her with a rush like a log-jam breaking in a river. It was like that magic trick of pulling the tablecloth out from under the dishes. You just remained motionless, tensing yourself, and then with one quick, fluid motion, you pulled out. That was the conventional wisdom.

She thought of the consequences if the conventional wisdom failed her. Thought of the fangs sinking into her flesh, here, miles from civilization. Would it hurt the baby? Would it kill the baby?

I have to. It was either that or wait for the rattlesnake to wake up.

She propped herself up on her elbows, making sure her legs didn't move. Thrusting her palms into the dirt, she tensed her muscles. On the count of three.

One. Two.

What if the bedroll was too tight? What if her knees came up and met resistance, and her legs were trapped? The rattler would be awake then, and very angry.

Tentatively she pushed at the blankets with her hands. They seemed loose enough. If she jackknifed her knees, the best thing to do was to lift her legs up and out as fast as possible. That meant that she might flip the blankets up in the air.

I can do it. The force built up in her again, her muscles taut as cables. Electricity seemed to quiver through her, sending messages to the muscles of her thighs, knees, legs.

One.

Two.

Three! She whipped her knees up and out, rolled and slithered through the dirt, amazed to realize she hadn't been bitten.

She stared at the bedroll. The mound remained motionless for a few moments; then the blankets rippled. As Billie watched in horror, the snake straightened into one long, thick lath. Still sluggish, it wound its way over to the saddle Billie had used as her pillow, and coiled up against it.

Even in the darkness, Billie could see the rattles on its tail.

Shaking with dread, she wrapped her serape around her and backed away from the blankets. She debated shooting the snake, but the gunshots might attract unwanted attention. The memory of the rifle shots this afternoon were enough to make her cautious. There were other people in these mountains besides Elliot and herself.

After putting on her boots and taking her gun—there would be no more nasty surprises tonight—Billie clambered up onto a broad, flat rock that overlooked camp. Huddled with her back against the hill, she waited for dawn.

She dozed.

Buttermilk nickered. Her eyes flew open. A

man stood over her, his large frame silhouetted against the indigo sky. Heart pounding, Billie reached for her gun.

"Better let it go," the man advised.

She raised her hands to show him she wouldn't touch the gun. Blood pounded in her ears, and her heart stampeded.

Suddenly the pins at her scalp came loose and her hair tumbled down around her shoulders. Now he would know she was a woman. Panic threatened to choke her. For the first time Billie realized just how foolish this adventure was.

"What the—?" The man broke off in the middle of his question and laughed.

"What's so funny?" she demanded, trying to keep the strain out of her voice. Something about him was familiar, but she couldn't see his features. His broad-shouldered frame was menacing enough.

Holstering his gun, the man walked toward her, tilting his face up so that the faint light of the dying moon played across his face. "If it isn't Billie Bahill. You don't look like a kidnap victim to me," the Arizona Ranger said, and laughed again.

Chapter Seven

Billie stared at the man she had last seen at La Zanja. A myriad of questions filled her mind, chief among them how the ranger had come to be standing here by her campfire in the Superstition Mountains in the early morning hours. And what did he mean by telling her she didn't look like a kidnap victim? Kidnap victim!

Suddenly it became clear. Her father must have made up some cock-and-bull story about her being abducted. No doubt he was too proud to admit she would leave him under her own steam. Trying to keep her voice from shaking, she demanded, "Is that what my father told you?" When he didn't reply, fury gripped her. "He sent you, didn't he?"

"I haven't seen your father since I spent the night at La Zanja."

"What were you doing sneaking around my camp in the middle of the night if you weren't looking for me?"

"I was looking for someone, but it wasn't you."

Was he telling the truth? Was it just coincidence that the ranger had turned up here in the Superstitions? "Who are you looking for?"

"I believe that's my business."

"How come you thought I was kidnapped?"

"I heard about it in Globe. Your father's burning the telegraph wires looking for you."

"Is there a reward?"

"Yes."

"Are you thinking of collecting it?"

"No, but I'd sure like to know what you're doing out here."

Billie couldn't help glancing toward the saddle, and saw with relief that the snake was gone. "I believe that's my business."

He nodded his acknowledgment.

It was cold. They stood in the clearing like two actors frozen in a tableau. He held her gaze, his eyes sparkling with something suspiciously close to amusement. Billie thought she must look a sight in her shirt, trousers, dangling suspenders and the serape pulled across her shoulders.

The ranger shifted his stance, his movements as slow as those of a stretching cat. He put one foot up on a rock, his gaze never leaving her face. The uncomfortable silence grew. Billie felt the urge to say something—anything—to avoid the silence. "I guess you'll be on your way, now that you see I'm not the one you're looking for."

He made no move to go.

"What's the matter?"

"Aren't you going to invite me to breakfast?" he asked.

"Breakfast?"

"It's morning, isn't it?" He motioned to the sky. In the span of time he'd been here, the heavens had lightened to pale lavender. Stars glittered in the broad expanse, and the moon had turned to a translucent eggshell. The desert itself was washed in a gray half-light, and the dark jumble of shapes around them began to take on identities—brush, trees, cactus and rocks. "Of course I can always go over the hill and start my own campfire. Seems a shame, though, when you've already got one here."

Nettled, Billie replied, "What do you take me for? I wasn't raised in a barn."

His grin widened a notch. Billie realized she looked as if a barn were precisely the kind of place she had been raised.

"I get the impression you'd rather be alone," he said.

"After breakfast is soon enough for me." She didn't know if she could trust him, but her sense of hospitality had been ingrained since childhood. No doubt the ranger suspected that was the case.

Billie's breakfast was a lot like the dinner she'd made the night before. She had always been a good camp cook. After spreading the bread batter thinly at the bottom of the iron skillet, she laid the pan on hot coals. When the bread formed a crust, she stood it on its edge, within baking distance of the coals, but far enough away so that it would rise. Next she cut bacon into the pan and fried it, afterward rapping the pan against a rock until the grease flew out. Transferring the bacon to a plate, she added water and coffee to the pan and let the water come to a boil. When the residual bacon fat melted in from both sides, the coffee was ready. Sam opened a can of tomatoes.

For the first half of the meal, they ate in silence, sitting cross-legged before the fire and occasionally warming their hands over the flames. Billie tried to hide her nervousness. The more she thought about it, the less likely it seemed that the ranger's presence was a coincidence.

"This is a pretty spot," Sam Gray said casually.

Suspicious, half expecting to see some of her father's men lurking in the bushes, Billie glanced around. She *had* chosen well, a small clearing sheltered from view of the trail. Beside her, a many-armed saguaro cactus towered into the sky. Desert zinnia was scattered in golden-green clumps across the desert floor, white flowers as fragile as moths. Mesquite trees, buckhorn cholla and burrobrush, haloed by the morning light, were feathered with delicate shadows. The sky had already been bleached by the fierce new sun to a greenish turquoise, dusted with stars. Around them, the desert mountains stretched like massive lions' paws, relaxed in sleep but potentially dangerous. On this quiet morning, it was easy for Billie to imagine that she and the ranger were the only people in the entire world.

Billie reflected that Sam Gray's presence somehow made the desert seem less menacing and more beautiful, perhaps because he looked at home here, and his comfort with their surroundings transmitted across the space between them, relaxing her.

The ranger spooned up more tomatoes. He gave her the impression that there was nothing more on his mind than enjoying a good breakfast, but was he trying to trick her into letting her guard down? Billie's hand touched the solid handle of her Colt .44. She would not go back, not now, when she was this close to finding Elliot. If Sam Gray tried to press her, she would hold the gun on him.

But could she shoot him? She swallowed. Surely the threat that she would shoot him would be enough.

She watched the ranger covertly, her mind racing. Could she believe him, or had her father sent him to find her? Ranger Gray said he was looking for someone else, but he could be lying. She scrutinized him from beneath her lashes. He didn't look as if he were hiding anything, but it didn't pay to take anything for granted. She hadn't come this far to be unceremoniously dumped back on La Zanja by her father's paid lackey. Billie decided on a fishing expedition. "The rangers go where they're needed, any place in Arizona. Is that right?" she ventured.

"That's right. You're a good cook."

She ignored the compliment and pressed on. "How does that work, exactly? Does the county sheriff ask for help, and the rangers send the next available man?" She pushed the heel of her bread around the tomato and bacon juices, tucked the dripping crust into her mouth, chewed thoughtfully, and swallowed. "Like now, for instance. Are you on a mission now?" Her voice held just the right tone of polite interest, but his expression told her she had failed. He stared at her, and she imagined he could read her thoughts as plainly as she could read a book.

"I already told you your father didn't send me."

"No?"

"No." He leaned back, setting his empty plate on the ground. "But if you'll take my advice, you'll turn around right now and head for home."

"Thanks for the advice."

"You're a woman alone on the most treacherous piece of ground in the territory."

"That's—"

"Your business. You've made that clear enough." He picked up the blue-speckled graniteware plate beside him, then abruptly reached across her. His shoulder, momentarily brushing hers, ignited tiny explosions up and down her arm. Startled, Billie jerked away.

"I thought I'd get your plate. Since you cooked, I'll clean up."

He could have overpowered and disarmed her

with that move, but he hadn't. Maybe he was telling the truth. Warily Billie handed him the plate and other utensils. Why had she reacted that way? Just the slightest contact with him—even through all her thick clothing—had sent a kinetic energy through her veins like electric wire. She could still feel the ghost of his touch on her arm, raising goose bumps. When Billie looked up, he was standing in front of her, watching her carefully. "Something wrong?"

"Other than the fact that I don't know if I can trust you? No."

He didn't move. His legs were slightly splayed, the Cuban-heeled boots planted in the sand not a foot from her. His spurs were the Mexican kind, with big rowels, and the light caught them. Billie was aware of his legs, the towering strength of him, but kept her gaze on his face. His eyes were searching, as if he were trying to figure her out. Billie couldn't really concentrate on his face, though. Some part of her wanted to look down and stop about eye level, where she knew his shotgun chaps cut away from his trousers. The place her father called—in animals—the business end. Some fiendish, horrible part of her wanted to examine that juncture, just to see if he looked any different from Elliot. . . .

Swallowing, Billie clutched her serape around her and stood up, almost dizzy. "Don't you think it's time you moved on? It'll get hot soon."

"We could ride together."

"I don't think that's such a good idea." She wished he would go away. He made her feel distinctly uncomfortable. The renegade thoughts she had just entertained made her feel dirty. And then another thought crossed her mind. Although she had been well for days, she felt a tad queasy. It was probably the bacon, but it wouldn't do to let him know too much about her. The sooner she got rid of him, the better. She had a feeling that if Sam Gray suspected she was pregnant, he would force her to go back. He did not impress her as the kind of man who would leave her out here alone if he knew.

His teal-colored eyes seemed to drill into her own, and as she watched they seemed to turn greener. "I could escort you back to the Bark Ranch. Jim Bark'll see you get safely back to Phoenix."

"I'm not going back to Phoenix."

From the corner of her eye, she saw something move.

Sam spun around. "Will you look at that?"

Billie followed his gaze. The rattlesnake had come out of hiding. With agonizing slowness it slithered through the sand toward a clump of burrobrush. Billie reached for her gun. She had a good shot at him. Sam caught her arm. "Let him go."

"How can you be sentimental about a rattlesnake?"

"I believe in live and let live."

Shaking, she pulled away from him. The memory of the snake's cool, heavy body pressed against her legs sent a wave of nausea over her. Her hand flew to her mouth and she clamped down on her queasiness with an iron will. Sam Gray was beside her in an instant, his hands on her shoulders. She felt him, his closeness, like shelter against a cold wind.

"Are you all right?"

She couldn't stop the tremor that ran through her body, and cursed her own weakness. Why was she reacting like this now, in front of this stranger? The danger was over.

"Sit down," he said. His voice was stern but gentle. He led her to a rock and pushed gently on her shoulders.

The nausea passed. "I'm all right now."

"I wondered why you weren't in your bedroll." His voice held the slightest hint of accusation. "He didn't bite you, did he? No. You'd be sick by now. What happened?"

She leaned her elbows on her knees, her head in her hands, and gulped a deep breath. "Nothing. I just woke up and it was sleeping right next to me. I got out," she added defiantly.

"You're lucky he didn't bite you!"

"Lucky? Luck had nothing to do with it!"

"You see how dangerous it is out here? You could be sick right now, maybe even dying. And if I hadn't come along—"

"You didn't save me! I got myself out of that situation! Because I know what I'm doing, and I don't need some patronizing, sanctimonious . . . cowboy to tell me what to do!"

His face was like granite. "You're only a day's ride from the Bark Ranch. Why don't you turn around now, before you get yourself killed?"

"Why don't you mind your own business?"

"If you don't care about yourself, what about your father?"

"My father?"

"If I were him, I'd be sick with worry."

She blurted out without thinking, "He doesn't care about me. He wouldn't care if I were an old maid forever, as long as I waited on him hand and foot!"

He stared at her. "What are you talking about?"

"Nothing!" She had let things go too far. If there was any hope that the ranger would leave her alone, she'd have to look and act reasonable. "As you can see, nobody has kidnapped me. My father tends to . . . exaggerate things. I can take care of myself. Why don't you just go on looking for whoever you've been sent to find, and let me get on with my own business?"

"What are you doing here?"

"I don't have to explain my actions to you. I can take care of myself."

"You think you're pretty tough, don't you? I know you can handle a horse and shoot straight, but that's not enough. Not out here. Do you really think that getup you're wearing will fool anybody?" He paused. Billie supposed he was waiting for what he said to sink in. She returned his gaze evenly.

"The men I'm trailing are killers. They robbed a payroll in Globe and they killed four innocent people. They don't care who they kill, either, because one of the victims was a pregnant woman.

If that doesn't make you want to go home, then you're crazier than I thought."

"Are you through?" she asked, her voice carefully bland.

"I'm through." He walked over to his horse, tightened the cinch with economical swiftness and swung aboard. Twisting around in the saddle, he added, "But I'd watch my back if I were you."

Then he led his mule up and over the little hill that had guarded her campsite, and was gone from view.

Billie was stunned. Was the ranger telling her the truth, or just trying to scare her? Fear, chill and numbing as creek water, spread through her vitals. She should go home, forget this madness.

But what did she have to go home to? Her father? Even if she could forgive him—which she couldn't—how would he treat her when he knew about the child? What kind of life would that be?

With or without Elliot, she would raise this baby, but he had the right to know about his child. She had to find him. Besides, he could be in danger, if what the ranger said was true.

The ranger was tough. He'd find the killers. As a matter of fact, there was a good chance they weren't anywhere around here. But she'd keep down in the canyons to be safe, and tonight she'd forgo the fire.

The dispirited-looking cottonwood tree and the copse of desert willow around it meant there was water under the sand. Fueled by thirst, fever and dementia, Elliot threw himself to his knees and started digging like a dog after a bone.

At last he was rewarded with a shallow dip in the sand, a tiny puddle of water. In his delirious state he thought the small, animal-like noises filling his brain must have come from somewhere else. But they came from his own throat, creaking like a rusty hinge. He thrust his face in the puddle and lapped at the water, dug some more with pain-blunted fingers, and drank again. Sand slithered down his throat with the water, but he didn't care. He could feel life swelling in him, and after he'd had his fill, he splashed the rest on his face and his throbbing arm.

He fell asleep beside the damp spot in the sand, and awakened in the late afternoon.

As he lay there, he saw the rusty pickax lying half-hidden in the sand near his face. Beyond it, high up on the hill, his blurred vision picked out a gouged hole, most of it boarded up with rotten timber. Directly underneath, Elliot saw uprooted bushes in a tumbled scree of rocks and dirt. It looked as if the hole had been deliberately covered up, but a recent rockslide had exposed it to view.

A mine.

A hidden mine. Julia's words: *You will find gold.* It had to be!

He'd found the Lost Dutchman Mine.

Sam was an hour down the trail before his anger wore off enough for him to think straight. He couldn't leave Billie Bahill alone out here.

He thought of Howard Daw, the slimy way he'd looked at Billie on La Zanja, and his stomach lurched. The men he was chasing were Howard Daw's brothers, and he doubted they would show her any mercy if she were to run into them. Like as not, they'd have their fun with her and then kill her.

His heart twisted in his chest. She might be a fool, but she was a brave fool. He couldn't let anything happen to her.

He glanced in the direction of the sun. It was around nine o'clock now. He could take Billie back to the Bark Ranch and be back out on the job by late tomorrow morning.

It wasn't as if he were hot on the killers' trail. After four days in the Superstitions, Sam hadn't found a trace of them.

The desert mountains were a maze of trails. Some had been well trammeled by shod hooves; others were little more than deer and javelina paths. Although this mountain range wasn't many miles across as the crow flew, there were hundreds of dead-end canyons, ridges, defiles and hills. Early on he had realized it would be impossible to find the killers unless he spotted them first.

They could be holed up in some canyon near a spring. They could have made it out of the mountains by now. They could be anywhere.

Suddenly he heard a distant rumble. Thunder? He looked up at the sky. It stretched above him, bright blue and cloudless. The summer thunderstorms were almost two months away.

Sam was surprised at the goose bumps on his arms. The eeriness of this place must be getting to him.

Damn it! He hated the thought of giving them even a day's more head start. It was like trying to find a needle in a haystack anyway, but the colder their trail, the less likely it was he would run across them.

But he couldn't let Billie Bahill stay out here. Sam reined Panther around and started back up the trail. What he was about to do would make her hate him forever.

Chapter Eight

As Billie reached the bend in the trail, Buttermilk shied violently. Startled, Billie looked up.

Sam Gray blocked the path, elbows resting on his pommel, rifle across his lap.

She knew immediately what he was up to. He was going to take her back. She reached for her gun.

"You point that gun at me, you'd better plan to use it," the Ranger said. He leveled his gaze at her, his dark blue eyes fathomless.

Billie's heart quivered like a covey of quail just before flight. He meant what he said. Her hand dropped away from the gun. Maybe she could talk her way out of it. "What are you doing here? I thought you were looking for robbers."

Sam leaned forward in his saddle. "I can't let you stay out here."

"*You* can't let me stay out here? Who are you? My guardian?"

"I'm a lawman, duly appointed by the governing body of this territory. I'm taking you back, so you might as well face it like the well-bred lady you are."

"You tricked me! You told me you were after robbers!"

His jaw had set and his mouth straightened into a grim line. "Let's go," he said.

"What are you going to do? Handcuff me? Hog-tie me? Is that the kind of man you are? You'd better do something, because I'm going on." She clucked her tongue at the mules and nudged Buttermilk's sides with her legs. She would go around him.

Sam Gray veered his horse to block her path, and the two animals collided. The lead mule crashed into them, and the second one veered around and started to kick. Buttermilk pivoted, his hindquarters crashing into the ranger's horse. Stirrups hooked. Billie's leg was crushed by the ranger's. All the time he stared at her, his eyes steely, the color of the ocean sparkling hard and dark in the sun. She kicked Buttermilk again, and the cow pony moved away from her leg, driving into the coal black horse, his head thrust up and over the other animal's neck. The ranger's horse was bigger than hers, and stood like a rock.

"Get out of my way!"

For answer, the ranger reached out and grabbed both of her hands. He held them up before him in an iron grip, his eyes boring into hers. She could feel the biting strength in his fingers, the bolt of energy that seemed to shoot up through the sinews of his arms to the coiled power of his muscles.

"Will you come peaceably?" he demanded.

"Get out of my way!" she repeated, trying futilely to jerk out of his grasp. "You're hurting me!" She kicked her heels into Buttermilk's sides, hoping to shove the ranger's mount off balance.

The horses drove into each other, their legs shifting in a melee of dust. The ranger transferred both of her wrists into one hand. Her fingers slick with sweat, Billie tried to worm out of his grip again.

Suddenly there was a loud snap. Metal, hard and unyielding, enclosed her left wrist. Handcuffs!

She watched in horror as the Arizona Ranger snapped a cuff on her other wrist. After plucking Buttermilk's reins from her grasp, he reached over and took her gun, sticking it in the waistband of his trousers. He snugged her horse up close to his right.

Billie almost sagged in the saddle, but pride held her upright. She glared at the ranger, letting the hatred she felt for him transmit across the space between them. He seemed unperturbed by her animosity.

Time stood still. The dust settled, and for the first time Billie was aware of the sun like a flatiron on her back, the odors of sweating horsehide, dust and the acrid smell of desert willow assaulting her nostrils. Buttermilk snorted. Billie tried to swallow, but her mouth was so dry she felt only a dry click in her throat. "What are you going to do now?" she asked, trying to keep the defiance in her voice but failing miserably.

"*We* are going to ride."

Not if she had anything to say about it! Handcuffed or not, Billie could still make a run for it. She didn't need reins; Buttermilk had been trained to respond to leg signals. She clapped her heels into Buttermilk's sides.

The gelding lunged forward but stopped abruptly at the pressure of the bit. Billie had forgotten that the ranger held the reins.

"You won't behave, will you?"

Billie paid no heed to the steel in his voice. Her gaze fastened on the headstall of the bridle. Even handcuffed, she could push the top of the bridle over Buttermilk's ears. The headstall would then slip uselessly to the ground, leaving the ranger holding a handful of reins but no horse.

Billie reached forward. The ranger's hand shot out and grabbed her wrist. His eyes drilled into her own, and she realized that he understood what she was trying to do. Before she knew it, he had clasped her around the waist and pulled her onto his own mount.

"Let go of me!" Facedown across the dark bay's neck, she thrashed her legs. Although she was strong, the ranger seemed unfazed by her efforts. She might as well have been a bug caught in a web, for all the effect her struggles had on the man.

With one hand on the waistband of her pants and the other holding her by the collar, he lifted her up into the air and plopped her unceremoniously down before him so that she sat astride his horse. He transferred one muscular arm to her rib cage beneath her breasts and pulled her back toward him, up and over the saddle horn until she was crushed against his length, at the same time sliding backward so that the two of them were wedged between the pommel and the cantle of the saddle. With an arm as unyielding as an iron bar, he held her tightly to him.

Billie felt as if the breath had been knocked out of her. How had she ended up in such an ignominious position? Surprise turned to fury. "Let me down!"

His voice was grim. "I can't trust you."

"You have no right to do this to me! Put me down at once!"

"Sorry."

"I hate you!"

"I don't blame you much," he replied evenly. "But like it or not, we're going to be pretty close for a while, so you'd better make the best of it." He clucked to his horse and they started forward. The sudden motion threw her back against his chest. She stiffened, trying to hold herself away from him, but it was impossible.

This part of the trail was well traveled and wider than most horse paths, so the two horses could walk abreast. The mules lined up behind them along the path, happy to be heading back in the direction they had last perceived as home.

The longer they rode, the more his presence disturbed her. She hated being forced into touching someone she didn't know, but there was nothing she could do. She could feel the firm musculature of his chest rubbing her shoulder blades through the material of their shirts; his body was disturbingly warm against her back. It caused a tingle that she didn't like. Her heart beat like a tiny fist against her throat, and a ticklish sensation burrowed deep in her stomach. Why did this man's touch bother her so much? Back at La Zanja she'd ridden double with one of the hands after the horse she was riding broke its leg, but it hadn't affected her like this!

It was almost as though she liked it. That certainly couldn't be true!

Sam Gray's masculine scent enveloped her. The hard line of his thighs pressed against the backs of her legs, and she was uncomfortably aware of where her backside ended and the fork of his thighs began. After her experience with Elliot, it was difficult to keep her mind from straying into forbidden territory. She tried not to think about it, but the idea that she was close to him—all of him—caused pleasurable frissons up and down her spine.

She tried to think of something else—like how much she hated him.

They rode in silence for a while. Billie simmered, glaring straight ahead. The faint timpani of thunder sounded. A thunderhead boiled up over the ridge opposite them. The cloud glittered pristine white against the sky.

"Looks like we're in for a storm," Sam Gray said. When Billie didn't reply, he continued as if she had. "You know, the Spaniards called these mountains *Sierra de la Espuma*, mountains of the foam. Maybe because of the way the thunderheads appear out of nowhere. That one there does look like foam. What do you think?"

She refused to answer.

The horse stumbled and the ranger's chin bumped her shoulder. Several days' worth of beard rasped against her cheek and she jerked her head forward. His voice rumbled softly in her ear. It seemed to come from his chest. "Superstitions run rampant here. A lot of people have been killed looking for that gold—if it exists at all. These mountains are sacred to the Apache, and so is gold. They believe it belongs to the sun, and they killed anyone who tried to take it out of here. Of course we don't have to worry about Apaches anymore, but Jacob Waltz did. Can you feel it? As if someone's watching us. The Pima Indians think this area is sacred, too. They believe that a giant worm lies under the earth, and gnaws at it from within. That's why the mountain changes so much, why it moves—"

A rock trickled down the ridge next to them. Startled, Billie jumped, then relaxed into the shelter of his body.

Sam grinned as she recoiled. "See? It does

move. You don't believe there's a worm under here, do you? No? I didn't think so. But sometimes at night it sounds like it, doesn't it? Ever lie under a mesquite tree at night and listen to the limbs creak? You can hear the whistling and moaning of wind through the holes in the rocks. It's enough to scare anyone."

Why was he telling her these stories? To scare her? Well, she didn't scare, and as soon as he delivered her to the Bark Ranch, she'd turn right around and come back.

For the next hour, the only sound was the scrape and click of shod hooves on rock, the snorting of horses, the creak of saddles. Sam Gray didn't seem the worse for wear, even though he had his hands full with two horses and three mules—and one furious woman. Was he a man at all, or some kind of machine? The silence was unnerving, as if something were wrong. Every once in a while Billie stared at the alien terrain and thought about what Gray had said about the Apaches.

Nonsense. The Apaches were long gone; they'd settled on the reservations for good. But the rifle shots she'd heard yesterday . . . a hunter? Or Reiney Petrasch guarding his part of the mountain? She wondered if Ranger Gray really believed a worm resided under the earth, or if he was just trying to throw a scare into her. There had to be some reason for this area's bad reputation . . . she thought of Elliot out here all by himself, and her resolve hardened. If only she could get rid of the ranger.

Once, Gray's horse spooked at something on the trail, and the ranger's arm shot out to steady her—completely unnecessary, since she was practically glued to the saddle and could ride any horse in her sleep. She couldn't help shivering, though, at the controlled power in the ranger's grip, the firmness of his fingers as they closed around her upper arm. Golden curls of hair glistened on his tanned forearm. Billie could clearly see the interplay of sinew and muscle that gave his hands their strength. She still couldn't believe the ease with which he had put her on his horse, lifting her as easily as if she were a feather.

The man was treating her like a tenderfoot, holding her like that! She jerked away from him, disgust in every line of her body.

He dropped his hand. Humor flitted like a shadow across the unruffled calm of his eyes. "Did I insult you?" he asked, his voice wry.

She clamped down on the retort that sprang to her lips. She would not boast about what kind of horsewoman she was; he'd only laugh at her.

Sam didn't pursue it. He had his own problems to think about. With every step Panther took, Billie's body rocked gently back against him. He could feel her tension just under the surface, and her anger. Billie Bahill was a taut bundle of energy, a fighter, and that made him admire her all the more. But it wasn't admiration that caused the quiver of excitement in his stomach. He realized after several miles that she was affecting him in other ways.

121

She was slender and light boned, and her curves fit against him as if she were made for him. Even the men's clothing looked good on her, although he didn't remember her being so flat chested. He wondered if she had bound her breasts to aid her disguise. The scent of her wafted up to him, a sage scent redolent of campfires in the open air and warm skin. Her complexion made him think of golden caramel, ripe and smooth. He was tantalized by the softness at the nape of her neck where a filigree of her blue-black hair had pulled out of its pins in tiny wisps. He ached to kiss her. Of course he wouldn't take advantage of her that way, but her proximity teased his senses, fanning his desire into a burning brand. The friction between them was unbearable. He was the tinder, and one spark from her would set up a conflagration he could not control.

He shifted back against the cantle, trying to create some space between her back end and his own increasingly mutinous body, but there was no relief from the throbbing heat. He wondered if she could feel his arousal. He doubted she would know what it was.

This could not go on. He would have to secure her some other way.

Billie was surprised when the ranger halted the horses.

He leaned past her to remove the coiled rope strapped to her pommel. A curious sensation bolted through the pit of her stomach when he brushed her arm with his sleeve. After dismounting, he helped her down. His hands spanned her waist for the briefest instant, causing an embarrassing outbreak of goose bumps. He lifted her onto Buttermilk. Her stomach surged up toward her throat and back down again, and the tickling feeling almost made her pass out. He tied the rope he'd taken from Buttermilk's pommel to her handcuffs with a deft series of knots. Buttermilk always wore a halter under his bridle, so it was a simple matter for Gray to remove Buttermilk's bridle, unknot the halter's lead rope from around the buckskin's neck and, on remounting, dally the lead rope around his saddle horn, along with the rope to Billie's shackles.

"What are you doing?" Billie demanded.

"Making you more comfortable."

Comfortable. She would not tell him that she'd grown accustomed to his body pressing against hers, and that the air against her back felt unpleasantly cold all of a sudden.

"You could thank me," he said as he gathered his reins.

"Thank you! Of all the bald-faced gall!" The tide of anger suddenly crested and broke over her in an icy wave. "Out of curiosity, why did you make me ride that way with you all this time? To break my spirit?"

"No," he replied grimly. "To show you what I'll do if you try to escape. I figure an hour like that is enough to make anyone think twice about trying it."

"Did you do that to Howard Daw?"

"No."

"Why not? Was it because he was a man and I'm a woman? Do you like to torture women, Mr. Gray? It hardly seems fair that you would treat a common criminal better than me."

He stiffened. His eyes seemed to sharpen to the intensity of steel rivets, and an angry shade of white bracketed his mouth. "I used other methods with him. You wouldn't like them."

"Or is it the only way you can get a woman to come near you? Is that it, Ranger Gray?"

That point hit home. Without a word, he started forward, pulling her along with him.

As they continued through the canyon, Billie realized that she had no chance to escape. He had her gun, he had control of her horse and she was handcuffed. The trail was too rocky for flight anyway. She would never achieve her aim by force. But she had found an Achilles' heel. The man didn't like to be considered unchivalrous to women. No doubt he fancied himself some kind of hero, galloping all over the territory, righting wrongs and dealing out justice at the end of a gun.

Billie had never played the part of the helpless heroine. She had always despised women who used their sex as a refuge from unpleasantness, who feigned frailty and stupidity to gain an advantage over men. It seemed hypocritical at worst, and at best a circuitous way of achieving their aims. But obviously the ranger was of the old school. He liked his women simpering and vaporish, liked to feel he was protecting their easily injured sensibilities. Perhaps she could reason with him, play to that chivalrous part of his nature.

"Must we move so fast? This heat is terrible," she said, her voice as soft and fluttery as she could make it.

He laughed. "You'd stoop to anything to get your way, wouldn't you?"

"I don't know what you're talking about."

"Miss Bahill, don't try to be something you're not. It only succeeds in making you look foolish."

Her face suffused with heat. What did he take her for? A complete tomboy? "Why are you doing this to me?" she said angrily.

"It's my duty."

"I thought you were after robbers."

"I am."

"Won't taking me back slow you down? What if you take me in and let the killers escape?"

Ah, she'd gotten him there. He met her question with silence.

She pressed her point. "Your first duty is to the Arizona rangers, isn't it? Aren't you shirking your responsibilities?"

The look he shot her seethed with anger. His face made her think of a mask, with two smoldering eyeholes. "We're less than a day's ride from the Bark Ranch. It won't slow me down that much."

"Please let me go. I'll pay you twice as much as the reward if you let me go now."

She should have known that would make him angrier. He stopped abruptly and swung around in his saddle. "You can forget trying to bribe me." His eyes searched hers. "For the last time, what are you doing out here?"

She swallowed. Maybe if he knew, he'd help her. It was a slim chance, but worth the effort. "I'm looking for my fiancé."

"Stevenson?"

"Yes. He . . . wants me to meet him here. So you see, I'll be just fine, as soon as I meet up with him."

"He wants you to meet him *here?* In the middle of nowhere? What kind of man would ask a woman to do that?" But even as he said the words, Billie saw comprehension dawn on his face. "He's not meeting you," he said abruptly.

"Yes, he is."

"Why don't you try telling the truth?"

She debated for a moment. What would it hurt if he knew? "He doesn't know I'm here exactly, but I can't let him come out here alone. He's only doing this for me."

An expression flitted across Sam's face, one she could not fathom. Was it pity?

"For your information, he's gone to find the Lost Dutchman Mine so he can support me when we get married!"

Sam's eyes narrowed, but he said nothing.

"I can't let him go out there alone. He's not used to this kind of country. He's completely . . ."

"Helpless?"

She wanted to slap the derisive expression right off his face. Instead she bit her tongue. At least he was talking to her, and there was a chance she could get him to capitulate.

"What about the rustlers?"

"The what?"

"Last time I saw you, you were set on saving La Zanja from rustlers. Now you're out here traipsing across the mountains after your fiancé. Don't you care about your ranch anymore?"

"It's none of my concern."

"Your father—"

"My father, if you must know, has cut me off without a cent. He's disowned me, so I can hardly mean that much to him!"

"Then why did he put out a reward for you?"

"For someone who isn't interested in the reward, you certainly talk about it a lot. You may pretend you're doing the honorable thing by taking me back, but you just want the money."

This time he didn't rise to the bait. He merely shrugged, his shuttered eyes lazy. "Think what you like."

"I'll just turn right around after you leave me at the Bark Ranch and come back out here. Why bother, unless it's for the reward money?"

"Once I leave you at the ranch, it's out of my hands. You'll be someone else's problem." He kicked his horse into a punishing trot, and Buttermilk followed.

"I'm not giving up," she said to his back.

"I don't expect you to."

Buttermilk's fast trot was naturally bumpy. It

was twice as bad when a person was handcuffed, so Billie was breathless when she spoke again. "What do you think this will accomplish, then?"

"Peace of mind."

"For my father?"

"For me."

"Have you ever been in love, Mr. Gray? Do you know what it's like to love someone so much that you'd walk to the end of the earth for them?" She gasped. A stitch in her side made her want to beg him to stop, but she refused to give in to it.

"Some people aren't worth walking across the street for," he replied, his voice even despite the fast trotting pace.

"You don't like him either! You're just like my father!"

"I don't have to like him. It's a free country."

She couldn't stand for another person to cast aspersions on Elliot. "Why?" she heard herself cry, and recoiled at the plaintiveness in her voice. "Just because he's not a cowboy. Just because he's not some brutish, gun-toting Philistine—"

Sam shot a grin at her. "Like me?"

"Like you! I should have expected you'd have the same opinions as my father. You're just the kind of oaf who would value brawn over brains!" She stood up in the stirrups, shoving her manacled hands onto the saddle horn to keep from being bounced to kingdom come.

He grinned again. "Want me to slow to a walk?"

"I'm fine the way I am."

"Suit yourself."

By late afternoon, the lone white cloud had turned into a mass of thunderheads, heavy with rain. Thunder shook the canyon walls, and lightning burst out of the darkness, twisted white wires connecting with the ground. Dust shuttled up the canyon, and the wind howled.

"We've got to get to higher ground," the ranger shouted as the first large splashes of rain hit them.

Billie nodded. To the north, she could already see a bluish gray veil of rain rolling along the mesa. It was only a matter of a few minutes before the dry streambed they'd been following would be a swollen river.

"Let's head for that outcropping up there. It might shelter us from the lightning," Sam called, urging his horse up the steep rocky slope. Buttermilk and the mules scrambled up behind him. Billie leaned forward, her head bent down to her horse's mane. They followed an invisible switchback up through the brush. Each time thunder boomed, Billie hunched her shoulders, certain that lightning would hit them. Rain lashed her, almost obscuring her vision. She could only cling to the saddle, huddled under her sodden poncho, and hope for the best. A couple of times Buttermilk slipped in the churned-up mud, or his shod hooves skated wildly on the slick rock faces. The mules clattered and skidded nonchalantly behind him. They were as agile as mountain goats.

At last they reached a level place up on the ridge. A giant boulder reared up above them, tilted forward so that it would give them shelter. The underside of the boulder was charred by fire.

"Looks like someone else had the same idea," Sam said, as he dismounted and kicked at the campfire ring. "We should be safe here."

She slithered down from Buttermilk, soaking wet, her hands bound together by the handcuffs. Shivering under the sparse shelter of a paloverde tree, she watched the ranger make the fire.

Because of the wind and the occasional snatches of rain that battered the sheltering boulder, Sam had difficulty lighting the fire. When it was going, he glanced at Billie.

"You'd better get out of those things," he said.

"How do you propose I do that?" She held up her hands, anger boiling up in her like noxious steam. The weight of the manacles on her rain-slick skin had already caused small red weals, and in the rain her hands felt cold and devoid of feeling. Water trickled down the back of her neck, she was shivering uncontrollably, and that cretin just stood there watching her as if he thought she'd try something else.

"Do you promise you won't try to escape?"

"Where am I going to escape to? All I see from here are canyons, and they're uncrossable."

"Passion has been known to win over logic."

"Hold your gun on me, then."

"That won't be necessary." Sam took hobbles

from his pack and hobbled the horses and mules, then walked over to her. "Hold your hands up."

She did, trembling with reaction. Why did being manacled make her feel like some kind of slave? As if her spirit had been broken? *I'm still Elizabeth Devereaux Bahill,* she told herself angrily. *A modern woman, not some sheep-eyed schoolgirl, flattered at the attention of a man— any man.* And yet, as Sam leaned toward her, she felt a thrill glide up through her vitals, and an absurd burst of gratitude as the handcuffs came free. Rubbing her hands, Billie glared at her captor. "Does it make you feel like a big man, treating me like this?"

"I wish I didn't have to."

"If my father hears about this, he'll have your commission!"

The ranger cocked his head to the side and regarded her quizzically. "I thought you said your father disowned you."

"Not so much so that he wouldn't want revenge. He'd feel that about any possession he once owned."

"Does he worry about the steer he consigns to the dinner table?"

"Of course not."

"Then you're more than just his possession."

She stared at him. This man had answered every volley with one of his own. It was getting harder and harder to categorize him as a stupid brute.

"Where're your clothes? I assume you have a second set," he said briskly.

She nodded to one of the mules. The ranger returned with a roll of her clothes: a divided leather riding skirt, a wool shirt and leggings. He untied the yellow slicker from her saddle. "I'm sorry we didn't have time to put these on," he said quietly. "But the way that lightning was striking—"

"I couldn't have done it anyway," she replied, holding up her hands.

He caught her meaning, but said nothing.

"Will you go away while I change?"

"I'll turn my back."

"Bastard!"

"Where'd you learn language like that? On the range?"

"I hate you!"

"Let me know when I can turn around again," he replied equably. He turned away from her, hands in his pockets, and stared at the rain.

Billie glanced to her right, where the horses and mules stood patiently in the drumming rain. The ranger's rifle was slung in its scabbard near the saddle horn. The coal black gelding was scarcely six yards away.

The decision made, she stepped in that direction.

"I took the precaution of unloading the rifle," the ranger said, still staring straight in front of him. "If I hear you make one more step toward those horses, I'm putting the handcuffs on you again and you can sit up all night in those clothes. Best just do as I say, and get changed. I'll count to fifty. One. Two. Three . . ."

Furious, Billie reached for her clothes. She stripped quickly down to her chemise and drawers, which were also wringing wet. She couldn't put dry clothes over wet ones—

"Seventeen, eighteen . . ."

Billie turned away and unbuttoned the chemise with numb fingers. She shrugged out of it, pulled the wool shirt over her head and shoved her arms into the sleeves. The shirt dropped straight down over her bandaged chest, falling to her thighs. She picked at the string that tied the rolled skirt, frustrated by the tiny knot.

"Thirty-five, thirty-six, thirty-seven . . ."

Muttering with impotent anger, she picked the last of the knot free.

She scuffled with the skirt, which seemed to have a mind of its own. At last she was able to pull it up. The joined leather at the bottom would have to serve as drawers.

The skirt, without the usual soft muslin of her drawers, seemed strange, alien. She felt naked below, except for one disturbing moment when the stiff leather brushed the juncture between her legs.

It tickled.

Billie's face flamed.

"Fifty."

Sam Gray turned and scrutinized her, frowning. "You look different."

"Oh?"

"What do you have strapped around your chest?"

"It's none of your business!"

"You looked better that night at La Zanja."

"Is that all a woman needs to make an impression on you? A . . . bosom?" Scandalized by her own use of the word, she blushed.

He grinned. "Not too long ago you swore like a sailor. Lightning won't strike you for saying 'bosom.'"

"I don't want to discuss it anymore," she said stiffly. She tried to stand perfectly still so she would not experience that tickling sensation again.

"Are you still cold?"

"No."

"Why don't we sit by the fire? This storm won't let up anytime soon, and you'll get wet again."

She saw the wisdom of his suggestion. Leaving the shelter of the paloverde, she stepped gingerly over to the boulder.

"You're not saddle sore, are you?"

"I can ride all day and leave you gasping in my dust," she replied automatically.

There it was again! Billie winced as the leather brushed against her all too pleasurably. Her face was hot and she tried not to look at Sam.

She sat down. The volcanic formation sheltered only a narrow ledge of ground, so she had to sit close to the rock face. At least she managed to sit so that the rough seam of leather didn't touch her body, although cool air funneled up through the long legs of the skirt, underscoring her vulnerability.

The ranger took out his knife and started stripping branches from the nearby paloverde tree. He seemed heedless of the lightning, although Billie thought that at any moment he would be hit. "What are you doing?" she asked nervously.

"We need more of a shelter than that."

She realized he was fashioning a makeshift lean-to of brush and logs against the boulder to keep the rain from coming in. In the short time it took him to complete the task, the rain started to abate, and the lightning didn't seem so close, to her relief.

Billie watched her captor covertly. He worked with casual grace, his motions swift and economical. She noted his deftness at cutting the branches, and his efficiency at placing them correctly. His lean, strong frame in action was fascinating to watch, and she found she couldn't keep her eyes off him.

Seemingly unaware of her gaze, the ranger tended the fire and started the kettle to boil. That done, he saw to their mounts. Billie observed the gentleness of the hands that rubbed the horses down thoroughly, despite the rain. Buttermilk loved to scare people by baring his teeth. It was all a bluff, but it served to keep strangers from touching him. To Billie's surprise, the gelding stood as calmly for the ranger as he did for her, completely relaxed. He even nickered when Sam approached him with the feed *moral* and strapped it on.

The traitor.

Billie had to drag her gaze away from man and horse. She looked instead toward the creekbed far below. She could see the muddy brown torrent from here, shuttling tree branches along its length like batons in a relay race. Although the rain was little more than a drizzle now, the canyon remained shrouded in gloom. Mist obscured the rocky ramparts and needlelike spires, making the mountains seem all the more menacing. Cholla studded the slopes, their clustered lobes glistening with raindrops, velvety yellow-gray. Billie could almost imagine a silent file of Apaches creeping through this country, ready to kill anyone who strayed here.

She shivered. This was a dangerous country, even now. Perhaps she *had* bitten off more than she could chew. But then her mind turned to Elliot. If the Superstitions were daunting to her, how much more alien they must seem to him. He could be in trouble right now, and she could do nothing about it, because of Sam Gray.

He returned to the fire and dished up their supper. "Here you go."

Even though the food looked and smelled enticing, Billie wouldn't give him the satisfaction. "I'm not hungry."

He didn't press her, although she sensed that he knew just how hungry she was. He set her plate on the ground beside them and tucked into his own meal with hearty enjoyment. She found her gaze straying to him, but every time he looked up she pretended her attention was elsewhere. Why did his every move intrigue her? It was hard to tear her eyes away from him. Every gesture—no matter how small—was stamped with his own brand of masculine grace.

Certainly he was a fine figure of a man. But Elliot was just as handsome in his own way. Perhaps it was the masculinity that seemed to roll off the ranger, an essence that caused a thrill in the pit of her stomach whenever they were close. No doubt he had in plenty what the Mexicans called *machismo*, and would lord it over any woman he happened to love. . . .

She shivered as she pictured him riding into the barnyard at La Zanja, riding in as if he owned it. As her husband. The idea both disturbed and fascinated her.

Sam was halfway through his meal before he asked again if she wanted to eat. "You sure you're not hungry?"

"Yes, I'm sure." He was so close to her; there wasn't much space under the lean-to. His shoulder brushed her arm and a tickle of excitement burrowed into her stomach.

"I didn't think you were the type to cut off your nose to spite your face," he said.

"What are you talking about?"

"If you plan on coming out here again after I leave you at Bark's, you'd better stoke up. You'll need your strength."

She wished he wouldn't look at her. She wished he weren't so close. It was difficult to keep her voice steady. "So you admit that taking me back is an exercise in futility."

"I'm hoping you'll get some sense between now and then."

"There's no chance of that." Her dinner was steaming beside her. The aroma teased her nostrils and made her mouth water. What was more, her foot was going to sleep. She shifted positions, and the seam brushed against her intimately. A frisson of pleasure rippled up through the center of her body, and she clamped her lips on a soundless moan.

Sam was looking straight at her. Did he guess about her skirt? The thought of losing control made her angry. Straightening her shoulders, Billie summoned her most withering tone. "You love to run other people's lives, don't you?"

His mouth straightened into a grim line and his face closed up like an abandoned house, but not before she caught a fleeting look of regret on his face. It was gone so quickly she might have imagined it. "Lady, you're in my way," he said brusquely. "I can't do my job with you out here."

She knew she was pushing him, but she didn't care. "I don't see why not."

He leaned forward. His gaze leveled across the space between them, and she felt the force of his conviction. "I'm after killers. I can't go after them and worry about you, too."

"I won't get in the way."

"How do you know? With you wandering all over the place looking for your boyfriend, you could run right into them."

"This is a big place," she replied, aware that she sounded flippant.

He didn't bother to answer.

"What about Elliot?" she demanded. "I should think you'd like me to find him. He'd be one less distraction."

Again he refused to rise to the bait. She took his silence to mean that he didn't care whether Elliot got in the way or not. "So that's the way it is. The knight in shining armor, looking for a dragon to slay and a maiden to rescue. I see your chivalry doesn't extend to men."

"Stevenson will have to look out for himself."

"I'm far better able to take care of myself out here than he is."

"You think I don't know that?"

"But because I'm a woman, you won't allow me the same rights as Elliot. That's what it comes down to."

"What you want is the right to get yourself killed."

"So?"

His eyes found hers again. "If I came across your boyfriend, I'd haul him in, too. I didn't run into him; I ran into you. For all I know, he didn't come out here at all."

"What do you mean by that?"

"Only that he might have come to his senses and stayed out of these mountains. As you should."

"Of course he's out here! I talked to the man who outfitted him. Besides, he wouldn't lie to me."

It was the ranger's turn to look away, and suddenly Billie felt a tiny stab of fear deep in her soul. Sam Gray acted as if he knew more about Elliot than he was letting on. But that was impossible.

It had to be her imagination. Gray had met Elliot only that one time.

"I guess I'll rinse these dishes," the ranger said.

She glanced at the food again.

He caught her gaze and diplomatically looked back down at his plate.

She couldn't stand it anymore. Her hand darted out to grab the dish. To his credit, he didn't say, "I told you so." As far as she could tell, he didn't seem to care one way or the other.

Chapter Nine

"I have to go chase a rabbit."

Billie could tell the ranger understood her meaning. She always used this euphemism when out working with the hands on La Zanja. Apparently it meant the same thing to the Arizona Rangers.

Sam nodded. It was the first interaction they'd had in over an hour. They had lapsed into uncomfortable silence after dinner, staring into the flames and studiously avoiding each other's gaze. Even so, Billie had managed to keep track of him under the dark sweep of her lashes. His face in repose had been closed, unreadable, and she had the feeling that he was alone in his thoughts.

She stood up and donned her slicker. The rain was steady; it had gone from the hard male rain of Indian lore to its softer, female counterpart. "You will let me go alone, won't you?" she asked, her voice heavy with sarcasm.

"You won't go far."

Billie's gaze dropped to the canyon below, to the raging torrent. He was right. He had all the cards.

She found a bush around the side of the hill and was back at the fire in a few minutes.

The firelight webbed Sam's strong jaw and cheekbones; the ridged shadows of the lean-to played over his broad shoulders. The brass-yellow glow of the fire made his eyes shine a deep blue-green. He stared into the flames, not bothering to acknowledge her return. Apparently he hadn't expected any surprises, since he remained in the same position as when she'd left him.

Billie removed her slicker, sat down and adjusted her skirt. She would be glad when she could wear her drawers again. At least she was dry. She wondered how Elliot was getting along in this storm. It seemed strange that the ranger had been out here for several days and not seen a trace of him.

What if he had run into Elliot, and for some reason kept the information from her? She remembered earlier tonight, how she felt he wasn't telling all he knew. Clearing her throat, she asked, "You said you doubted Elliot had come out here at all. Why?"

"I don't have a reason to think he is or isn't here."

"But you said—"

"I said I hoped he had enough sense to stay out of these mountains. Just like I hope you'll give up and go home where it's safe."

She ignored the lecture. "You haven't seen him?"

"No."

He sounded sincere. But why did she have the feeling he was keeping something from her? "Please, if there's something you know about him, don't spare me. I have to know." Suddenly dread filled her like a cold wind. "He isn't dead, is he?"

"Dead?" Sam Gray laughed. "Why would you think that?"

"You keep telling me how dangerous it is out here. I thought maybe you'd come across him . . . dead."

"I'll say this once. When I answer a question, I make a practice of answering it honestly the first time."

There didn't seem to be a reply for that. But it still didn't explain why he disliked Elliot. She needed to know why a complete stranger had such a low opinion of the man she loved. She needed to know so she could bring the demons that plagued her out into the open and fight them, refute any doubts she had, once and for all. "Why don't you like him, then?"

Sam said nothing. After that circus in Nogales, he couldn't say much without putting Elliot in a bad light.

"Why?" she persisted.

143

He shrugged, trying to keep his expression bland. "Some people just rub each other the wrong way."

"That's no answer."

"It's my answer."

It was obvious she wanted to get something off her chest. "My father says he's after my money."

He wasn't about to fall into that trap. He'd been party to this kind of feminine fishing expedition before, and nothing a man said was right.

"Is that what you believe, Mr. Gray?"

"Could be." He kept his voice noncommittal.

"What makes you think so?" She speared him with her gaze.

"I didn't—"

"You only met him once, over a card game. And yet you have a very low opinion of him." She harped on the same note, like the bass pedal on a dirge. Pretty she might be, but Billie Bahill was maddening, too. He couldn't imagine spending the rest of his life arguing with her. His brain would turn to mush in a month.

She'd make a damn fine lawyer, though. Disarm a man with those clear aquamarine eyes, then move in for the kill.

"Did my father talk to you about him?"

He was tempted to tell her the truth, but it wasn't his place. Billie would not thank him; she'd hate him even more. "Miss Bahill, your father did not say anything to me that you didn't hear. I know of no reason why he'd be after your money. You're a beautiful woman, a darn sight too pretty to be—"

"Well, thank you for that candid observation."

He changed the subject. "Since your fiancé is so set on finding it, do you know the story of the Lost Dutchman Mine?"

"Jacob Waltz—that German they call the Dutchman—had a mine in the Superstitions. He killed his partner for it. Everyone knows the story."

"Apaches killed his partner."

"I heard he was as mean as they come. He made it look like Apaches, but it was murder sure enough. Shot him in the back."

"Where'd you get that? From a dime novel? I knew the man, and what you're talking is hogwash."

"It's common knowledge."

She'd argue with a stone.

"You shouldn't be so quick to take on someone else's opinions," Sam told her. "There are people who can't stand it if someone's prosperous. They have to make up all kinds of things about him, to show that even if he's rich, he kicks his dog or beats his wife or cheats at cards, that underneath he's just as unhappy as they are."

"If he was so rich, why didn't he live in high style?"

Sam grinned as he remembered the old man. "He liked his life the way it was—thrived on all the attention. He'd go out into the mountains every few months with his burro, and people would fall over themselves trying to follow him. Old Jake was as wily as a coyote."

"Are you saying there really isn't a mine?"

"Oh, he had some gold. I saw it. But it could have come from anywhere, and he wasn't telling. It was all a big joke to him."

"A big joke? Elliot's risking his life to find that mine!"

"He should have learned something about it before he ran off half-cocked." As soon as the words were out of his mouth, Sam realized his mistake.

"You certainly know him well, for someone who only met him one night."

"I know his kind."

"And what kind is that, Mr. Gray?"

He'd done it now. He'd have to head her off at the pass if he wanted any peace at all. "A lot of prospectors who come out here are so excited about the idea of the gold mine, they don't bother to find out what the dangers are."

She looked mad as hell at that one, but he could tell she was too honest to argue. It was clear he'd only said out loud what she herself had been thinking.

"The rest of the legend is very interesting. Do you want to hear it?"

"Not especially."

"Well, you're going to hear it anyway. Arizona Rangers don't get to talk to people that often. I've got a captive audience, so I'm going to take advantage of it."

"It's nice to know you've got a sense of humor

under that lone-eagle exterior," she replied dryly.

Man alive, she was a paradox. One minute she could come up with a cool retort like that, knock him for a loop, and the next, he could swear she was afraid to look at him. He supposed that she wasn't used to being out in the middle of nowhere with a strange man. He launched into his story, hoping to put her at ease. "The Peraltas were a Spanish family who had a mine here in the Superstitions."

The Peraltas and their peons, Sam told her, were massacred by the Apaches, who didn't care about gold for riches but wanted to keep it there in the sacred mountain. Only one of the Peralta family escaped the bloodbath: the young Peralta heir, who grew to adulthood.

Years later, the young man was saved from death by a couple of prospectors who had decided to try their luck south of the border. "It happened in a cantina in Mexico," he told her. "A card game gone wrong. One of the Mexicans drew his gun on Miguel Peralta. Waltz and his partner, Jacob Weiser, came to his rescue. Peralta rewarded them by deeding them the mine. That is, after one final trip of his own to refill the family coffers."

"And it was after that that Weiser was murdered."

"Right. Sometime in the seventies. Waltz and Weiser had been in the mountains for a long time, when Waltz went into town for more supplies. When he returned, he found Weiser dead, killed by the Apaches."

Billie asked him a few more questions, but gradually drowsiness overcame her interest.

Her shoulders were tipped back against the boulder, her feet flat on the ground, knees bent. As he watched, her chin sank toward her chest and her eyelashes lowered. The incessant hiss of the rain filled his ears, but aside from that it seemed, despite all the pressing troubles each had brought to this moment, that they were alone in a quiet world of their own making. It was like a magic spell, one he did not wish to break. The cool air blew in between the slats of the lean-to, redolent with the fresh sweet scent of creosote bush. Billie Bahill was as beautiful in slumber as she was awake. Her skin was soft and glowed in the dying firelight, her lips lying together in a graceful line. There was a blush on her cheeks, whipped up from the cool air. Her hair had been loosed from its bonds and slid like twin dark rivers down her light wool shirt. The top button was undone on the shirt and his eye was drawn to warm caramel skin, smooth and satiny in the flickering light. He couldn't keep his eyes off her, the way her chest rose and fell under the soft material.

Sam moved closer, thinking to wake her. He had already laid out her bedroll. He touched her arm. Still asleep, she slid gently sideways, tilted her body toward him and curled up against his shoulder.

The first shock of her touch bolted through

him. He could feel her chin pressing against his shoulder, her hand on his arm, her even breathing. Maybe he'd let her stay that way for a while. What could it hurt?

If she grew heavy, he didn't notice. His thoughts made him uncomfortable enough. She elicited a number of sensations and emotions in him. He felt protective. He wanted to stroke her hair, comfort her even in sleep. He wanted to tell her that she would always be safe with him, even though he knew that was impossible. Tomorrow he would deliver her to Bark's Ranch and that would be it. But the yearning was too great. The muscles in his arms contracted and played out in fractions, as if on creaking pulleys, as he settled his hand gently on her head, on the soft and shining hair that slid like silk beneath his palm. His heart opened, spreading warmth through him, and he wondered how he could feel so strongly for this prickly young woman who had been nothing but trouble. He smoothed her hair, once, twice. Fearing to wake her, he drew his hand back, and was surprised at the ghostly sensations that itched against his palm.

She stirred. Thunder rumbled in the distance. Rain tapped on the shelter. Her lips parted, and she moaned.

Like an arrow, desire quivered through him. He felt the stir of arousal and immediately crushed the thought from his mind, a boot grinding the life out of a rose's bloom.

And woke her.

For a moment she looked startled as a fawn.

149

Her eyes were wide and dark in the firelight, and it twisted his heart to see her mouth part in horror. Immediately she blushed pink and drew away from him. "I'm sorry," she stammered, and her breast rose and fell with obvious agitation, even under all those bandages.

He tried to make his voice steady. "It's all right. I'm known for offering a shoulder to lean on." A poor attempt at humor.

"You should have said something," she said, obviously embarrassed.

"It didn't bother me."

She must have believed him, for she skimmed the heel of her hand across her eyes. "I think I'll turn in."

He did not argue.

After she was asleep again, Sam listened to the falling rain, his heart aching. Maybe it was the rain. Maybe it was because he'd known, briefly, the warmth of another human being. A lot of people thought he was a loner, but Sam often longed for human companionship. Rangering was a lonely life, but he had chosen it. Hadn't marriage proven even lonelier? His mind veered away from the memories that haunted him; he had good practice at that. He didn't want to sully this night with the ghosts of the past. God knew, he'd spent enough of his life floundering in that dark sea of pain.

But the furies that plagued him night and day would not leave him alone. They screeched at him, demanding his attention. *Joey—*

No. He wanted to be selfish, just for tonight.

Just for tonight he wanted to forget his responsibilities. Just for tonight he wanted to pretend that his life was his to start afresh, that he had not yet known how quickly the sweetness of love could curdle into disappointment and pain. Just for tonight he wanted to believe that love was new and clean and natural again—even if that love was only an illusion. He would watch over his sleeping beauty, and fool his mind into believing that she was his.

Billie awoke to the cool breath of night fanning her cheeks. She peered up through the crevice between the lean-to and the boulder, expecting overcast skies, but the heavens had been washed clean except for a few silvery clouds that clotted the sky like mattress ticking. To the west it was clear, however, and the sky made Billie think of navy velvet sewn with tiny winking diamonds. She glanced at Sam's bedroll. He was gone.

Inexplicably, her heart started to pound. Her first reaction was fear that he had left her. But wasn't that what she wanted, for heaven's sake? She *wanted* to escape.

Rising to her feet, Billie wiped the sleep from her eyes, inhaling the fresh air. A chorus of crickets vied with the bleating tenor of Colorado River toads, who had come out from their hibernation under the sand.

Billie's gaze strayed to the horses. Perhaps now was her chance. But what if Sam had just gone to chase a rabbit? She rubbed her wrist. She sure didn't want to be handcuffed again!

She bit her lip. A breeze ruffled her hair. Straining her eyes against the darkness, she tried to make out shapes.

She took a tentative few steps toward Buttermilk.

There was a scrape of boots on rock. She glanced up and saw the black silhouette of the ranger on the boulder above her, hunkered on his heels and holding the rifle across his lap.

Relief claimed her. It was the opposite of what she should be feeling, but Billie decided not to analyze it. "How'd you get up there?" she called.

"You want to come up?"

"Yes."

"Go around to your left."

She did as she was told, and saw that there were several boulders piled up, along with some easy handholds. He was down beside her in a few jumps, and held out his hand.

She put her hand in his and was surprised at the welcome feel of his palm, vibrant and warm. His hand clasping hers made her feel protected, secure. He helped her up until they were both at the top of the towering rock formation, breathless and glowing from the exertion.

When his arm dropped to his side, she felt a vague disappointment. "Like the view?" he asked her.

"It's beautiful! I could be on top of the world." They were up high enough that she could see over some of the other ridges, and down into the canyon, where the rushing funnel of floodwater caught the starlight. The water ran with such muscular force that the sight of it caused the tiny hairs on her arms to stand up.

"Are you cold?"

"A little." She didn't object when he placed his arm across her shoulders.

"My sister said she could always stay warm on the coldest night as long as she was warm enough right here." His hand rested on Billie's upper arm, just below her shoulder.

Billie felt the sensation of warmth steal through her. "You have a sister?" she asked, trying to ignore the disturbing feelings that gripped her as Sam's fingers gently rubbed her skin through her shirt.

"Two of them. The one who likes to keep her shoulders warm is called Lily. My other sister's named Addie."

"Nice names," Billie mused. Her skirt was creeping up on her again. She tried to ignore it, but with Sam's fingers caressing her upper arm, it was difficult to keep the two sensations from melding together into one forbidden temptation. . . .

"Lily was always particular. When it came to putting fresh bedclothes on their bed, Lily would bully Addie into making the bed while she lay in the middle, with the sheets and blankets pulled up to her chin, just so. Then she'd direct Addie to tuck the blankets in at the bottom." His fingers touched the pulse of her throat and she nearly jumped out of her skin.

He withdrew his hand, and Billie wondered why she ached for him to touch her again.

"She just couldn't stand it if the bedclothes came up too far, like to here," he tapped her nose, "Or if they were too short, like here—" He pointed to her breastbone, but didn't touch her there. Just the thought of it caused goose bumps to ripple over her arms.

"What happened to her?" she asked softly, wishing her legs would stop trembling.

"She got married. Don't know how such a headstrong girl managed it, but she did. I wonder if her husband has to make the bed around her."

Concentrate on the subject at hand. Billie broke loose from his grip on her shoulder and turned to face him, trying to make the move appear casual. "And Addie? What happened to her?"

"Ah, she was the sweet one. Never said a cross word, always did what she was told." He shrugged. "She never married."

"But the bossy one did."

"That's right. The bossy one did. Maybe there's a lesson in there somewhere."

Billie tilted her chin up to look at him. He must be awfully tall to be taller than she. "What lesson?"

"Well, Addie was the boy-crazy one. She was always trying to please boys by pretending to be interested in what they did, waiting on them hand and foot, acting dumb when she's really smart. Lily, well, she just pretty much did as she pleased. Maybe men liked Lily better because whatever she was, she was herself."

Billie thought that one over. "That's not right,"

she said at last. "Everyone knows that men fancy a certain kind of woman. Soft, feminine . . ." She paused, realizing that she was neither. The women of Harshaw had always pitied her, thought of her as some kind of freak. She'd overheard a number of catty remarks that had cut her to the quick. *That girl will never find a husband if she doesn't stop riding around the country like a cowhand.*

Sam was staring at her. All she could see was the reflection of starlight in his eyes, but his scrutiny was palpable. "Something wrong?" he asked.

"Not if you don't count being held prisoner against my will," she retorted quickly. Why did she feel guilty for her remark? After all, he was the person in the wrong, not her. But suddenly she wanted to return to a more civilized subject. Swallowing her pride, she asked, "How old are your sisters?"

"Addie is . . . let's see, she'd be twenty-eight. Lily's a year younger."

"They live in Arizona?"

"Prescott."

"That's where your parents live?"

She saw the shadow cross his face, and suddenly realized she knew so little about this man. "It's a pretty night," he said.

So he didn't want to discuss his parents. She'd abide by that.

For a moment, silence reigned. An errant breeze touched her skin. Sam's hair, silver-edged in the darkness, licked the wind. One of the horses snorted.

"I sure do admire that buckskin of yours," Sam said.

"Broke him myself when he was four."

"You ride broncs, too?"

"Why not? A man's just as breakable as I am." He whistled softly.

She felt defensive. "I'm better at busting broncs than just about anyone on La Zanja."

He grinned. "I don't doubt it."

"You're making fun of me."

"No, I'm not."

"If Lily busted broncs instead of bossing her sister around, do you think she'd still have a husband?" Billie challenged.

"I think he'd love her no matter what she did. He might even love her because she broke broncs."

"That's ridiculous. Men—"

"Like their women to be soft and feminine." He parroted her own words. "Maybe some men. But I think a lot of us like women who are most like ourselves."

Now that was a truly alien concept. What kind of a fool did he think she was? "How do you know?" she demanded. "Have you ever been married?"

She felt, rather than saw, his withdrawal. "Yes," he said at last.

"And she thought like you."

This time Billie couldn't miss the hardness in his eyes. "No." Abruptly, he turned from her and walked to the edge of the boulder, looking out on the black expanse of mountains. From the stiffness of his back, she knew he didn't want to talk anymore.

So he'd been married. Obviously it had ended tragically. Billie wanted to know if his wife had died or if there had been a divorce . . . now, that would be a scandal.

Everything about marriage intrigued her. It seemed to be such an interesting state, elevating the most romantic love to a higher level. A love sanctioned by God . . .

She wondered what it would be like. Mrs. Elliot Stevenson. She already knew part of it—no doubt once they were married, it would get better—but did it really change you? Were you one person on the morning of the wedding and another that afternoon? Did people look at you differently, with more respect, maybe? All of these questions clamored for attention, but she could not ask the ranger. Occasionally marriages were unhappy, and obviously he had suffered from this greatest of all disappointments. She felt sorry for him.

Abruptly, a cicada's loud, sustained buzz sounded in the brush just below them. The moon had risen above the cliffs opposite, its reflection shining in silver-edged puddles of rainwater on the rocks. The breeze was chilly, and Billie longed for Sam's arm around her shoulder. Lily wasn't the only one who could feel the cold. But she could tell he was in his own world, and sensed that he wished to be alone with his thoughts.

She sat down on the rock, watching him. He stood straight and tall, his head tipped up to the stars, legs slightly apart, his strong fingers loosely curled at his sides. Billie was surprised at the longing that shot through her, for something she could not define. Perhaps it was the waste of such a romantic setting. Elliot should be here, kissing her . . .

But that idea left her cold.

What did she want? At this moment she didn't know. Maybe it was enough to enjoy this beautiful night, absorbing its scents and sounds, and appreciate the sight of a handsome man.

After a while, by unspoken consent, the two of them returned to camp. Billie fell asleep almost right away.

They awoke to a heat lightning display and more rain. It was obvious that they wouldn't be going anywhere, at least for the morning. After a breakfast of flapjacks and "spotted pup"—a rice and raisin pudding—Sam brought out a worn pack of cards and they entertained themselves by playing poker, using pebbles for chips.

"You're a good poker player," Sam said after Billie won her second hand.

"Thank you. My father taught me."

"Is there anything you can't do?"

"I can't play the piano. I can't sew."

"Do you want to?"

"Not particularly."

"I'll bet you can't shoe a horse."

She couldn't keep the triumphant smile from spreading across her face. "Wrong."

"You can shoe a horse?"

"You bet."

"Good, because I can't. If Panther throws a shoe, you're the person I'll ask to help. How many?" he asked, referring to the cards.

Billie held up three fingers. Her face was impassive when she picked them up. He found himself hoping she wouldn't beat him again. He looked at his own cards and threw in four pebbles.

Billie upped the ante.

She was bluffing. Had to be. Sam added to the pot. Billie bet accordingly, but he knew she was bluffing. He permitted himself a moment of triumph as he spread out his cards: a full house.

Billie frowned, sighed. She studied her cards, lifted one up and slid it back into the left side of the fan of cards, then hesitated. Sam couldn't keep his eyes from her bosom, which heaved gently as she sighed again. Her eyelashes lowered, her lips pressed together, glowing pinkly in the gray light. The rain came down softly, tapping on the shelter, perfuming the air with its fresh scent.

She was beautiful in defeat.

With quiet deliberation, Billie set down four jacks and a three.

"Who'd you learn to play poker from? Doc Holliday?"

Billie smiled, looking like a cat who had gotten into the cream. "Why don't we raise the stakes?" she challenged.

"What? Play for boulders?"

She laughed. "No. We can play for my release. I win the next hand, you let me go. You win, you can take me in."

"That's no bet. I can take you in anyway." Some devil in him spurred him to add, "What else do you have to offer?"

Billie blushed crimson. Apparently she, too, had heard of the poker games that went on in Gay Alley, the prostitute section of Tucson, where the soiled doves and their customers often amused themselves by stripping off an article of clothing each time they lost—until they were naked as the day they were born.

At last Billie said, "What about a colt? We have some very fine animals on La Zanja. You could have your pick."

Ah. She'd neatly sidestepped that trap. Sam leaned back and lit a rolled cigarette. "Too risky," he said. "What if I let you go and you got lost? Or killed? How would I collect?"

Billie shivered. The thought that she might actually get lost or killed had been brought home to her recently, after traversing this menacing landscape. It could well turn out that way. "I'd write you a chit for it."

Sam grinned. "Do you think I'd relish being the one to tell your father you aren't coming back? You overestimate my courage."

It was obvious he was toying with her. "I take it you won't play for my release."

"You take it right."

"Then you'd best deal the cards," she said briskly.

His next words disarmed her. "Did anyone ever tell you how much you look like your mother?"

"How do you—Oh." Flustered, Billie remembered the portrait at La Zanja. "But I don't think so. I've always thought she was very beautiful."

"So are you."

Was this some kind of trick to get her mind off the card game? She knew she was pretty, but beautiful? "Would you just deal the cards?" she demanded.

"Did your father raise you all by himself?" Sam asked as he snapped the cards facedown.

Billie tried to turn it into a joke. "If he hadn't raised me, and Panther threw a shoe, you'd be out of luck."

"True enough. But it must have been tough, just you and your father."

Billie gathered up her hand. "I sometimes wonder how different my life would be if my mother had been alive."

Sam caught her gaze and held it, an ironic smile touching his lips. He had the strangest effect on her sometimes. It was the way he looked at her, as if she were the most interesting person in the world. Such attention was flattering, yes. But it was also disconcerting.

"How do you think it would be different?" he asked.

"I—I don't know. Maybe I would have been

161

more interested in clothes and dolls and things."
Suddenly it seemed important that she put it
into words, although she never had before. "I
had a school friend in Harshaw. Sometimes I'd
spend the night in town with her and her family.
I'll never forget one time when the colonel
dropped me off and I went in the house and
Becky and her mother were both ironing. Her
mother had a regular sadiron, and Becky had a
little one—it even had a tiny sleeve. I always fantasized that maybe it could have been the same
thing with my mother." She rushed on, closing
her eyes. "I could picture us painting—she'd
have a big easel and I'd have one just like it, only
my size, and we'd be painting a still life, some
flowers in a vase. . . ." She shook her head. "Silly,
isn't it?"

Sam didn't reply.

"But life isn't fair. What's done is done. That's
what the colonel says. He believes you have to
be tough to get on in this world. It all comes
down to survival of the fittest. My mother was
weak, and she didn't make it."

"It's as simple as that?"

"As simple as that." She felt suddenly angry at
her mother all over again for being so weak, so
. . . ill. For not being there when she was needed.
"Only the strong survive, or deserve to. The colonel says—"

"Have you always called your father the colonel?"

"What else would I call him?"

*   *   *

162

They played until lunch, which consisted of more spotted pup, canned peaches and biscuits. After eating, Sam went to check on the horses. The rain kept up steadily, and lightning forked the sky.

Billie took the opportunity to look at the portrait of Elliot and herself. She tried not to think about what Julia Thomas had said. Surely a simple photograph couldn't cause their engagement harm. That was just an old wives' tale.

Returning from the horses, Sam caught her eye as she tenderly wiped the bubble glass of the photograph with the hem of her skirt. "How did you meet Elliot?" he asked.

"He came to the ranch one day looking for work." Billie smiled fondly. "He tried to hire on as a cowboy. That was a mistake."

"Let me guess. The hands gave him a rank bronc to ride."

"They always do that. Haze the new man. But it wasn't fair. The colonel had no intention of hiring him."

"Because he was a tenderfoot?"

She felt a bit like a traitor, but couldn't help laughing. "It was obvious. He dressed . . ."

Sam's eyes sparkled with mischief. "Don't tell me he wore a bowler."

"No! It was just . . . well, he wore cowboy clothes, but they were new. His boots were brand-new. And even though his clothes were regular enough, they just didn't look right on him."

"So the boys hazed him."

163

"We have this old claybank bronc named Yellowjacket. No one can ride him; the colonel has collected a lot of bets from cowboys who thought they could. The colonel—Father," she amended hastily, "didn't need to go that far. Any half-broke horse would have done. Elliot could have been killed. He broke a finger. It got caught in the reins."

"You nursed him back to health?"

"I splinted his finger, if that's what you mean."

"So he stayed on La Zanja?"

"Yes, and after my father had his fun, he did hire him on, to paint scenes of ranch work. Fortunately Elliot broke the finger on his left hand. F-Father thought a whole gallery of paintings of his ranch would look very impressive."

"I didn't see anything like what you describe."

"He didn't like them. Something about the colors, I think. He called them prissy."

"Were they?"

"Were they what?"

"Prissy?"

She thought back, and then giggled. "Yes. I guess they were."

They played cards again. This time Sam won more often than he lost. Billie realized that she'd revealed a great deal about her private life, but Sam had avoided talking about himself. It was time to even the odds. "What was the war like?" she asked him.

Sam looked grim. "Ugly."

"But it must have been exciting, too. Imagine

being in the same company as the future president of the United States. To be one of the Rough Riders."

"It wasn't exciting. It was revolting. Men riding into direct fire, knowing they'd be blown to bits. A lot of good men. A lot of good horses. All because we wanted to bully our way into the limelight as a world power."

She glanced at Buttermilk, and thought of him being torn to bits. Somehow the idea of an animal being killed for man's aims made her sadder than the fate of the humans who understood the danger. Still, when duty called, there was no excuse to turn away. "The Cubans were horribly oppressed by the Spanish. We couldn't just stand by and let that happen. We had to intervene. Besides, to give your life for your country is an honorable thing."

"Where'd you get that?"

"Why, it says so in my history book."

Sam took two more cards. "Your history book. I guess that kind of education will make sure there will be cannon fodder for the next generation."

"You're not sorry you went?" she asked, appalled.

"Some wars are unnecessary. This was one of them. It was trumped up from the beginning by expansionists who used it for their own aims."

"But what about the *USS Maine?*" Billie demanded. The Spanish had sunk a United States battleship. How could the U.S. not respond?

"Some think that *we* blew up the *Maine.*"

"How could you say such a thing?"

Sam revealed his hand. "I win," he said, and scooped up the pot.

Billie ignored the game. "Well, you may have had your doubts, but you did go. You didn't run away. I find that admirable." She wondered, as she spoke, if Elliot would have done the same. Apparently not, since he was of an age with the ranger. Maybe, she thought defensively, the war happened during the time he'd spent in Paris. "You should be proud that you went," she insisted.

"I went because I was as ignorant as everybody else."

"But you'd do it again."

He paused. "No, I wouldn't. Maybe if everyone refused to go, there wouldn't be any wars."

She'd been about to make a hero out of him. "You sound suspiciously like a pacifist."

"Anybody who's been in battle must either be a pacifist or a fool."

That was as personal as the ranger got. Although Sam Gray was easy to talk to, Billie noticed that he turned away any reference to his family, other than his sisters, whom he obviously adored.

She, on the other hand, continued to bare her soul, despite conscious attempts to hold back. They talked about the way the kids had made fun of her at school in Harshaw, her father, horses, cattle auctions, roundups; they argued about squatters, statehood, the Cattlemen's Association, the evils of liquor, the merits of single-rig saddles as opposed to double rigs, and politics. He was a Democrat; her father was a Republican. Of course, she added acidly, *she* wasn't really anything, because women weren't allowed to vote.

Through it all, Sam Gray's past remained an enigma. Billie sensed there was a nasty wound that remained just under the surface, in danger of reopening. Something terrible had happened to the ranger, and it wasn't just the war.

Maybe it had to do with his wife. . . .

Billie couldn't help shivering deliciously. What would it be like to be married to the ranger? She clamped down on this treacherous thought with a will, but could not deny the new and frightening sensations the Arizona Ranger caused in her.

It had happened sometime in the long afternoon of card playing.

When they were talking, things were fine. But if he went off for some reason—to get wood, see to the horses—and came back, her heart started pounding in her chest and her throat turned dry as sawdust. She felt just the way she had at thirteen, when she first discovered boys, and one in particular: Charlie Roberds. She'd suffered a full-blown schoolgirl crush on Charlie Roberds. To her dismay, her treacherous body was responding much the same way to Sam Gray.

Sometimes he'd brush her in passing, sending her mind cartwheeling and sheathing her skin in static electricity. Billie wondered if she was making a fool of herself around him, if he knew how his touch affected her. He gave no sign.

Once, when Billie walked off to "chase a rabbit," she became painfully aware of her body as she walked away from him; her posture, her arms, her legs. She knew he was watching her and it made her feel awkward. Did she look all right? She took mental inventory. Was her skirt caught on her boot? Had he been staring at her because she'd had some food between her teeth? Was her face dirty? Out of his sight, she had used spittle on her handkerchief to wipe her face, and then pinned her hair back up.

Excitement whirled around inside her like a hot wind, making her legs tremble, her face suffuse with heat. What was happening to her? She'd never felt this way around Elliot. Billie was powerless to stop the sensations that bombarded her, the need that rushed headlong through her body toward him, as if drawn by a magnetic force. One minute she'd despised him; the next she was acting like a lovesick pup.

She needed to pay attention to the important things. Like finding Elliot. It would be wise to remember just whose side the ranger was on.

Toward late afternoon, the rain finally abated. Thunder grumbled off like a disgruntled guest. The sky started to clear a little toward the west, although a few thunderheads remained over the mountains, their boiling tops carnation pink in the sunset, their bellies leaden blue. It was an awe-inspiring sight.

The ranger had become quieter the last few hours, and Billie could see that something both-

ered him. He'd get up and pace around, looking
at the rain. Now that it was over, he looked vis-
ibly relieved. "Let's hope it doesn't happen again
tomorrow," he muttered.

"What doesn't?"

"This storm pattern. It's fouling me up. God
knows where those outlaws are now."

"I see what you mean. Maybe you ought to
leave me here and—"

His voice was brittle with anger. "Don't think
you can wriggle off the hook. We're going back!"

Stunned into silence, she stared at him. Why
was he angry with her? *He* was the one being
stubborn about this! For all she cared, he could
turn her loose right now.

Sam continued to pace. "I guess it can't be
helped. I couldn't get across that river down
there even if I were alone."

"Well, cheer up. It looks like the storm's going
away, and you'll be rid of me soon enough," she
said, her voice coldly furious.

He didn't reply, but glared at the fire.

Billie decided it was time to pull herself together. Obviously the ranger saw her only as a
nuisance, a duty. She had to put a rein on her
feelings. Otherwise she'd look like a fool. Even
though they had enjoyed a nice day together, it
was clear that Sam Gray didn't like her as much
as she liked him.

She couldn't let him know how much his rejection bothered her, and how much she desired
his approval.

The strained silence grew like a chasm between them. Billie vowed that if she got a chance, she'd get away from the ranger. And when she did, just maybe she'd be able to get away from these strange new feelings, as well.

The opportunity came sooner than she'd expected.

Billie had taken a nap after supper, since she hadn't gotten that much sleep the night before. She awoke to a strange voice and more rain.

"Much obliged. This is the only dry spot in the whole canyon."

Billie opened her eyes and looked up.

A man in a yellow slicker stood next to the fire. Water dripped from his Stetson onto his shoulders. He was short and compact, with narrow shoulders and a big head. His enormous round eyes made him appear very young. He sported a handlebar mustache with twisted ends. Hunkering down, hands over the fire, he glanced at Billie.

"Your partner looks all in. Are you prospectors?" he asked Sam.

"No."

Tucked in the way she was, her hair pinned up and the blanket over her ears, Billie realized she must look like a boy.

The stranger grunted. "I don't suppose you'd tell me if you were. You never know who to trust."

Sam didn't reply.

"Name's Mac Monroe," the man volunteered, shaking hands with Sam.

Sam motioned to Billie. "I'm Sam and that's Billie. Any luck?"

"I'm getting close. Can't tell you anything else. You understand."

Sam nodded.

Was it Billie's imagination, or did Sam dislike their guest? He probably didn't want anyone to know that he had a woman prisoner, that he had mistreated her in such a manner—

Suddenly she realized that this man could help her escape. Surely if she told him how she had been handcuffed and humiliated . . .

But how could she get to him? It would be impossible under Sam Gray's watchful eye. If she made a fuss, he would tell his side of the story. Most people, she reflected, shied away from confrontation. They needed a very good reason to interfere. Who would the stranger be more likely to believe? An armed man—an Arizona Ranger who was the official law in this territory—or an obviously deranged young woman dressed as a man? Mac Monroe would listen to Sam.

Unless . . . She thought of the reward poster Sam had shown her. She could offer him a reward of her own. She had a lot of money. If he helped her escape, she'd pay him well.

Well, she couldn't do anything now. Not until Sam was asleep, or away from camp. Maybe tomorrow, when he went to gather wood for the fire. She'd find a way.

What if the man refused to help her?

He couldn't. She'd heard the way he talked

about the mine. He needed money. That was the great equalizer, the thing she had that Sam Gray did not.

Another hand had been dealt, and this time she had some cards she could use.

Sam didn't trust Mac Monroe. He had seen the type before. They combed the Superstition Mountains looking for a quick, easy way to get rich. "Gold fever" was a real condition, infecting otherwise amiable people. They looked feverish, with flushed skin, overbright eyes, their expressions paranoid. Sam could see all these symptoms in this man, whose eyes gleamed as hard and bright as the gold he sought. His boyish features didn't fool Sam. Mac Monroe was trouble.

Maybe Monroe's paranoia would win out, and he'd be gone before morning, after covering his tracks. If he didn't shoot both of them in their sleep. As Sam settled into his bedroll, his hand closed around his gun. He wouldn't take any chances.

Sleep did not come easy to him. He glanced at Billie. Apparently she had no trouble sleeping. He liked the way her long, dark lashes curved against her cheek, which glowed softly like a firm and perfect apricot in the flickering firelight. How could Monroe mistake her for a boy? It was hard to believe she was so tough. He had seen other women who could ride and shoot like Billie Bahill, but they were mannish creatures devoid of grace or beauty—like the infamous Pearl Hart, whom he had seen when she was incarcerated in Florence after an attempted robbery. Billie was another type altogether.

Was he doing the right thing? Billie had every right to hate him, but it was his duty to protect her from herself—and the highwaymen.

After all, what did she have to look forward to? If she caught up with Elliot, she'd have a rude awakening.

His heart twisted as he remembered the prostitute sitting on Stevenson's lap.

Suddenly Sam had a disconcerting thought. Was he really just doing his duty, or did he have an ulterior motive? He thought of the way he had responded to her the night before. The tenderness he'd experienced, holding her as she slept, his futile longing for his own life to start anew. Could it be that he wanted her for himself?

No. His reaction to her had been purely physical—and perfectly normal. After all, he wasn't a eunuch. She was a beautiful woman, and their enforced closeness would have driven any man to distraction. But the leap from lust to love was a large one, and he was not prepared to make it. What he felt for her was more along the lines of protectiveness than love.

Admittedly, he didn't want her to meet Stevenson out here, but not because of jealousy. Stevenson might gamble on the notion that Colonel Bahill would be so happy to get his daughter back, he would accept the marriage. In the long run, marriage to that spineless weakling would hurt Billie more than the cruelest rejection. But would Billie feel that way?

Sam hated to interfere in situations like this. He knew from experience how complicated things could get between a man and a woman.

He knew how love could turn to hate in an instant.

Sam raised his arms above his head, listening to the hissing rain. He shouldn't get involved. It was none of his business.

She was a grown woman. A strong woman. She would have to sort things out for herself. All he owed her was to make sure she got back to civilization safe and sound, and out of his hair.

But as he lay awake in his bedroll, Sam wondered if he really wanted her out of his hair at all.

Chapter Ten

The aroma of coffee and bacon woke Billie, and for a moment she forgot where she was. She loved the smell of coffee perking on a campfire. The air was fresh and washed clean, the dawn sky amethyst. Suddenly she realized exactly where she was—and why.

Well, she thought, Sam Gray would be grateful for the clear sky. He could deposit her at Bark's Ranch and go off to chase his precious outlaws.

She'd see if she could put a crimp in that plan. Warm and cozy in her bedroll, Billie stretched her legs, then rose upon her elbows, her hair tumbling down around her shoulders.

Mac Monroe, sitting cross-legged before the fire, almost dropped his coffee cup. "Why, you're a—a woman!"

Billie couldn't help smiling at his shocked expression.

Monroe glanced at Sam. "You called him Bill."

"I called her Billie. It's a nickname."

"I'm right sorry, ma'am," Monroe said, removing his hat. "I just assumed—"

"It's quite all right," Billie said.

"I met another man and his wife out here one time. Begging your respect, ma'am, she was a hardcase. Not at all like you."

"I'm not his wife," Billie said, as regally as possible.

Sam blushed to his roots.

"What she means to say," Sam interjected, "is that she's not here with me of her own free will. She's under my protection. I'm taking her out of here."

"Oh." The stranger looked confused.

"I'm his prisoner," Billie said, trying to keep the sarcasm out of her voice and failing.

"Well, maybe I'd better get going." The prospector rolled up his bedding hastily.

"Why don't you ride along with us?" Billie asked sweetly. She smiled as she saw the ranger's expression.

Sam glared at her.

"I thought I overheard you talking about heading in to Phoenix for supplies," Billie continued. "I, for one, would love to have some company."

"Well, I—"

"We're riding the same trail."

Monroe glanced nervously at Sam. "I reckon I could," he said diffidently.

Thrill to the most sensual, adventure-filled Historical Romances on the market today...

FROM  LEISURE BOOKS

As a home subscriber to Leisure Romance Book Club, you'll enjoy the best in today's BRAND-NEW Historical Romance fiction. For over twenty-five years, Leisure Books has brought you the award-winning, high-quality authors you know and love to read. Each Leisure Historical Romance will sweep you away to a world of high adventure...and intimate romance. Discover for yourself all the passion and excitement millions of readers thrill to each and every month.

Save $5.00 Each Time You Buy!

Each month, the Leisure Romance Book Club brings you four brand-new titles from Leisure Books, America's foremost publisher of Historical Romances. EACH PACKAGE WILL SAVE YOU $5.00 FROM THE BOOKSTORE PRICE! And you'll never miss a new title with our convenient home delivery service.

Here's how we do it. Each package will carry a FREE 10-DAY EXAMINATION privilege. At the end of that time, if you decide to keep your books, simply pay the low invoice price of $16.96, no shipping or handling charges added. HOME DELIVERY IS ALWAYS FREE. With today's top Historical Romance novels selling for $5.99 and higher, our price SAVES YOU $5.00 with each shipment.

AND YOUR FIRST FOUR-BOOK SHIPMENT IS TOTALLY FREE!

IT'S A BARGAIN YOU CAN'T BEAT! A Super $21.96 Value!

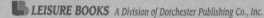 **LEISURE BOOKS** *A Division of Dorchester Publishing Co., Inc.*

The ranger seemed to deliberate for a moment, then shrugged. If he suspected anything, he didn't let on.

"It's settled, then," Billie said. She glanced at the chemise and drawers draped over a couple of creosote bushes near the horses. How had the stranger missed those? He wasn't very observant. "Ranger Gray, I would like to change my clothing. Would you two gentlemen do me the favor of going away for a few minutes?"

Sam flicked a glance to the underclothing. "We'll go for a walk."

Mac Monroe looked at Billie. For a moment his gaze lingered on her, making her feel uncomfortable. But his eyes were wide and innocent. How old was he, anyway? Eighteen?

Sam Gray was careful to take her firearms; then he led Mac Monroe down the ridge and out of view.

After they were gone, Billie debated saddling up Buttermilk and hightailing it out of there. But she knew she'd need a head start if she wanted to lose the ranger. The mules would slow her down. She'd have to take them; no one would make it far in this country without water. He'd catch her easily.

No. The best thing to do was to be the model prisoner and bide her time. Taking the reward poster, she scratched a quick note on it with a muddy stick, then put it in Monroe's saddlebag. With any luck he'd see it when they stopped for lunch. With better luck, he'd know how to read.

She hoped he wouldn't show his surprise—if he understood her message at all.

The note said: "Help me escape. I'll pay you well." She struggled into her chemise and drawers, grateful when the divided skirt no longer rubbed her. When Sam and Mac Monroe returned, she sat demurely by the fire, drinking her second cup of coffee, even though her heart was hammering a mile a minute, and when she looked at the ranger a spark seemed to jump across the space between them.

I'd better get away from him soon.

They didn't leave the canyon until late morning, when the creek had dropped enough for them to cross. By that evening, no doubt the creekbed would be dry as a bone.

The air was hot and steamy. Billie rode quietly behind Sam, wondering if she was doing the right thing.

The swaying of the horse combined with the smothering wet heat began to make her feel ill. Of all the times for her morning sickness to return! At last she couldn't stand it anymore. "Could we stop?" she asked with a gasp.

Sam Gray wheeled his horse around, his expression concerned. "What's wrong?"

"I—I feel a little sick. It's the heat." The sour taste filled her mouth. "I've got to get down—I think I'm going to—"

Before she knew it, Sam was at her side. He eased her off Buttermilk and helped her over to the brush, where she was violently ill. Billie was embarrassed, yet grateful for his calming presence. His big hand cupped her forehead to steady her. When she was finished, he gently wiped her mouth with his bandanna and smoothed her hair. His gaze found hers, and Billie felt her heart open up like a hothouse flower. The concern in those dark eyes was for her. It was obvious he cared. He was so strong, so reliable. There was something about him that made her feel safe. Again she found herself comparing him to Elliot. Sam Gray would never take off in the middle of the night, no matter what the provocation. Sam Gray wouldn't leave her to wait and wonder almost a month before sending her a message. She knew in her heart that if Sam were her fiancé, he would never desert her, never let her down.

Billie clamped down on that treacherous line of thought. Elliot hadn't failed her. Elliot was just a different kind of person. He was an artist, and artists never fit into the common mold. Elliot had proved in a thousand ways how much he loved her. Right now he was risking his life for their future.

Sam Gray was the enemy. She must remember that.

Mac Monroe appeared at Sam's elbow. "Are you all right?"

Billie nodded. Shaking, she tried to stand up. Sam steadied her as her feet almost slipped out from under her, and the familiar shock of pleasure arrowed through her body as his hand closed around her arm. "Do you want to rest?" he asked.

"For a minute." She couldn't look at him. If she did, she'd melt. Pulling away, Billie tottered over to a paloverde tree and sat down in its sketchy shade. Still a trifle queasy, she stared at her toes.

He had seen her like that, sick as a dog, and it didn't bother him.

As Sam loosened the cinch on Billie's horse, Monroe rummaged through his saddlebags, declaring he was hungry and wanted some jerky. Billie watched him carefully. His back was to her, but she thought she saw him stiffen.

He didn't let on that he'd seen anything, but as they sat in the shade of the tree, Billie caught him staring at her. He had a permanently ingenuous expression, perhaps because his eyes were sky blue and as round as saucers. It was hard to tell what he was thinking, because his expression didn't seem to alter much. But as Billie mounted Buttermilk, he winked at her.

Billie tried to hide her nervousness. She still felt ill, and now she had the disturbing impression that Monroe was watching her all the time. Come to think of it, that grin of his was quite unpleasant, and a couple of times he rode too close to her. Sam didn't seem to notice anything unusual, but Billie knew his casual grace hid a sharp mind and lightning reflexes. Perhaps he already suspected Monroe, but was too smart to show it. All of a sudden she hoped that was the case.

Billie desperately wanted to call back the note she'd written. What if Monroe killed Sam? How could she live with herself if she caused his death?

It was too late for that. Monroe was out of her control. She had started a juggernaut, and it would roll over anything in its path.

Billie wanted to warn Sam. A couple of times she almost spoke up, but two things stopped her: If Monroe wanted her money, he would have to do as she said. He would help her overpower the ranger, then take the money and move on. They could take Sam's firearms and leave his horse farther up the canyon. He'd have plenty of water, food and shade.

Grimly, she bit her lip. She had to find Elliot. He could be in danger. Besides, if she were around Sam much longer, she might end up making a complete fool of herself. She had to get away, had to throw her lot in with Mac Monroe, and hope that she could handle him.

Elliot held the rock up into the hard glare of the sun. The host rock was some kind of quartz, he guessed, its opaque white spikes embroidered with a thready filigree of gold.

The legend said that the gold from the Lost Dutchman Mine was to be found in white quartz. This was it. It had to be.

Elliot lifted his head to get his bearings, and the movement caused him to stagger. He still suffered from the effects of dehydration. Shielding his eyes, he scanned the canyon. The scene before him blurred and wavered, but finally resolved itself into land and sky. Elliot had made so many turns he was completely lost, but now he was not worried. He was meant to survive. Why else had he stumbled on the mine that hundreds of seasoned prospectors hadn't found after years of searching?

The legend centered around a tall peak—the peak everyone assumed to be Weaver's Needle. Elliot didn't see Weaver's Needle from where he was, but there was another, shorter spire nearby. The mine itself was high up on the ridge, and if he hadn't seen the pick and then looked up, straight at it, he would never have noticed it. A giant boulder looked as if it had been rammed into the canyon wall about twenty-five feet directly above the mine entrance. He certainly couldn't miss *that* again. Not to mention the old stone ruins at the mouth of this canyon.

He had to memorize the way this area looked, pay attention when he walked out. This was very important. He would fill his pockets and shirt with as much gold as he could carry, drink his fill from the spring, then head out.

But he'd be back.

The heat and his thirst were forgotten as Elliot grabbed the rusty pick and started chipping away at the dirt-clogged hole in the mountain.

Sam, Billie and Monroe could only ride single-file on the narrow path. Sam had managed to make sure that Mac Monroe rode in the lead, his pack burro behind him on the trail. Billie followed with her mules, and Sam and his mule took up the rear.

Just after noon, Billie's second mule stumbled and fell. Sam's horse, veering off the trail to avoid the fallen animal, brushed a chainfruit cholla with its chest. Squealing, the gelding jumped into the air, all four legs leaving the ground at once, and landed bucking. All hell broke loose. The mule, struggling to its feet and frightened by Sam's horse, almost pulled its companion and Buttermilk down as it bolted. Sam managed to stick with Panther, but the dark bay tried to run away from the excruciating pain. It took some horsemanship before the ranger could calm the horse and dismount. Billie had to worry about keeping her seat and getting her mules untangled.

Sam was off Panther now. Soothing the animal with gentle hands and quiet words, he took a stick and dislodged the cholla lobe from the horse's quivering hide.

"Don't do anything you'll be sorry for," Monroe said. He had guided his mount within a few feet of the ranger. His gun was leveled at Sam's chest.

Billie froze in her saddle. In the confusion, she had forgotten all about Monroe. Her heart thumped, and blood roared in her ears.

"Billie, get his guns," Monroe commanded.

This was what she'd been waiting for. Why did she feel so wretched? Her head throbbing, Billie slid down from her horse and collected the ranger's revolver, his rifle and her own firearms.

"I'll take them," Monroe said. He was grinning again, and his big blue eyes held a crazy gleam.

183

Momentarily, Billie thought of arguing.

"Hand them to me now," Monroe said, "or I'll shoot his horse."

She gave him Sam's gun and rifle, and started to put her own rifle in Buttermilk's saddle scabbard.

"Better let me have 'em," Monroe said.

"But they're mine."

"I'll hold 'em. For safekeeping."

Billie wanted to argue, but the hard light in Monroe's eyes dissuaded her, especially when he trained his gun on Buttermilk.

He unloaded her rifle and threw it down the slope, her revolver after it, and kept the ranger's firearms.

Billie realized with horror that she had made a terrible mistake. This man was unhinged. Would he kill Sam? "Don't hurt him," she cried.

"You want me to spare his life?"

"Please."

"Hear that? The lady has a soft spot for you. You know this is her idea, don't you?"

All through the ordeal, the ranger had stood still, his face like granite. He didn't show any surprise at Monroe's revelation.

"Seems she don't like you that much," Monroe said. He raised his gun and sighted down the barrel at the ranger. "She prefers me."

"Please!" Fear shot through Billie. Unmindful of her own danger, she reached for Monroe, blocking his aim. She grabbed at his gun hand.

Monroe shook her off. "I seen you before, Ranger. Out near Whitlow's ranch. You was trackin' someone. That wouldn't be me, now, would it? You aren't looking for my claim?" His voice was high, almost hysterical, and the mad glitter of his eyes threw a real scare into Billie.

"I'm tracking robbers."

Monroe snorted. "Likely story. You're after my mine, just like everybody else. Give me one good reason I shouldn't plug you right through the heart right now."

The ranger said nothing. He merely stared at Monroe, his expression grim. Didn't he know the meaning of fear? Why didn't he try to explain?

"He isn't after your mine!" Billie shouted. "He's an Arizona Ranger, and he's looking for the men who robbed the Old Dominion payroll. Please, let him go. All I want is to get away. We can tie him up, leave his horse down the canyon. I have lots of money. I'll pay you!" She realized the futility of her argument as soon as the words left her lips. This man had just thrown away her firearms. If he wanted her money, he had only to take it, and kill her along with the ranger.

Mac Monroe leaned his arms on his pommel, considering. "How much money you got?"

Billie halved the amount automatically. "Two hundred dollars."

He whistled. "You think this pissant ranger's worth a poke that big?"

"There's no reason to kill him." Billie tried to keep her voice calm. "You don't want a murder on your conscience, do you? You know the kind of attention that would draw. He's a ranger. Rangers take care of their own. Do you want the

185

whole bunch of them down on your neck?"

"No one would know who did it—if you didn't talk."

A chill ran up Billie's spine. Was he implying that he would kill her, too? She tried to make her voice sound hard, cold. "He's not worth it. Even if no one knows you killed him, this mountain will be crawling with rangers. They might even find your claim."

That caught his attention. His gun wavered.

"You know I'm telling the truth. It's up to you," she added dismissively. "Killing him would only create more problems. To me he isn't worth it."

Billie thought she saw the corner of Sam's mouth twitch slightly, as if he wanted to grin.

Monroe looked at Billie, his round eyes calculating. "If I killed him, you'd be mad at me, wouldn't you, Billie?"

"I would think you were a fool."

"You really believe the rangers would come looking for him?"

"You can bet on it."

"I sure don't want that. Get away from that horse!" he ordered the ranger. He threw Billie a coil of rope. "Tie him up good."

Billie slid down from her mount and secured Sam's hands behind his back with the rope. When she touched him, it felt as if a series of firecrackers exploded up and down her arm. Grimly Billie closed her mind to the attraction she felt for him, and concentrated on the task at hand. If she could convince Monroe that the ranger was no longer a threat, Sam's life would be spared.

Billie was adept at roping and tying, and knew several types of knots. Purposely, she tied the kind of knot Sam would be able to get out of, if he worked steadily for twenty minutes.

"Not so tough now, are you, Ranger?" Monroe taunted.

Sam's body stiffened. His broad shoulders grew taut, and Billie felt his resistance, his anger. Being near him at this moment made her remember the range stallion her father had caught once. Even though the horse had been blindfolded, its head snugged up against the snubbing post, one hind leg tied up so he couldn't go anywhere, she had still felt its dangerous power. Her father had urged her to touch the animal's quivering neck. As her hand came into contact with the wild animal, she'd experienced a shock. The stallion wasn't quivering with fear, but with rage.

That was the ranger.

I should be happy, she thought, tugging on the ropes. After all, he had done the same thing to her. Now he could discover just how uncomfortable and humiliating it was to be trussed up like this. But try as she would, Billie couldn't summon up the self-righteous anger she'd expected to feel.

"Legs, too." Monroe motioned with his gun barrel. Sam sat down.

Billie looped a rope around his legs and pulled it together. She could feel the whipcord strength of his thighs through the corduroy material, the tensed muscles. He didn't say a word, but Billie imagined that the irony of her tying him up wasn't lost on him.

"Here." Monroe threw Billie an old sock. "Gag him. We don't want to have to listen to him scream for help."

The sock was dirty. Tears ached behind her eyes. "I'm sorry," she whispered.

Poised over him, she made the mistake of looking into his eyes. They were impassive—neither angry nor disappointed—the emotions she'd expected. But his eyes took her measure, and found her wanting. That, more than anything else, cut her to the quick.

A lump formed in Billie's throat, and she blinked back tears. She felt diminished in his presence. Even tied up, Sam Gray remained undefeated. He radiated a powerful aura of dignity and pride, as that stallion had so long ago.

The stallion, never tamed, had been destroyed. The colonel couldn't let him back out on the open range to rival his own purebred stud, and a horse that couldn't be broken was useless on a ranch. The stallion's pride had killed him. Would Sam Gray's pride do the same?

Monroe was unstable. The challenge in Sam's eyes could be enough to set him off.

Billie swallowed. Suddenly she wanted to get away from here before the situation escalated. A crazy man like Mac Monroe would kill Sam Gray just to prove a point.

Hastily, she secured the gag.

She left him a full canteen within reach and took the reins to his horse. "We'll leave him up the canyon a ways," she told him. "Your mule, too."

"Come on! Let's get out of here!" Monroe motioned to her horse with his gun.

Relieved, Billie mounted Buttermilk. As they rode back in the direction they'd come, she willed herself not to look back.

But her heart ached with grief.

Chapter Eleven

Elliot spent the whole day digging out the loose ore from the mine. He tried to pace himself, drinking frequently from the spring and forcing himself to rest in the shade during the hottest part of the day, but exhilaration burned inside him like a fever. How could he rest when he had found the Lost Dutchman Mine? All that gold! Lying there on the ground, his for the taking!

He filled his pockets, shirt and pants with the broken rocks. Every time he thought he had enough, another rock would tumble out at his feet and its enticing mellow golden color would cast its spell over him. Finally, when he was so loaded down he could barely walk, Elliot decided to call it quits. He'd be back. Hastily he covered up the mine, and after drinking his fill from the spring, he started out in the cool of the evening.

By morning he realized he was lost again. As the sun rose and his thirst grew worse, Elliot started to panic.

He was in exactly the same position he'd been in before he'd found the spring and the mine.

His skin burned painfully wherever the sun touched it. He thought the remaining spines from the cholla had infected his arm, because it throbbed unbearably and raged with fever. He hadn't noticed it at the mine. It was almost as if he'd been in a daze the whole time; the only thing that had mattered on this earth was the gold he could gather up.

Thirst filled Elliot's throat like a hot, insistent wind. His fingers and toes began to tingle, and his head felt as if it had been locked into a vise. He'd been sick twice this morning, vomiting what little water he had in his stomach onto the baked ground. Now the headache was worse, and he began to weave as he walked, stopping every few minutes to lie in the shade of whatever bush or tree was handy.

Delirious, nearly blind, Elliot didn't notice the sky darken with clouds. He didn't hear the distant thunder, nor connect it to the possibility of rain—the stuff that would offer him salvation. He knew only that he was lost again.

Billie realized she was in great danger. She had willingly placed herself in the hands of a man who was completely unpredictable.

Fortunately, Monroe seemed oblivious to her as he rode on ahead. They left Ranger Gray's horse and mule in the next canyon, tethered to a mesquite tree. Her mind kept returning to Sam Gray. Would he really be able to get loose? Or had she condemned him to die in this barren desert?

If she had, she'd never be able to forgive herself.

The realization caught Billie with the suddenness of a dust devil, whirling through her soul. After she got rid of Monroe, what was to stop her from going back and checking on the ranger herself?

Billie could barely contain her eagerness to be rid of Monroe and carry out her plan. She found the opportunity as they reached a fork in the trail.

Nervously she cleared her throat. "Mr. Monroe, I know you were headed back to Phoenix when we met. I'll be fine from now on."

"I couldn't leave a woman alone out here. Besides, you don't have a gun."

Billie bit back the comment that flew to her lips; *he* was the one who had deprived her of her weapon. "I can't expect a perfect stranger to give up his own plans just to ride with me. I have the money—"

Monroe wheeled his horse around to face her and removed his gun from the waistband of his pants. He grinned. "Oh, I'll take the money, all right. I earned it, taking on that ranger for you.

Shouldn't have let you talk me out of killin' him, though. When he gets loose he'll come after me. But if I have a hostage, well, he'll think twice about pickin' me off from some ridge. Ain't that right?"

"Hostage?"

His blue eyes widened. "You know how long I've been in these mountains?"

"No." Billie tried to keep wraps on her runaway heart.

"A year. A year of working myself to the bone on some puny little claim, and you sail in here with more money than I got this whole time! Here you are, an answer to all my problems. A beautiful woman and enough money to make all my dreams come true."

Billie tried to keep her voice steady. "You gave us the impression you'd found a good claim—"

"I will now. Two hundred dollars will help me outfit a major expedition. Enough money to keep me in these mountains for another year or more. I can really look for the Lost Dutchman, instead of just trying to break even. I want to thank you for that."

Billie swallowed. "Just let me go. You'll have the money. I would only hold you up. Someone else could find the mine before you get back to Phoenix and put together your outfit."

"What will you do for me if I let you go?"

Billie stared at him. His smile was angelic, his round eyes innocent, but his words sent a shiver through her.

"I like you. You're right pretty. You be good to

me, we'll go our separate ways right afterward. But you got to be real good to me."

Revulsion flooded her. How could such evil lurk behind that boyish mask? Without thinking, she clapped her heels into Buttermilk's sides and took off at a gallop.

Gunfire burst behind her. The lead mule catapulted forward into Buttermilk's flank, then collapsed to the ground. Its dead weight brought Billie and her horse up short. She fumbled with the lead rope looped around her saddlehorn, but by that time she saw that escape was fruitless. Monroe had caught up, still grinning. He pointed his gun at her second mule. "First I shoot your mule, then your horse. You want that?"

Even if she managed to escape, without a mount she'd be dead in this country.

"You goin' to do as I say now?"

She glared at him.

His gun shifted to Buttermilk.

"No!" she cried. "I—I'll do as you say."

"Good." He giggled maniacally. "Let me see the money."

She tossed her saddlebag at him.

He rummaged through it. "There's got to be five hundred dollars here!" He threw the saddlebags at his feet, and the madness in his eyes glittered like shards of glass. "You lied to me, you crazy bitch!" He grabbed at her leg, yanked her out of the saddle and onto the rocky ground. "You're gonna learn not to lie to me! I'll teach you good!"

He shoved his fist against her mouth to keep her from screaming, and started pulling at her shirt. His hand found the tightly wrapped bandages and he cursed. His hungry mouth slithered over her lips, repulsive and wet, like snail tracks. Billie clamped her teeth together and tightened her lips against his tongue. She tried to push him off her, but he was too strong. She couldn't stand the thought of him doing what Elliot had done—couldn't even fathom such a horrendous thing.

She kicked him. He grunted. "Bitch!" His grimy hands snared her hair, pulling it painfully so that tears leaped to her eyes. The pressure of his chest against hers was smothering.

"I like spirit," he muttered. "And you're gonna like me." One hand fumbled with the buttons on her skirt, ripping them off and laying her bare except for the flimsy muslin drawers, which he quickly tore aside. He raised up a little, and Billie shuddered. Grinning demonically, he straightened his arms and lay poised above her. "Now you'll see—"

A neat round hole appeared in the middle of his forehead. Still grinning, he slumped onto her, just as the sound of the gunshot tore through Billie's ears.

Chapter Twelve

The unseasonal thunderstorms that had taken
Billie and Sam by surprise saved Elliot Stevenson's life, but they carried a hidden danger. Heat
and thirst had weakened him, but his real enemy
was hypothermia.

When the thunderstorm broke on the afternoon following his fabulous find, Elliot's body
was slick with sweat. As the wind picked up before the storm, the sweat began to chill him.
Rain lashed down, soaking him to the skin. He
filled the crown of his big Stetson with water,
drank so eagerly that afterward cramps
squeezed his stomach like a fist. His thirst
slaked, Elliot managed to find shelter under a
paloverde tree, but he was too far gone to remove his sodden clothes. He curled up into a

fetal position and lay shaking, miserable and feverish.

Elliot would never know how close he came
to death, there in the rain that had seemed such
a blessing.

He heard voices. He'd been hearing voices all
along, but these were different. They came
closer.

He wished they'd leave him alone, let him
sleep. Everything about him was cold except for
his throat. His throat was an entity in itself. He
imagined it as a fire-breathing dragon.

"Is he dead?" a voice asked.

The other voice spoke loudly beside his ear.
"Damn! Will you look at that!"

Someone shoved him roughly. Rocks spilled
out of his shirt. They were important rocks, but
he couldn't remember why. He scrabbled weakly
in the dirt, trying to hold on to one of them as it
rolled out from under his palm. The men talked
over him, but he didn't register the meaning of
the words.

". . . the real thing, all right. You reckon he
found the mine?"

"What mine?"

"The Lost Dutchman!"

"You think that's a true story?"

"Better ask him quick. He's about gone."

"Gimme that canteen."

Rough hands propped his head up. The back
of his skull felt as if it would fall off. His neck

trembled and when the first drop of water touched his lips, his throat locked.

"Where you been, fella?" one of the voices asked. "Where'd you get that gold?" Elliot couldn't see who was talking. He didn't know if he was blind or if his eyes were closed, and he didn't much care.

"He cain't talk. Get some of that water into him. Little bit at a time."

"Look at that gold! Hot damn! There must be a thousand dollars' worth of ore here!"

"Get his shirt off! He's shaking like a leaf. He'll die on us if we don't warm him up. Rub his arms."

"Kind of makes up for everything, don't it?"

"There's more. You can bet on it. Lots more where that came from."

"Did he drink any?"

"I think so. Went in and didn't come out."

"Don't choke him, now. We need him."

"Wonder where he's got it stashed."

"Ask him."

"You deaf? I said he cain't talk. Man, he's cold as the grave. Lie down with him."

"Are you kidding me?"

"You want him to tell us, don't you?"

"You do it."

"Do I have to do every damn thing myself?"

Their words drifted around and through him. He just wanted to be left alone.

Someone was lying with him. The widow? What was she doing out here? Did she want his gold? Well, he wouldn't give it to her. But he had to admit she sure felt warm. Her weight pressed against him, warming his back, and her hands rubbed his arms. He cried out loud as her hands brushed against the cholla spines. But her body warmth seeped into him.

"Don't you look cute!" one of the men said with a laugh. "Comfy as two spoons in a drawer."

"Shut up! You want him to live, don't you? There's only one way to do it when a fella's this far gone."

"He's as pretty as a girl, ain't he? Bet he'd like more than a hug from you."

"Dwight, shut your damned mouth!"

Elliot slept.

The Arizona Ranger stepped around the dead mule. He didn't even glance at Mac Monroe.

Billie felt as if all the air in her body had gone out of her in one expelled breath. She pushed the dead man off her and slid back in the dust, her limbs shaking uncontrollably.

Gathering up Billie's underclothing and skirt, Sam draped them across her, keeping his eyes level with hers to show he wouldn't look at her nakedness. "Do you want some water?" he asked quietly.

Unable to speak, she nodded.

Sam took his time retrieving it, giving Billie time to dress. She struggled into her clothing and sat back in the dirt, unable to remain standing.

Sam walked back and knelt beside her.

Billie should have felt embarrassed, mortified. Instead, a strange, bittersweet relief spread through her limbs. It had just been brought home to her how a man could overpower a woman. Even a weakling like Mac Monroe had more physical strength than she did. And yet this virile man—overwhelmingly, heart-stoppingly male—treated her with respect and kindness, his touch as gentle as if she were a piece of bone china. His very presence reassured her, filling her heart and soul with thankfulness and awe.

After she'd drunk her fill from the canteen, the ranger soaked his bandanna and handed it to her. Gratefully, Billie ran it over her face, trying to rub out the odor of Mac Monroe that clung to her nostrils.

"You're all right now," he said, his voice as gentle as it had been when he'd soothed his terrified horse. Nonsensically, Billie's mind grasped and held on to a tiny, unimportant detail. Sam's hair had come out of its short ponytail. It caught the sun; pure dark gold. She wanted to touch it. She wanted to touch the strong line of his jaw, bracket the breadth of his shoulders with open arms. Feel with her fingers, her arms, her chest, her face, the strength of the man who had saved her life.

"Billie?"

Her mind veered back to the close call she'd just had. To imagine that slimy, grinning creature doing to her what Elliot had done. She rubbed her arms, feeling sick. Sam brushed her hair from her face. When he withdrew his hand she grasped it in her own.

"He tried to—"

"I know."

"I'm sorry! I'm so sorry!"

Sam folded her into his arms. The sense of completion was overwhelming. "I know you are. It's all right."

"He could have killed you, and it was all because of me!" Her chest heaved; her eyes stung. She felt the tears come, the tears that her father had never let her cry. Sam—big and strong—held her to him, stroking her hair.

Billie felt as if her sobs were wrenched from the core of her body, from some bottomless well she did not know she possessed. Crying was a sign of weakness, but Sam didn't seem to mind. He just held her, and Billie was glad to be in his arms, glad to be with him at all. She had betrayed him, but he still cared enough to hug her when she cried. Still cared enough to come after her and save her life.

"Are you all right now?" he asked eventually. His face was only inches from hers, and Billie realized again how handsome he was. There was such strength in his features, strength and compassion. His eyes were like quiet pools of blue-green, clear and cool on a hot day. He tilted his chin slightly toward her, his fingers cupping her chin.

Billie shivered. She knew in her bones that he was going to kiss her. Oh, how she wanted him to. Wanted the feeling of his firm lips against hers, comforting, warm, enticing. It would be wonderful to immerse herself in him, let the brand of Sam's mouth obliterate the obscenity of Mac Monroe. She felt her own chin rise a fraction of an inch. They seemed to strain toward each other, like metal to magnet. Her breath hitched, still drowning in the tears she had cried, but the fluttering of her heart was due more to the possibilities opening up to her than to pain and fear.

His mouth hovered over hers. There was an invisible thread between them, pulling them toward each other. Billie was transfixed by his closeness, caught in his spell. Goose bumps ran up and down her arms. She could feel the layer of air between his face and her own, wanted to bridge the gap. The powerful feelings Sam's touch had unleashed would not be denied.

Slowly Sam lowered his head until their mouths brushed. As their lips pressed together, Billie couldn't believe the thrill that raced through her. It felt right. Their lips molded to each other, deepened, and Billie's arms came up to clasp him around the neck, pulling him closer.

And then she remembered Elliot.

Her hesitation was small, but it was enough.

Sam drew back as if burned. "I'm sorry," he said. "I shouldn't have done that."

Everything in her exhorted him to kiss her again, but she remained silent. There was such a thing as honor. As much as she wanted to kiss

Sam, she knew the attraction she felt for him was wrong.

"You've had a shock," Sam said after a moment. "We'll camp here."

Billie nodded. She certainly didn't feel like going on, not after what had just happened. Her gaze shifted to Monroe's body. "What about him?" she asked, her voice tinny in her own ears.

"I'll bury him."

"I'd rather you bury the mule." Billie knew she sounded bitter.

"I'll bury them both."

She sat in the shade of a paloverde tree, surrounded by a thicket of buckhorn cholla, burrobrush and prickly pear, and watched Sam dig the graves. His shirt came off early; the sun gleamed on each rippling muscle. A fine sheen of sweat oiled his bronzed skin. Occasionally he'd join her under the tree and drink from the felt-covered canteen she proffered him.

At these times his closeness was disturbing, exciting. Even the scent of his perspiration was clean and thoroughly male, redolent of the hot dried tops of wild grass, dust on horse hide and the salty tang of warm skin. His chest heaved only slightly from exertion and his body seemed larger than life in the velvety warmth of the tasseled shade. She couldn't keep her eyes off him: the solid musculature of his chest, the corded steel of his arms, the hard planes of his back. Every muscle and sinew was carved and beveled by outdoor work, honed and forged by the fierce desert in which he had dwelled.

It seemed that in those moments she had to fill her eyes with him, memorizing his every move and putting it away deep in her heart as a keepsake.

This was the man who had saved her life.

At last Monroe and the mule were each buried under a cairn of rocks.

"Would you mind—please say some words over the mule," she asked him.

Sam noted that the strain had made her face a dull paper white. He suddenly realized how strong a blow Monroe's attempted rape had been to a woman who was used to controlling her own life. He doubted Billie had ever been bested before.

Sam stood by the mule's grave and cleared his throat. "Some people think animals have no souls, but I never did hold with that. This mule was a good animal and he's earned a Christian burial. He gave his life for his mistress on this trail in the Superstition Mountains, April sixteenth, 1902."

"Thank you."

He pointed several hundred yards up the canyon. "Let's make for that cottonwood over there. It's a nice spot to camp. That way you won't have to look at these rocks and be reminded of . . . you just won't have to think about it."

Billie stood up, swayed and almost fell.

He caught her in his arms, and was surprised at the emotions that bolted through him—fear for her physical health, sorrow for what had happened to her and an affection so deep it wounded him. "You've had a nasty shock. Let me carry you over there."

"I'm not an invalid!"

"For once in your life, Billie, why don't you lean on someone?"

She didn't reply, but neither did she fight him. As he lifted her gently, she clasped her arms around his neck. He was aware of her cheek resting against his, the lightness of her body, the sweet scent of her. Her hair had come loose again and fell over his arm, a swatch of shimmering black satin. Its softness brushed against his skin, tantalizing, and he remembered how it felt to kiss her. For a moment he wanted to lower his mouth to hers again, to run his fingers over that peachy soft complexion, and tell her that he would take care of her. He would keep her from harm.

He took her over to the cottonwood tree and laid her in its shade. The leaves fluttered and pinwheeled on their stems, casting dapples of dark shade on the ground. Above them the rusty rock face towered into the sky, pocked with holes and chiseled into rippled strata. A few saguaros clung to impossibly narrow ledges, like pale green candles set into wall niches. Water from the rain had collected in shallow pools among the rocks of a stream that many times of year would be flowing strongly. Long grass grew beneath the mesquites. Ranchers called it six-weeks grass, because that was how long it was tender and edible. The grass was still tinged with green, although Sam had to choose a spot carefully for Billie to rest because the foxtails of the grass left needle-sharp burrs. Nonetheless, it was a beautiful spot in a hard country, a place that filled him with longing. He remembered a picnic with Marisa in a canyon like this, long ago.

"I'll get the mules and horses," he told her. "When I shot Monroe, his horse and burro took off. I'll look for them later."

When he returned, she seemed much better. He hobbled the animals and sat down nearby.

"I put your gun and rifle with your horse," Sam said. "Reloaded them from the ammunition box in your pack."

"Thank you."

"It was a lucky thing he threw your guns where I could get at them."

"I thought he unloaded them both."

"He wasn't very careful. There was one bullet left in your Colt."

"Thank the Lord you're a good shot." Her lackluster voice didn't match the fervency of her words.

They lapsed into silence, which quickly grew uncomfortable. At length, Billie spoke. "I guess you were right," she said softly. "I was a fool to come out here."

"You've just had some bad luck." Sam didn't know why he was suddenly making excuses for her, taking her part. But it was true. Billie was a good hand, and he had little doubt she could handle herself out here under most circumstances. He knew she'd survive better than a tenderfoot like Stevenson, if it weren't for the fact that there were always men who would prey on a woman alone.

"No, you were right all along. I almost got us both killed."

"You could use some practice tying knots."

"I meant you to escape!" she blurted out. "That's why I tied you like that."

"That's more like it. You were starting to sound like one of those helpless females who couldn't do anything without a man to help them."

She glared at him. "You don't know me very well, do you?"

He'd really gotten her goat. Color was back in her cheeks now, and she'd temporarily forgotten her own fragility. "I'll admit you shouldn't have trusted Monroe, although I can understand why you did it. But I have to know: Are you going to try to escape again?"

"You mean, did I learn my lesson?" she asked bitterly.

"You just said—"

"I know what I said!" She sighed heavily. "Maybe I have been foolhardy, coming out here."

"What about Elliot?"

She was quiet for a long time. He could see the anguish in her eyes. "I don't know," she said at last. "It seemed so simple . . . before. I thought it would be easy. Elliot went into the Superstitions. I'd just have to go in and get him.

I never expected . . ." She trailed off, her eyes dull, as if she were staring at some inward, unpleasant landscape.

He put his hand on hers, offering her comfort he knew was inadequate. Billie had just faced her own mortality, just learned that she was not completely in control of her life. That was a hard truth to swallow.

At last she turned her face to him. Her eyes glistened with unspilled tears. "I don't know what to do."

"It's dangerous out here. For anyone."

"I know! That's why I feel so . . . torn. How can I abandon Elliot, when he's even more helpless than I am?"

Sam had no answer for that.

Billie walked around the bend in the canyon. Sam had told her there was a deep pool of water there, collected from the last two days' rain. She needed a bath. The imprint of Monroe's fingers felt embedded into her skin, and she fancied that the smell of him covered her like a noxious film.

Sam had ridden off to find Monroe's horse and burro, making himself scarce for her benefit. Obviously he trusted her not to run away. Not that she felt like it. Apathy had replaced determination, at least for now.

The afternoon sun gleamed off the rocks, making them hot to the touch. Canyon ragweed smelled bitter and dark and secret in her nostrils, an age-old smell. Billie removed her boots, careful to put some of the money that had so enticed Mac Monroe into the toe of one of them. It was the safest place she could imagine; she doubted anyone would think to take off her boots to find money. Then, in quick succession, she removed her grimy leather skirt, her shirt, the torn chemise and drawers, peeled off the bandages around her chest, exulting in the freedom of her unfettered breasts. Was it her imagination, or were they just a little bigger? She felt the urge to touch them, cup her hands under their solid weight and see. Of course, that would be wrong. But the urge to explore her own body, especially now that she was on the brink of change, was irresistible. Self-consciously, Billie ran her fingers lightly over the white skin of her belly. She became braver, smoothing her hand once more over her flat stomach; then she let her hands rest at the juncture of her breasts and chest wall, allowing the firm globes to rest gently on her closed fists. Slowly she opened her fists, lightly furrowed a thumb into the groove between her breasts, opened her hands and let her fingers fan out briefly across the tight, soft skin, one forefinger gently flicking against a nipple as Elliot had once done. It hardened immediately with a sweet burst of pleasure. Billie's hand jerked back as if she'd touched a hot stove. What was she thinking of? The sun must have addled her brain. Only her husband should be able to touch her that way.

But a tiny voice inside her head spoke up. Why should she not touch her body? It was hers, wasn't it? During her baths she would run a washcloth with businesslike proficiency over the same area. What was wrong with taking pleasure in herself, the curves, the smooth expanse of creamy skin?

Tentatively, Billie's hands returned to her body. She ran them over her strong, lean thighs, down her legs to her feet. She placed one hand on the opposite arm, felt the long muscles that ran from shoulder to forearm to wrist. Women's arms were supposed to be white and soft and plump, but she liked the hardness of hers, the resilience and gleam of her skin over the firm contours.

She ran her hands back down to her stomach. Her mind wandered to the ranger, and his mouth on hers. She felt as if something were melting inside her, deep in the center of her body. The place where only Elliot had been.

But she pictured Sam, not Elliot. His tanned, muscled arms, his broad chest, the breathtaking power in his body, and wondered if his legs were muscular, too, beneath the shotgun chaps he wore. . . .

Right now, with the sun warm on the top of her head and the light breeze teasing her skin, she felt renewed. Yes, Mac Monroe had almost raped her, but he hadn't. Sam Gray had saved her from that fate.

Billie shivered deliciously. Sam made her feel safe. Safe and . . . valued. Just the way he listened to her, as if she had something important to say. He didn't ever patronize her, as some of the cattlemen did when she had business to discuss. She closed her eyes and pictured him as he had looked in the shade of the paloverde. Felt again the ghostly impression of his lips on hers.

She looked down at the water, but her eyes saw only the Arizona Ranger.

A minnow flashed in the tarnished gold shallows, then darted away. Initially, the air breathing upon her naked body felt cool, almost seductive, but the sun's heat on her skin quickly grew uncomfortable.

Billie stepped thigh-deep into the pool. The water was searing in its coldness. It sucked at the warmth in her, rolling up from the placid depths that glimmered brown and amber like the tortoiseshell combs she had left behind at home. Below, among the speckled rocks, she could see green moss furl and unfurl with the movement of the water. She dug her toes into the silt, gaining purchase on the slippery-smooth rock beneath it, leaned forward and dove into the bright water, feeling it rip at her hair and body. The dashing cold cleansed her, laved Monroe's filth away.

After washing with Pears' scented soap, Billie swam for a while, then floated, drifting in the tingling water as her black hair fanned out around her. Nearby, a cottonwood trailed its bright green leaves like a feather boa onto the water. With each breeze, little bits of white fluff detached themselves from the cottonwood branches and snowed down on the placid surface of the pool. Billie closed her eyes and let the gentle current of her own paddling feet carry her into another world, where the sun bloomed rosy gold against her eyelids and joy lay cradled deep inside her. A sweetness pervaded her body as she dwelt on the memory of Sam's kiss, his lips pressing against her own . . . shouldn't think that . . . it was wrong . . . but she let the lapping water take her along, and it was impossible to resist.

Sam came across Billie by accident. He'd found Monroe's horse and pack burro in the next canyon. That canyon had looped around a spur of high ground, taking him back to where he'd started. He had forgotten that Billie had gone up this part of the canyon for her bath.

He let his pony pick its own way along the rocky ridge, once in a while glancing down at the water, which reflected the sun occasionally like strands of a silver necklace draped along a gleaming white collarbone of rock.

He caught a flash in the rocky pool below.

Billie.

Sam felt his breath leave him, as if he'd been punched in the stomach. She was beautiful. More beautiful than he had imagined. Her slender body cleaved the water, broke the surface, then glided backward, her hair as dark as midnight as it rippled around her. One shoulder arched up out of the shallows, as smooth and polished as a bar of soap.

No man could remain unmoved by such a sight. He wanted her. Every bone in his body resonated with that primal need. He felt himself stiffen, felt the drive begin that jarred him out of his mind and into his senses.

She flashed like an otter at play.

Sam swallowed. He wanted to be with her, hold her, kiss her, take her. Even though he knew it was wrong, he found himself dismounting from Panther, found himself on the path down to the pool, his breath coming in gasps.

She didn't see him. She was oblivious, floating on her back, eyes closed.

Sam could barely contain himself as he shucked his clothes, hands shaking. He entered the water like a knife, and the coldness jarred him back to reality. What was he doing?

Startled, Billie jerked upright and flailed as she tried to maintain her footing.

"Sam!" Her face was white against the dark water and the water-shiny black of her hair.

He kept his distance, treading water. "I didn't mean to startle you. It was hot and I saw you swimming—it looked so inviting—I had to come in, too." He didn't say what had been the most inviting.

To his surprise she didn't argue. "I suppose you have as much right as I do to be here. But I'll have to get out." She turned away. "I trust you'll turn your head."

He reached out and grabbed her hand. He felt a kinetic energy as their fingers touched, and he shivered. "Please don't go. We're both in now. I won't touch you." Silently he added, *If you don't want me to.* "The harm's done."

She hesitated. Now that she was used to the

water, she didn't want to leave it. The silky liquid was soothing, and there were several more hot dusty hours until sunset. Sam was a man of his word. A gentleman. Besides, if she kept under the water he wouldn't see anything. . . .

Of course he already had. He had seen Mac Monroe preparing to rut on her like a mad bull, had seen her skirt torn away from her legs and the torn drawers.

She blushed, her face radiating heat.

"I can't see anything," he said, as if reading her mind. "Besides, all men are the same to one degree or other, and so are women. I've seen plenty."

"No doubt you have," she said dryly, thinking that a handsome man of his age must have experience with a number of women. Suddenly it seemed quite humorous. She started to laugh. Sam joined her.

"Are you laughing at me?" he said at last. "Don't you think I could get a woman to look at me twice?"

She tried to hold on to her mirth, not even knowing what struck her so funny. It was impossible. She let out another giggle.

"You *are* laughing at me! I'll teach you not to make fun of an Arizona Ranger."

"How will you do that?"

"Like this!" His arm arced as he skimmed a hand across the pool's surface, splashing water in her face.

She splashed him right back, and soon they had a war going. She forgot that they were naked, forgot that this whole incident was sordid and unseemly. Closing her eyes and shoving water at him, ducking his salvos, she felt free and happy, like a bird on the wing.

Suddenly she felt something grab her leg. She let out a scream and kicked out. Sam surfaced right beside her. "You're not easy to trip up," he said.

She was neck-deep in the water, but Billie could feel the heat of his body close to hers. She looked into his eyes, and her heart seemed to twirl once before settling into her stomach. The water's reflection noosed his dark shoulders in wavering golden light, bounced off his square chin and brought a sparkle to his teal-colored eyes. He was staring at her, his gaze serious. A shock of his dark golden hair fell over his forehead, and Billie thought lazily that the ranger was still dangerous.

And then, as if by tacit agreement, they came together. One moment they were looking into each other's eyes; the next, it seemed to Billie that they surged through the tiny space that separated them, lips melding together like twin flames as she entwined her arms around his neck. She felt the solid wall of his chest against the cushion of her own breasts, smelled his warm skin, the masculine scent of him, drank in every sensation with a thirst that seemed unquenchable.

She felt as if she had come home. His mouth was made for hers—the curve of his lips, the way his tongue teased at the corners, making her think of rich, forbidden honey.

She wanted more. Her need drove her, clamoring for a more satisfying kiss. Their tongues mingled, danced, melted together, binding them closer. But she wanted even more than that, could feel the aching at the core of her body, feel the desire surge through her as it had never done with Elliot.

Billie knew that Sam wanted her as well. She could feel him, hot and insistent in the cold water, and it almost drove her mad.

This is wrong.

She was helpless to stop it. She might as well have been on a runaway train. Closing her eyes, she gave in to desire.

His body pressed against her, shutting out the water, so that their flesh moved together in delightful friction, sparking a flurry of glorious sensations, silk on satin. But there was one part of him that was not tender.

Billie gasped out loud as she felt the heat of him, the adamant press of flesh against her hip. Succumbing to the whirlwind of sensation radiating from her core, she shifted her stance slightly so that he came up against her most tender place. She knew his power then, like a spring, coiled and ready, waiting to be unleashed. Waiting for her to unleash it with a word.

The words hovered behind her lips, breathless but unspoken. *Yes, please, yes!* He drew back slightly and looked into her eyes. The question there was plain to read, and she was surprised that he had the self-control to ask it. "Billie, are you sure you want this?"

It was that question that stopped her. Reality collided with desire. She remembered her duty, and the trust that had been placed in her. Before she could censor them, the unwelcome words hurtled through the space between them. "But what about the baby—"

She saw something in his eyes then that made her flinch. A flash of brilliance, quickly extinguished. Sam Gray's eyes became hard as sapphire, reflecting back the sun from their brittle surfaces. "Baby?"

She couldn't answer. It was too hard to catch her breath, and she felt a moan growing in her throat for what might have been. She clamped down on the sound, but her body buzzed with pleasure denied, and despair that there was no chance for it now.

"What baby?"

Wretched, she pulled away from him.

His arm was like an iron bar as he pulled her around to face him. "Answer me!"

She quailed at his anger, his anguish. Defiantly she lifted her chin. "Elliot's. That's why I have to find him. He has a right to know."

Sam's eyes darkened, and she saw the pain there. His hand dropped from hers. "I'm sorry," he said roughly. Then, without a backward look, he swam to the edge of the pool and pulled himself out.

She saw him stand there briefly, his back to

her, as he bent to pull his trousers on. He picked up his boots, shirt and hat, and walked into the brush above the pool.

She wanted to reach out to him, but held back.

What was wrong with her? How could she have given in to her carnal desires like that? She had never felt like this before, never been pulled by such a strong current into such deep water. It was as if she were another person altogether. Certainly Elliot had never elicited such a response in her.

Sam, at least, had a clear head. But she . . . she was little better than the whores on Canal Street in Nogales.

Stunned, choked by self-revulsion, Billie waited for a long time after she heard Sam ride off. The water had lost its buoyancy. It felt as dull as dishwater against her skin. Nothing could wash the filth from her body this time, since it came from within.

Sam unsaddled his horse, trying to put a brake on his careening thoughts. The fact was, he didn't know who to be angry with: Billie, Elliot or himself.

He wanted to strike out, destroy, tear something apart. Beat his fists bloody against a rock. How could she have come out here at all, knowing what she did? How could she expose her unborn child to such danger?

He closed his eyes as he saw in his mind's eye Mac Monroe, poised above her. How close the man had come to raping her, maybe even hurting the child—

Damn her! Damn her for putting the life of her child in jeopardy, damn her for making him feel like a fool, damn her for being so beautiful, so cooperative, so loving. . . .

A hollowness filled his soul. He felt as if his legs had been kicked out from under him. For a brief instant he had found himself letting go, letting this woman into his heart. Found himself hoping that maybe this time he could give his love openly, and that that love would be returned.

But no matter the reason, he had taken advantage of her. He'd thought her inexperienced, a virgin. Yet he'd tried to seduce her. His craving for her had overtaken common decency. He had wanted her so badly that, for a split second after she'd told him about the baby, he'd wanted to continue. Block out her words from his mind, make love to her and damn the cost.

Pain crushed his heart, and despair whistled through the cracks in his soul like wind through an abandoned house.

He had already started supper when a chastened Billie Bahill returned to camp. He tried to ignore the fresh scent of her skin and the way her raven hair, still wet and smelling of Pears' Soap, fell down her back in a tangled skein. And the two enticingly damp patches on her shirt where her hair had lain on her breasts.

Sam held out a plate, the action stiff and abrupt.

"I'm not hungry."

"Don't give me that," he said, his voice curt. "You have to eat."

She didn't answer, but accepted the plate almost meekly.

They ate in silence. At last Sam couldn't stand it anymore. "You could have told me."

"Why?"

"Because I had a right to know."

"*You* had the right to know? You have nothing to do with it."

"You should have told me," he insisted stubbornly.

"Why? You were dead set on making me go back. If I told you it would only make things worse—I'd never be able to talk you into letting me go."

"I wouldn't have let you go anyway. I told you before, these mountains are no place for a woman alone."

She looked at him, her eyes clear. "Then it didn't make any difference."

His fury, simmering all evening, boiled over. "Yes, it made a difference! I never would have touched you if I knew!"

Her skin turned shell pink, and she looked away. "I'm sorry," she said at last.

Her apology took the wind out of his sails. What she'd done was understandable, he supposed. Billie was determined to find Elliot and tell him about his child, and she would do anything to achieve that aim. He was more angry with himself for wanting her so much. "What now?"

"What do you mean?"

Damn, he wished she wouldn't look at him like that. He could get lost in those eyes in an instant. "Do you still want to find Elliot?"

"Yes." Her gaze held steady.

Do you still love him? The words crouched behind his lips like a troll under a bridge, but he did not say them out loud. "Why don't you hire someone to find him?"

She paused, thinking about it. "I suppose I could do that." The relief in her expression indicated that she would give him no more trouble. It must have finally sunk in how dangerous it was out here.

"When we get back to Bark's Ranch, I'll find you someone good."

"Thank you."

There was a formality between them now. They had gone too far, seen too much of each other's souls, and then been yanked back into stark reality. It was too much to hope for them to be friends now.

"We'll be able to make it back tomorrow," he said into the awkward silence.

"I guess it's the best thing."

"Are you feeling all right?" He floundered, grasped at words. "I mean, when Monroe pulled you from your horse . . . ?"

Her gaze was level. "I'm fine."

"Good."

There didn't seem to be anything else to say.

A short while later, Billie stood abruptly and walked to the edge of the creek. Sam could barely see her in the gathering darkness, but he could tell from the way she stood, shoulders slightly bowed and hands clasped, that she was unhappy. Before he knew what he was doing, he had walked over to where she was. A shiny tear tracked down her cheek.

"You all right?" he asked, knowing it was a foolish question.

Billie smiled, her expression ironic. "Don't worry about me."

"Anyone can see something's bothering you."

She shook her head. "You were right. I could have hired someone to find Elliot. But instead I had to come out here myself. When I think what might have happened . . ." She shivered. "How could I have been such a fool?"

"You did what you felt you had to do."

She turned to face him, her expression grim. "I didn't even let myself think of doing it another way. And do you know why? Because I wanted to look him in the eye when I told him, because I was afraid he might not . . ." She faltered. "Might not come back. I thought that if I could only talk to him, make him see how important it was to both of us, he would be as happy as I am."

"It could still be that way," Sam said, but he knew his voice lacked conviction.

"No matter what," she said fiercely, "I will not forget my duty to this child. Whether he marries me or not, we'll survive. I made up my mind about that a long time ago."

"I know you will."

Her eyes searched his. "You really mean that, don't you?"

His throat was suddenly dry. "You have a great deal of courage. You'll do what you have to, no matter what happens with Elliot."

She frowned. "It will be tough, though. For the child. You know how people are. They'll make things hard for her."

"Her?"

"I want a daughter."

He couldn't help but grin. "Do you always get your own way?"

Her expression turned bleak. "Not this time. This time I have to admit defeat and go home."

"Sometimes that's the most courageous thing a person can do." He reached out and took her hand, looked into the calm sadness of her eyes. "We'll find Elliot, I promise. I'll look for him myself, after I bring those outlaws in."

"He said he wanted children."

"He'd have to be a fool not to want your children." The words tumbled out before he could stop them.

Her eyes mirrored her surprise. "You are too kind," she said at last.

"No. I mean it. You are a fine person. A brave, fine person."

She smiled again, but the smile didn't reach her eyes. "A fine person doesn't get herself into situations like this."

"You're too hard on yourself."

She pulled away from him. "You don't understand! First I let Elliot have his way with me, and then—this afternoon . . . I don't know what's wrong with me!" She averted her face, but he knew she was crying silently.

He took hold of her shoulders. "There's nothing wrong with you! I was the one who tried to seduce *you*. If there's any blame, let's lay it at the right door."

"But I was willing. Oh, you'll never know how willing! How could I do that to Elliot?"

"What happened was momentary madness. It won't happen again." But even as he spoke, he felt the current of excitement between them, burning through his fingers. How badly he wanted to tell her he loved her, that they would have a good life together.

But he, too, had his duty.

She leaned against him, and he found himself stroking her hair. "Don't think about it anymore," he said soothingly. "You were scared; you had a nasty shock. It was only natural you'd turn to me for comfort."

She sighed, and it was as if a great burden were lifted off her shoulders. "It would kill Elliot if he knew," she said. "He's a very proud man."

"I won't tell him," Sam replied, his heart aching. "Everything will be all right. You'll see."

They walked back to camp, hand in hand. Not long after, Billie went to sleep. Sam lay in his bedroll, too, but his eyes remained wide open.

*   *   *

Billie woke to the sound of clattering hooves on rock. A vague feeling of shame followed her into consciousness, and with it the remembered scene at the pool with Sam. Her stomach constricted with revulsion at her own actions.

She heard a low nicker.

The ridge opposite rose up black against the indigo sky. Stars speckled the heavens, so close that Billie imagined she could touch them. The dank odor of canyon ragweed, which had become so familiar to her in this desert, ladened the membranes of her nostrils; she could almost taste its bitterness. A light breeze touched her skin, and the cottonwood's leaves rustled.

The sound of hooves again. Out of the corner of her eye Billie caught a movement; something pale floating over the trail farther up the canyon. As it approached, the pale thing materialized into a horse—a white horse. The whole scene held a dreamlike, surrealistic quality. The creature's mane and tail were very long and streamed down in shimmering skeins. Something silver at its head glinted in the moonlight. A bridle?

The animal arched its neck as it picked its way along the base of the dark cliff, stopping here and there to graze or to drink from the water.

Billie couldn't believe her eyes. *I must be dreaming!*

She heard the scrape of boots on rocks, and glanced over at the other bedroll. Sam sat up, his gaze fixed on the white horse.

Sam's gelding whinnied.

The horse approached, its coat the color of moonstone. The light from the moon glanced off its pinkish white eyes.

The horse was an albino. Billie remembered the men at the Red Indian Mercantile telling her that Elliot was riding an albino. "Elliot!" She gasped.

At her voice, the horse raised its head, sniffed the air, then wheeled and took off down the canyon.

Billie threw back her blankets and started to pull on her boots.

"Leave it," Sam advised. "The horses are tired and it's too dark to see all the rocks. The horse will still be here in the morning. It's the only water for miles."

"That was Elliot's horse." When Sam didn't reply, Billie said, "Don't you understand? Elliot could be hurt!"

"If you ride now, you might get hurt, too. It can wait until morning."

Suddenly all Billie's doubts about Elliot disappeared. She couldn't go back to sleep now, not knowing that he might be hurt—even killed!

She had to do something. Struggling into her boots, she went over to get Buttermilk.

Sam Gray was at her side in a flash. His hand closed around her arm. Billie felt a shock run through her body. His touch was like electricity. "Are you crazy?" he asked her. "If Buttermilk stumbles, if he throws you into those rocks, do you know what might happen? You've had a close call today."

Billie knew he was right. She pulled away, try-ing to ignore her body's betrayal. "He could be dying! If he lost his mules, if he's without wa-ter—the horse had its bridle on. It must have thrown Elliot. I can't wait. Every hour counts!"

"I'll go."

"Now? You won't wait until morning?"

"Going now doesn't make any sense."

"Please!"

Sam's mouth straightened to a grim line. "Promise me you'll stay here. For the baby's sake if not your own."

"I will."

Sam squeezed her hand. He walked over to his horse, saddled and mounted him, then rode off down the canyon.

That same night, Elliot lay in his borrowed bedroll, staring at the moon. Although his stom-ach was full and he had almost recovered from dehydration, the fear that consumed him was greater than before.

Dwight and Phin were going to kill him. He knew it in his bones.

Once he was in his right mind again, Elliot had recognized the good Samaritans who had rescued him. The day he'd left Phoenix he'd seen their faces in the newspaper. Dwight and Phin Daw had attempted to rob the Old Dominion Copper Company payroll, murdering four peo-ple in the process.

They were killers.

It naturally followed that these were not the

kind of men who'd save a life out of kindness. Oh, no. They were keeping him alive to find the gold, and after he found it for them, they'd dispose of him.

We'll be partners. Fifty-fifty. You show us where the mine is, and we'll haul it out on the mule. We'll all be happy. You'll get a lot more gold than you could carry out on foot, and we'll get our share for saving your life and providing the mule. You owe us.

Elliot was no fool. Once he located the mine, his life would be over. For the last day and a half—they didn't give him a whole lot of time to recover—he'd purposely tried to throw them off the trail, buying time. But now they were getting impatient. They might be thinking he couldn't find it at all, and consider him a liability.

The fact was, even if he wanted to find the mine, he doubted he could. The canyons all looked alike, and for the life of him he couldn't remember where it was.

He was scared, down deep. So scared he couldn't sleep, couldn't think. The only thing keeping him alive was the promise of more gold. He didn't dare tell them he'd picked up most of the loose stuff, that if they wanted more, they'd have to mine it like everybody else, by drilling and blasting it out with dynamite.

Telling them that just wouldn't be prudent.

Sam rode through the darkness, trying to come to grips with his feelings about Billie.

He had lost all sense of honor from the moment he saw her in that pool. He had gone after her with single-minded purpose, thinking with the lower half of his body, unwilling even to consider her feelings.

The savage attraction they'd shared aside, Sam should not have tried to take advantage of it. Billie had been through a bad experience, and she had been fair game for him. He was her rescuer, the man who had saved her from rape. Human emotion, he'd realized early on, could be pulled every which way if the pressure was right. When control was taken away, people did strange things to affirm that they were still alive. He'd heard of many a female hostage who had married her Apache captor. Billie's desire for him had seemed genuine, but Sam doubted she would have let him touch her under other, less stressful circumstances.

He had a lot to answer for. He couldn't forget the anguish in her voice tonight. *A fine person doesn't get herself into situations like this.*

He had to find Stevenson. All their troubles would be over once he found the artist. Billie and Elliot would be reunited, return to La Zanja to start a new life together, and he could walk away with a clear conscience. He tried to convince himself that Billie could be happy, even married to a con man like Elliot. No doubt the colonel would see Elliot differently, now that Billie was pregnant. And Elliot himself would have to be good to her—she was the golden goose.

Sam winced. He couldn't bear the thought of

Billie marrying a man who didn't love her. But what else could he do? She was determined to find Elliot; she must still love him.

He had no right to interfere, since he could offer Billie nothing. Even if she did love him, he couldn't see any way out of the ties that bound them both.

He found the albino early in the morning, grazing along the dry streambed in another canyon. The horse didn't look so impressive in the light of day. There were festering saddle galls all along its back. One rein dangled free; the other had snapped off. The Mexican spade bit had torn hell out of the horse's tender pink mouth.

It was one sorry-looking animal.

Sam removed the silver-embossed bridle, put his spare halter on the albino and led it along with him. The horse would never last out here on his own.

The ranger found no sign of Elliot. He had looked for tracks, but seen no footprints. No mule tracks, for that matter. Only the albino's prints, which were easy to tell because they were much bigger than the average cow pony's.

Sam judged that the albino had been loose for several days. He supposed that if he followed the gelding's tracks long enough, he would find the place where the white horse and Elliot had parted company, but it would take a long time. A loose horse didn't walk in a straight line the way a ridden horse did; it wandered where its fancy took it, stopping to graze whenever it felt like it. There was no way of telling how far the albino had come, and its trail would more than likely lead Sam on a lot of wild-goose chases.

After following the aimless path through two canyons, Sam decided to turn back. The albino's feet were tender and it stumbled often, holding Sam up. He'd leave the white horse with Billie, then come out again.

That was when he saw the red stuff. It hung on a limb of creosote like a tuft of bright red fur. Angora. Cowboys up north used angora in their chaps.

Could Elliot be stupid enough to wear something like that out here? He thought of the silver-encrusted bridle, the fancy Spanish bit. It was obvious Elliot liked to put on a good show.

Sam squinted against the glare. All up and down the canyon he could see the red stuff, snagged on anything prickly. Out here, that described most of the plants.

He hobbled the albino and followed the angora trail for a while.

Around noon, Sam came to a dead-end canyon wedged between vermilion cliffs. In the shade of the cliffs grazed a mule. The contents of its pack littered the canyon: shiny new camping gear, prospecting equipment and a box of art supplies.

Sam had found Elliot Stevenson's mule.

Chapter Thirteen

Billie never did like to wait. Hours had come and gone, and still Sam didn't show up.

The sun rose above the cliff face. It was beautiful here, an oasis in the dry desert, but Billie couldn't appreciate it. Worry nagged her, made her nervous. Her heart hammering in her chest, she prayed fervently for Elliot to be all right, for Sam to find him. If anyone could save Elliot, it was the strong, capable ranger.

She tried not to think about how good it felt to be held by Sam Gray, or how his kiss still resonated within her soul. Instead she took out the photograph of herself and Elliot and stared into its depths, as if by doing so she could return to the person she'd been before this adventure. Despite the hardship of tracking Elliot down, her life had been an uncomplicated one until three days ago.

Billie realized that she could stare at the portrait until she was cross-eyed, but it wouldn't arouse the tender feelings it once had. Too much had happened since then. But she was certain that when she saw Elliot in the flesh again, everything would be all right. She loved him, didn't she?

Hooves clopped hollowly on the rocks downstream. Billie turned her head in that direction, her heart soaring. But it wasn't Sam.

Strangers rode toward her: two scruffy-looking men on bay horses leading a mule, and one even scruffier companion on foot.

Billie was frightened. The man in the lead, riding the blaze-faced bay, had the severe expression of a preacher, with piercing eyes. A tangled beard and mustache hid his mouth, which, judging from the man's clenched jaw, was compressed tightly. The younger of the two horsemen was small and wiry, with a long drooping mustache. Jug ears stuck out beneath the grimy hat. A domed forehead combined with a long face and small round chin made Billie think of an inverted pear. His eyes did not blaze like the other man's; they were sunk deep in dark sockets. He didn't look too bright. Both horsemen shared the same broad, flat nose. They looked mean.

Billie sidled over to Buttermilk and stretched her hand toward the scabbard for her rifle, her eyes never leaving the men approaching her. After Mac Monroe, it paid to be wary.

The man in the lead raised his hand, halting his party. He leaned forward on his pommel. "Well, well. What have we here?"

She glanced at the third man, the one she had initially dismissed because he was afoot, and therefore less dangerous. He, too, looked vaguely familiar. Lank black hair hung in his face; his beard was bushy. Black eyes glittered madly in his skull. He wore ridiculous angora chaps, bright red. Threadbare and almost bald in places, the chaps looked as if some madman had torn out giant hanks of the wool by the handful.

Billie's hand closed over the rifle stock.

Suddenly the man on foot stopped. "Elizabeth!" he shrieked, and lunged forward, his arms wide.

Billie's hand dropped, her rifle forgotten. Shock bolted through her. How did this filthy ragamuffin know her name?

The man stumbled just before he reached her and grabbed at her legs as he fell. His hands clutched her skirt as he hugged her around the knees. "Elizabeth, oh, Elizabeth, I'm so glad to see you!"

It was Elliot.

Billie staggered and almost fell as the man clasped her legs. She couldn't fathom this turn of events. Elliot. The man she loved, alive and safe. He was holding her right now, and yet the only emotion she felt was embarrassment. She couldn't move because he clung to her knees. It was almost as if he were abasing himself for her. Why didn't he stand up?

Such an uncharitable sentiment was unlike her. Did she have a heart of stone? Elliot was obviously in very bad shape. He needed her now more than ever, and here she was showing her distaste for him just because he was too weak to stand!

Billie dropped to her knees beside Elliot and hugged him hard. He was a bag of bones. "Elliot, I was afraid you were dead!"

"What's going on here?"

Billie glanced up. The older man had taken off his hat and smoothed thin chestnut hair flat across his squared-off head. He reminded her of Howard Daw, although he didn't look much like him.

Elliot's face was pressed into her neck, his fingers hooked in her hair. He said her name over and over, his body racked by giant sobs. Billie felt another stab of annoyance. She felt smothered.

It had all happened too fast. One minute she was looking for Elliot, sure that he was injured or killed, and the next, here he was. And these two men—how had he hooked up with them?

Apparently they were as much in the dark as she. "Do you know this man, lady?" the stocky man demanded.

Billie tried to keep her voice calm. "Who are you?"

"Shut your mouth! I'm askin' the questions!"

"Now, Phin, that ain't no way to talk to a lady." The pear-faced horseman looked at her, his gaze gentle. Out of the harsh sunlight, whose shadows had given his face a brutish cast, he looked much younger. His eyes were a softer blue than the leader's, and he seemed genuinely friendly.

"Oh, God, Elizabeth . . . I can't believe it. . . ."

Billie ignored him. She concentrated instead on the two men and tried to determine whether they were dangerous. "This is my fiancé. I found his horse last night. I'm very grateful to you for saving his life."

"Her fiancé, eh? What do you think, Dwight? Do you believe that?"

The younger man grinned. "Elliot don't look the type to have a pretty girl like her. A pretty boy, maybe."

The slur was not lost on Billie. "I assure you that it's true. Elliot will tell you if you don't believe me."

Elliot detached himself from her arms. "It's true," he said. He sat down in the dirt and passed a hand over his face. Billie saw for the first time how sick he really was.

"You traveling with anyone?" the man called Phin demanded. He was looking at the mules and horses.

Something warned Billie not to give anything away. "Nope, just me."

"That's a saddlehorse," Phin said, pointing to Mac Monroe's sorrel.

"I found him on the trail. His owner had an accident."

"What're you doin' out here?"

The truth would serve as well as anything. "I was looking for my fiancé. Now that I've found him, I imagine we'll be heading back." She tried to sound confident, breezy. "Thank you again for saving his life. If there's anything I can do—"

"Not so fast. We have some unfinished business to take care of. We're partners with your friend here."

"Partners?"

"Business partners. We own a fifty-fifty share in a mine. Elliot was just taking us to it when we came across you."

"A mine?" Confused, Billie glanced at Elliot. He was sitting cross-legged in the sand, and despite his bedraggled appearance, looked more like the old Elliot. "Is it true? You have a mine?" she asked him.

Elliot shrugged. "I did find some old workings. There were a few pieces of loose ore."

Something told Billie that Elliot wasn't telling the entire truth.

"You said it was the Lost Dutchman!" Dwight glared at Elliot. The gentleness in his eyes had fled as if it had never been.

"I'm prone to exaggerate." Elliot glanced at Billie, his demeanor calm now. "You know how I am. I get excited about things, even when they're not important. It's the artist in me."

"He led us on!" shouted Dwight. "I ought to kill you right now!" He reached for his gun.

"Dwight, you buttonhook, can't you see he's lying? He just doesn't want to share the wealth."

Phin withdrew his own pistol and leveled it at Elliot. "You going back on our deal?"

Elliot's coolness disappeared. "No, Phin, you know I wouldn't do that! If I misled you in any way, I'm sorry! But really, that mine was just an old working."

Heart hammering, Billie edged toward Buttermilk's saddle. Her hand was almost to the scabbard when Dwight trained his gun on her. His grin was apologetic. "Phin, she was goin' for her gun."

"That ain't very ladylike, now, is it? Dwight, you snub up those mules. We'll take the girl with us."

"Yes, sir. 'Scuse me, ma'am—I mean, miss—but you'll have to get away from that horse."

Billie's heart reached a crescendo as Dwight put a hand on her arm. She recoiled as she saw that the third finger of his right hand was little more than a stump.

"Don't worry," the man named Phin told Billie. "If you cooperate, we'll let you go as soon as our business is finished. Maybe you can persuade your fiancé here to stop fooling around and find that mine."

"We're no use to you!" Billie cried. "You heard what Elliot said. The mine is worthless!"

"Feisty thing, ain't you? Dwight, tie this young lady up. She might cause some trouble."

Billie winced as Dwight knotted her hands together. His actions were tentative, almost reverent. "Sorry about this, miss."

"What's taking you so long?" Phin shouted.

"Just doin' a good job," Dwight called out, then lowered his voice. "That okay? It don't hurt too much, does it?"

"Hurry up!" Phin walked over to where Elliot sat and grabbed him by the hair. "You still our business partner?"

Elliot nodded, his eyes wild with fear.

"Let me make it real clear. You care about your ladylove, don't you?"

Elliot nodded again, obviously too scared to speak.

"You'd better play it straight with us this time, or buzzards'll be picking at her carcass by nightfall. You wouldn't want that, would you?"

Elliot shook his head. He reminded Billie of a rodent caught in the jaws of a predator. Why didn't Elliot stand up to him? The least he could do was face him like a man, even if he didn't say anything. Sam certainly wouldn't allow himself to be cowed like that.

"If you try to cheat us, she's dead." Phin thrust Elliot away in disgust. "Better put him up on the sorrel horse. We'll make better time," he instructed Dwight. "Leave the burro here."

Soon the party was strung out on the trail. They put Elliot in the lead, with Dwight behind him. Billie was third, and Phin brought up the rear. Each rider had a mule or two. Dwight kept twisting around in his saddle to look at her, and he asked her often if she was comfortable. It didn't take a genius to realized that he was powerfully attracted to her.

Captive again, Billie tried to keep despair at

239

bay. Dwight and Phin were just like Mac Monroe, only worse. She had little doubt what would happen to the two of them after they located the mine.

Billie found herself praying that Sam would follow them. But she'd better come up with a plan of her own, just in case.

Sam stared at the churned-up mud.

The horses were gone. Billie was gone.

Her betrayal stabbed through him, taking his breath away. The unbidden words whispered through his brain: *Just like Marisa.*

But another part of him battled back. The logical part, the part that knew what kind of person Billie was. No, Billie wouldn't have gone without letting him know she was all right.

Sam's anger was quickly replaced by fear as he realized that there were other hoofprints besides those of their own horses and mules.

If she had not gone voluntarily, who had taken her?

He tried to stem the rising tide of panic that filled his chest. Maybe Colonel Bahill's men had found her—maybe she hadn't had time to leave him a message.

He breathed a sigh of relief. That was it. He had no doubt that Bahill had sent a posse after her.

Then he saw the scrap of red clinging to a desert broom along the riverbed. There was a lot more of it, snarled threads among the hoofprints.

If Sam had been right, and Stevenson was the one who had the angora chaps, the artist had been here. Along with some horsemen.

Sam knelt beside the hoofprints. One print in particular interested him. There was a notch in the indentation where the frog of the hoof would be.

When Sam had first set out to find the robbers, he had stopped at the mining town of Silver King, where the robbers had stolen the mule. Sam remembered asking the proprietor of the livery stable if there was anything unusual about the animal; if its feet were identifiable in any way.

The mule had been recently injured, the frog of its hoof cut diagonally by a tree root. A cut that might look like this.

Swallowing his fear, Sam left Elliot's mule, the burro and the albino hobbled at the camp and mounted Panther. He had no time to lose.

Elliot couldn't find the canyon. Hour after hour in the broiling heat they traveled aimlessly through the maze of basins, ridges and draws. With every mile Dwight and Phin became more impatient. Billie thought that before long the outlaws' patience would wear out completely, and they would kill them both. Although Dwight seemed infatuated with her, she knew he would follow Phin's orders. It was obvious in the way the two men interacted with one another. They reminded her of a dominant dog and a submissive dog. She could almost imagine Dwight lying down on his back and yipping to show his obedience, should Phin demand it.

Billie had no chance to talk to Elliot. He still didn't know about her condition. As she rode single-file behind Dwight, Billie tried to analyze her feelings toward her fiancé.

She was puzzled by her own lack of feeling. Where was the wildly beating heart, the joy she'd always felt before in Elliot's presence? Am I that superficial, she thought, that I can't see beyond clean clothes and good grooming?

The poor man was weak from thirst and hunger—and surely not in his right mind. Could she blame him for that? Who knew what he had suffered? No wonder he was afraid of his own shadow.

If they did manage to escape, she'd make sure he got the care he needed. Billie had no doubt her feelings for him would return, with time.

She had to stop thinking about the Arizona Ranger. That episode in her life was over. Elliot was her future. Elliot was the man she loved.

Late in the afternoon, one of the mules fell down and wouldn't get up. The horses were exhausted, and wouldn't be able to go much farther in this heat. Reluctantly, Billie's captors decided to make camp.

"One more day," Phin told Elliot. "If you don't find that mine tomorrow, you're a dead man."

Billie watched them numbly from astride Buttermilk. The constant motion of the horse had caused the rope to saw against her wrists. Her eyes felt like grapes dipped in sand, and her body ached all over. When they stopped for water, she could barely open her mouth to drink it. Buttermilk was tougher than the other horses and seemed the least tired, but she knew that another couple of days of this would wear him down, too.

Despite her weariness, Billie nudged Buttermilk toward Phin. Her voice cracked, but she spoke with as much dignity as she could muster. "I might be able to convince Elliot to show you where the mine is . . . that is, if he knows, himself."

"You think he's lost, or pulling my leg?"

"I think he's lost. Maybe I can help him remember."

Phin pondered her request for a moment.

"Aw, have a heart, Phin," Dwight interjected. "They're in love. They ought to be able to talk to each other."

Billie shot him a swift smile of thanks, and he grinned with pleasure. She pressed on. "When we find the mine, you'll let us go. Won't you?"

A look passed between the two men.

Dwight said, "A woman and a tenderfoot crybaby won't give us much trouble. Come on, Phin. She's a lady; can't you tell? A lady gives her word, it's as good as gold."

Phin stared at Billie as if he were weighing her mentally. "You make sure he tells us where the mine is. If you don't . . ." He let the threat hang in the air.

Billie walked over to sit down beside Elliot a

little way from the fire, out of their captors' hearing. Dwight kept his rifle pointed in their direction.

It was the first chance Billie had had to talk to Elliot since they had met in the desert, and all of a sudden she didn't know what to say.

He sat cross-legged in the dirt, pulling on a piece of jerky with his bound hands. For a moment Billie wondered if he would acknowledge her at all. Every bit of his energy seemed focused on the food, which he gnawed at like a savage.

"Elliot," she said softly.

Still chewing, he glanced at her, then resumed tearing at his jerky.

Here it was. The moment she had been waiting for. She had strapped herself up like a boy, stolen her father's money and run away from home, ridden into the forbidding maze of mountains that had killed many an experienced prospector, risked rape, death and miscarriage to bring this news to Elliot. Now that he was here before her, she felt strangely numb. The words she had planned to say—*Elliot, I am carrying your child*—seemed oddly flat.

She cleared her throat. "I have something to tell you."

Elliot's eyes darted furtively toward her again. He set the food down carefully in his lap and covered it with his hand, as if he were afraid she would steal it. "We're in some fine mess, aren't we?"

"I guess we are. But we can't give up hope yet."

"A real mess," Elliot continued, as if he hadn't

heard her. "They're the Daw brothers, Billie. The outlaws that robbed the Old Dominion payroll. They've killed four people already. They'll kill us, too."

So these were the men Sam was tracking. She should have realized who they were the moment she saw them. She should have shot them on sight.

But it was too late for that now.

"They're meaner than a nestful of rattle-snakes," Elliot added bleakly.

Billie couldn't be bothered with self-pity right now. "Elliot, look at me. This is very important. I have some news that . . . concerns you. I know it looks bad right now, but I think this will make you feel better. And if we are able to escape—"

"Escape?"

"It's possible. We have to try . . . but I think you should know . . . it's wonderful news—"

"Yes, yes, go on!" he said impatiently.

"I don't know how to say it." Now that the time had come, she felt strangely awkward.

Elliot looked at her, his expression hopeful. "You know something. Something good."

"Yes." She took a deep breath. "Elliot, I'm going to have a baby. Our baby."

"Is this some kind of a joke?"

Stunned, Billie realized Elliot didn't believe her. It was probably a shock to him—anyone would have trouble believing such a thing, especially in this situation. "It's true. We are going to have a child."

"What are you babbling about?" he demanded, not bothering to hide his impatience.

Billie had expected many reactions—surprise, joy, perhaps sadness that the child was doomed from the beginning. She did not expect annoyance.

Elliot glared at her. "Don't you see what a mess we're in? We're going to be murdered just as soon as I find that mine! Who gives a damn if you're going to have a baby!"

Billie felt as if she had been thrown from a horse into a pile of rocks. Stunned and bruised, she tried to catch her whirling thoughts, but they seemed to fly around just beyond her reach.

He turned away. "Just leave me alone. I don't want to think about it. I don't want to think about anything. If you can't offer me something constructive about how we're going to get out of this mess, don't talk to me at all."

For a moment she could only stare at him. Then it sank in. Elliot didn't care that she was carrying his child. He didn't care about the comfort she had tried to offer him. He made it quite clear that he found her effort to console him woefully inadequate. She supposed, considering what they faced, his was a practical position, if utterly heartless.

Unable to fathom his rejection of her gift, she quietly stood up and walked back to the campfire.

Billie ate her dinner with the outlaws. If Phin Daw hardly spoke to her, Dwight was solicitous, offering her the extra biscuit and trying to include her in the conversation. Billie wondered again if she might be able to use his interest in her in some way.

When Dwight went to hobble the horses for the night, Phin glared at Billie. "My brother likes you. I don't want to see him hurt."

"How could I hurt him?"

"You never mind. Just get this straight. He does what I tell him. Always has, always will, and no fool girl will keep him from doing what is right by his own family."

"Right?" Billie said bitterly. "What do you call right? Holding hostages, robbing payrolls, killing women—"

Phin shook a finger at her. "You think you know a lot, girl, but you don't. Not by a long shot. No one ever talks about how our family was cheated out of our land by the Old Dominion mine, how they run off our cattle. A sheriff on their payroll shot our pa in the back."

"But that doesn't excuse—"

" 'The Lord God is a jealous God. An eye for an eye, a tooth for a tooth!' " Phin quoted. "That's what we believe. Now you listen to me. Dwight's always been what you might call the chivalrous type. Ma's Bible-learnin' really sank in with him, the way it never did with our brother Howard. I don't want you foolin' with his feelings."

"He's a grown man. I'm sure he can take care of himself."

"Let me tell you a little story. You saw he lost his finger?"

She nodded.

"Happened when he was eighteen. Dwight always did have an eye for the ladies. Real shy, but he knows what he wants. Well, there was this old Mormon lived near us, had himself four wives. One of 'em was a fifteen-year-old girl that Dwight was sweet on. Ol' Dwight, he up and kidnapped her one day, took her up into the mountains. Tried to get her to marry him. He figured if the old man could marry four women, the girl could marry him."

Shock jolted through Billie. Suddenly Dwight didn't seem so gentle.

"He didn't know her in the biblical sense, or anything—didn't even touch her. Wanted her to marry him first. But you ought to know how seriously he takes things, and why you shouldn't lead him on."

"What happened?"

"That little girl didn't want no part of him. One day she got holt of his rifle and laid for him. Missed by a mile, 'cept for his finger. Now Dwight, he's a hothead. He killed her with his skinnin' knife, and the thing is, I don't think he even knew he did it. Came to, kind of, afterward. Felt real bad after that, but it was too late then, wasn't it?"

Billie tasted fear like copper in her mouth, tried to shut out the horrible picture Phin had drawn in her mind.

"Go easy with Dwight, missy, for your own good."

She nodded, completely numb.

Dwight returned a short time later, complaining about Buttermilk. "Damn horse almost kicked me!"

"He's particular about who touches his feet," Billie said.

"Well, he better become unparticular or we'll all be eatin' horsemeat!"

"I'll handle him next time," Billie said, stemming the revulsion and fear that fought their way up into her throat.

"You'll do no such thing," Phin said. "I saw how good you ride."

Billie had no chance to reply. She heard the crunch of boots, felt displaced air against her face. Elliot squatted down before her, his bound hands held out as if in supplication. "Elizabeth— Billie—I want to talk to you."

She stiffened. "I don't want to talk to you."

"Please. I have to tell you how sorry I am." His voice was urgent.

Billie shook her head. She felt as if her heart had turned to stone. Elliot had rejected her, rejected her child.

"Hey, what're you doin'?" shouted Dwight.

"I want to talk to my fiancée alone."

"It don't look like she wants to talk to you."

"We're just having a lovers' quarrel," Elliot explained.

Dwight put his hand on Billie's arm, the fleshy stump of his finger pinning her through the light wool of her shirt, pressing into her skin. "You know you don't have to go with him, you don't want to."

"Thank you, Dwight, but I think it would be wise to hear what he has to say," she replied, her mind still roiling with grisly visions of the Mormon girl.

Elliot and Billie walked over to the ironwood tree where they had sat earlier. "I'm sorry, Billie, about what I said. I—I've had a lot of problems."

Problems. Billie wanted to tell him that she'd had a lot of problems, too. And so had Sam Gray. But that didn't turn Sam into a sullen stranger. It didn't make him lash out at others and treat them like dirt. It didn't make him reject his own child.

"What can I do to make it up to you? I love you, Billie. It was just such a shock—something I never would have expected—it took me by surprise."

She didn't answer.

"I really am sorry. I don't think I understood what you were saying." He kicked the dirt with his boot. "It's just that I'm so scared. They're going to kill us, Billie. It's hard to think about anything else."

Billie still refused to reply. Let him dig himself in deeper.

"I know you must hate me. It was unforgivable. But I didn't know what I was saying. I swear to the Lord above, I didn't. I—I've been sick."

"Is that all you have to say?"

"Well . . ."

"Because if it is, I'd like to go back to the fire."

"Don't turn your back on me! I need you! I need you and our baby! It's the only thing that will keep me going!"

"That's not what you said a minute ago."

"I swear I didn't know what I was saying! I've been sick. Look! Look at this!" He held up his hands, showing her his bare arm, which was the color and texture of red meat. "I fell into some cholla; it's infected. I've been delirious, Billie. I was almost dead when these men found me. I know it's no excuse, but if you knew what I'd been through . . . Oh, what's the use? I've done the unforgivable. I know I can't expect you to forgive me, but I swear that I love you and I love our child. I swear it!"

Could he mean it? Billie studied his face. He looked sincere. Could he have just struck out because he'd been through so much? She didn't think she could trust him, but she wanted to. How she wanted to!

"Please believe me. I'm sorry. If I could take back those words—I'd sooner cut my tongue out than hurt you." Awkwardly, he looped his arms over her head and pulled her to his chest. "I love you," he muttered into her hair, and hugged her hard.

Billie let him hold her as confusion whirled around in her soul. She tried not to think of the other man, the man who had always made her feel safe and loved when he hugged her.

Her compliance was not lost on Elliot. "Let's talk," he said eagerly.

Did he really think all was forgiven with a few sweet words and a hug?

"We have so much to catch up on. I'm going to be a father! I've got news for you, too. I really *did* find the Lost Dutchman Mine. You won't believe it. . . ."

He helped her sit down on the sand, talking all the while. He told her about the mine, the fabulous Lost Dutchman. He talked about fatherhood, and how he'd always wanted a son. Elliot rambled on and on while Billie listened numbly, too exhausted to take exception to the strangeness of his sudden about-face. When he asked her a question, she answered it, feeling strangely detached. After a while she realized that the questions had a pattern.

"The Arizona Ranger will come after you, won't he? He would suspect foul play. You know him pretty well. He wouldn't give up, would he? Perhaps we can find a way to let him know where we are. . . .

"Do you think your father is looking for you, too? We might get out of this yet. Then we can get married and I'll make an honest woman of you. . . ."

Billie knew he was pumping her for information. The knowledge that Elliot was just using her again settled in her heart, her bones, her blood. It drained her energy.

Billie had fallen in love with a fantasy. She had been a starry-eyed fool. Her father was right; Sam was right. Elliot wasn't free-spirited;

he was undependable. He wasn't sensitive, but weak. He wasn't possessed by love; he used it as a weapon.

"I love you, Billie. I love you more than anything in the world." Elliot's words passed through and over her, leaving her unmoved.

"Who knows? Sam Gray might come in handy after all." Elliot patted her hand. "You know that Howard was Dwight and Phin's brother." He giggled. "Quite a coincidence, isn't it? The ranger arrested their brother, and now he's after them. Their mother—they call her Ma, talk about her as if she were the Virgin Mary herself—she's the brains of the whole bunch. She masterminded the holdup. Dwight and Phin wanted to go after the ranger who brought in their brother, but she said they'd need money. Money first, revenge later. That's her motto." He giggled again. "Howard was a bad one. The man he killed in Bisbee? It was a miner. That whole family hates miners. Miners like to wear red shirts, did you know that? Ol' Howard, he got drunk one night and shot a man in the stomach for wearing a red shirt."

Billie hardly heard him. Her mind felt as dull as a butter knife. She couldn't think about it now; it was all too much to sort out. This Elliot was so different from the Elliot she had fallen in love with. As hurt as she was, she wanted to believe he wasn't lying completely. That somewhere inside him there was a little of the man she had thought him to be.

She closed her eyes and let his words wash over her.

"Can you imagine that?" Elliot mused. "He killed a man for wearing the wrong-colored shirt."

Chapter Fourteen

In the clear light of morning Billie felt more in-
clined to forgive Elliot, if not forget. He had been
put through a horrible ordeal—an ordeal that
might break anyone. And Elliot had never been
a strong man.

Hadn't he told her over and over how excited
he was about the child? Didn't she owe him the
benefit of the doubt?

She would just put it out of her mind for now.
There would be plenty of time to question Elliot's sincerity after they escaped from the Daw
brothers.

There was a reason to be hopeful this morning. Dwight Daw was sick. They would be getting a late start, because the outlaw spent most
of his time running back and forth to the bushes.

Phin had to saddle the horses himself. He

hardly noticed Billie and Elliot. He was too busy grousing. One of the mules gave him trouble as he loaded the pack. "Dwight, get out here and give me a hand!" he shouted.

"In a minute!" came the reply from down the brushy slope.

Billie gauged the distance to Buttermilk and Phin's bay horse. They had already been unhobbled. Dwight had been about to saddle Buttermilk when the call of nature came again. The bay stood as a good cow pony should, ground-tied, his reins dangling loose on the ground. Better yet, Dwight's rifle rested in the scabbard.

This was their chance. Billie glanced at Elliot, then at the horses. He caught her gaze, looked puzzled.

"Damn you! Hold still!" Phin jerked on the mule's headstall.

Billie leaned toward Elliot, watching Phin's back. Phin cursed a blue streak, his voice loud enough to cover Billie's whispered directions. "You jump on the bay horse." Buttermilk might buck with Elliot aboard, and she doubted he could ride bareback. "We'll go on the count of three. You'll have the rifle. If you have to use it, make sure you don't miss."

He held up his hands. "I can't use a rifle. I don't think I can even get on a horse without my hands being free."

Was he that much of a coward? Here was their chance—their only chance. "On the count of three."

"They'll kill us for sure!" Elliot whispered.

"They'll kill us anyway!" she hissed savagely.

Phin had moved on to his own mount. His gun was thrust in his pants. He stooped to grab at the cinch ring that hung down from the horse's far side, and missed.

"Now!" Billie dashed for Buttermilk, clasped his crest and a handful of mane in her bound hands and sprang onto his back. One touch of her spurs and the buckskin bounded forward.

From the corner of her eye she saw Phin's horse dance away. In a reflex action, Phin, completely caught off guard, yanked at the cinch ring as if it were the gun he sought. He yanked so hard the saddle slid off the other side and under the horse's belly. Phin dropped the cinch and reached for the gun in his pants just as Dwight came crashing through the brush like an enraged bull. Elliot stood helpless for a moment, losing any advantage that could be gained from the confusion, then gathered the reins of the bay and tried frantically to step into the stirrup as the confused animal wheeled around him in a circle.

"The rifle!" Billie screamed. "Hold it on them!" She kicked Buttermilk forward, mortally certain that at any moment she would feel a bullet slam into her back.

A gun barked in the morning air. Billie looked back, saw Elliot standing next to the bay horse, his joined hands held up. "I give up!" he shouted. "Don't shoot me!" The rifle sat in the scabbard beside him, within easy reach.

The idiot! He could have made it, if he hadn't been so cowed by the outlaws!

Undecided, Billie pulled up for a moment, then kicked Buttermilk forward again. She couldn't think about Elliot now. She'd find Sam, and they'd come back for him. One thing was certain: she wouldn't do him any good if she were captive, too.

"You come back here!" Phin shouted.

For answer, she leaned over Buttermilk's neck and urged him headlong up the rocky trail.

"You come back or we'll shoot your boyfriend right now!"

"He means it, Billie!" Elliot squealed like a terrified rabbit in a cat's mouth. "Don't let them kill me!"

The urgency in his voice tore at her like claws. She could feel his abject fear.

Buttermilk's pace faltered, as if he sensed her indecision.

"I'll kill him!" Phin shouted. "Don't think I won't!"

Logic vied with panic, and won. They wanted the mine. They wouldn't kill Elliot.

"Please! Oh, God, please, Billie, he's going to kill me!"

Billie jerked a confused Buttermilk to a halt. Wheeled him around to look.

Don't listen to them. They need Elliot to find the mine, a voice said in her head, loud and clear. She kicked Buttermilk forward again. But it was too late. That split second of indecision had sunk her. Hoofbeats sounded behind her, and she heard the whistle of a rope just before it settled over her shoulders.

The rope tightened around her chest and arms, yanked her off the horse and onto the rocks.

Billie and Elliot sat side by side under a mesquite tree, tied to the limbs above them. Dwight and Phin had gone over the hill to decide what to do about their captives. As their voices rose, Billie's spirits sank.

Phin's voice drifted over to them. "He doesn't know where the mine is! I say we kill 'em both and stick to our original plan. There's enough gold already to get us out of the territory. We can make a new start anywhere."

"Kill him, then, but not the girl."

"Dwight, she's trouble. Can't you see that? Besides, what'll Ma say?"

"I don't care what Ma says!" Dwight said stubbornly. "I want to marry her."

Phin's reply was muffled; he'd lowered his voice. Straining her ears, Billie could make out only a few words: ". . . have to . . . away they'll lead 'em right . . . You can have . . . first, but after that . . . Don't cross me!" Phin's voice drifted away, as if they were walking away from camp. Soon they were too far away for her to hear.

"I'm so sorry, Billie," Elliot said mournfully. "It looks like they're going to kill us both."

"It doesn't matter now."

"But it does. Now that I know there's no hope . . . I want you to know how sorry I am."

She didn't know whether to believe him or not. Was he still trying to dupe her? If so, what was the point? They'd be dead within the hour. There would be no escape now.

"You should have run, Billie. Why didn't you?"

"I did run."

His voice was heavy with self-pity. "You waited for me. I slowed you down. If I'd grabbed the rifle like you said—"

"It's too late for recriminations. We tried, and we failed."

"You tried. I'd already given up." He sighed. "I'm just so tired. I can barely stand up, and so many times I don't feel as if I'm really here. It's as if I'm outside my body, looking down at this . . . stranger. I guess what I need to say is that I've betrayed you. And not just today."

"I know that, Elliot," she replied quietly.

"What?" He stared at her, nonplussed.

"You wanted my money. That's why you asked me to marry you."

To his credit, he didn't try to deny it. "I wanted you, too."

"You don't have to lie."

"It's not a lie." He held her gaze unflinchingly. "You're everything I'm not. You live on one of the finest ranches in the West. I wanted that. The prestige, the . . . power. The way men look at your father when he walks down the street, the respect they show him. Even you, a woman . . . you have all of those things. You can ride and rope and shoot—all the things I'd like to be able to do. I wanted your courage, Billie. Your self-respect." He closed his eyes and Billie could see his pain. "I have none of that. I thought having money would make me respectable, make me feel less small. But I found out that even with all the gold I found, I didn't have any more courage. I wasn't any better a man than I was without it."

Billie's heart went out to him. His good looks were gone. His fine Roman features had turned hawklike with hunger. He was gaunt, light as a scarecrow, and his eyes were sunken in their sockets. The snarled black beard and the stringy hair obscured the once-elegant features she had admired beyond reason not so long ago. But Billie realized that right now she liked Elliot better than ever before. He was being honest now—truly honest—for the first time in his life. He was admitting things about himself that she had never expected to hear. "It's all right," she told him, her voice low. "I think you are a better man."

Tears brimmed over his eyes. "God, Billie, if I could just take back the things I said to you! I hurt you so much! If we do by some miracle get out of this alive, I want to marry you. I want to give my child a name."

She murmured her agreement, partly because she wanted to comfort him, and partly because she wanted to believe that he really had changed.

Elliot's proposal—much more honorable than his last one—was certainly something to think about. If he was sincere about wanting to be a father, how could she deny him that opportunity? It might prove to be the turning point in his life.

Anyway, in a few minutes it probably wouldn't matter one way or the other. Boots crunched on rock. Dwight and Phin were coming back.

Sam lay stomach-down on the ridge, concealed by brush, as he watched the outlaws' camp. He'd left Panther back at the mouth of the canyon, afraid that the horse might catch the scent of his own kind, whinny to his comrades and give their position away. Sam's gun was drawn; he was ready to attack if necessary.

His heart went out to Billie, who sat, back arched, against the thorny mesquite tree, arms raised above her head and hands bound tightly to one sturdy limb. Elliot, similarly bound, was beside her, his face a mask of fear. The outlaws were nowhere in sight.

Every moment that Billie suffered cut Sam like a knife. She must be scared to death. He wondered if they'd hurt her.

If they had, he'd kill them.

He couldn't bear to think about it now. All he could do was wait for the outlaws to show up.

Billie's heart pounded as she saw the top of Phin Daw's head rise above the hill and into her line of sight. His rifle rested on his shoulder. He looked as if he were out for a simple day of hunting.

Hunting us, she thought. *He's decided to kill us now*.

She glanced at Elliot, whose face was soaked with sweat. His eyes glittered hard and bright as obsidian with a fear so sharp that Billie fancied she could smell it on him.

The two outlaws stood before them, their legs slightly splayed, rifles pointing at the ground.

"Please let us go. We won't tell anyone we saw you. Please!" Elliot begged.

"Shut up!" Phin kicked Elliot hard. "You had your chance."

Dwight shouldered his rifle.

Billie shut her eyes.

A cocked gun hammer split the morning air.

Chapter Fifteen

Sam Gray pointed a gun at Phin Daw's head. He had come up behind Phin just as his brother had been about to shoot Stevenson. "Drop it!"

Phin nearly jumped a foot, and dropped his rifle. Dwight's rifle, too, clattered to the ground.

"What do you want with us?"

Sam nudged the rifles with his foot, let them tumble down over the lip of the ravine that bordered the camp. "You're under arrest for the murder of four people in Globe, and attempted robbery of the Old Dominion payroll. Put your hands on top of your heads. Do it now!"

"This is a mistake!" But Phin clasped his hands on top of his head. Dwight stepped toward Sam, his stance menacing.

Sam raised his gun muzzle, pointing it at Phin's chest. "Best tell your brother to do as I say, or I'll drop you where you stand," he said, keeping his tone conversational. Sam had learned long ago that if you didn't put emotion into your voice, a threat carried more impact. "Get closer together."

The two sidled up to each other, hands still on their heads. "Sit down." Sam's gaze never left Phin and Dwight. "Keep your hands on your heads and sit down."

The outlaws crouched, then sat cross-legged on the ground, their hands never leaving their heads. Still training his gun on them, Sam stepped over to Billie and cut the thongs that bound her with his knife. She untied Elliot.

"Billie," Sam called, keeping his attention on the killers, "I have two sets of handcuffs in my saddlebags. Just over the hill."

Billie was back in an instant. She held out the cuffs.

Something caught the corner of his eye, a slow, stealthy movement near Billie, but he had to concentrate on the killers. It had to be Stevenson, probably going to collect the rifles. Good. He needed all the help he could get.

Then he heard a squeal, and all hell broke loose. A gold and black whirlwind suddenly tore through the camp.

It was Billie's yellow horse, bucking and kicking his way through the cold campfire before flattening out in a run into the desert, Elliot Stevenson clinging to his back like a limpet.

In that split second, Dwight Daw lunged at Sam. Sam stepped sideways and hit the outlaw a blow on the head, but the force knocked his gun out of his hand. Dwight came at him again. Sam jerked his other gun from his holster and aimed it at the enraged outlaw, planning to deflect him with the threat.

"You kill my brother, and I'll kill her."

The words pierced his consciousness. Sam turned his head slightly and felt his legs go weak. Phin Daw was holding Billie by the arm, Sam's own gun aimed at her head.

Sam clutched his revolver, his mind reeling. A tidal wave of fear rose up in him, momentarily blacking out all thought. Through the dark haze that almost obscured his vision, he saw Billie's eyes, sparkling hard and angry in her white face, saw her mouth move but could not understand the words. The blue-gray metal of the gun against Billie's head caught the light, cold and deadly.

"I mean it. Throw your gun down!"

Billie's voice came to him, as if from far away. Her words burned through his consciousness. "Don't listen to him, Sam! Don't let him get your gun!"

He could not believe how brave this woman was. More courageous than anyone he had ever known. Perhaps she could face death, but he couldn't let her face it. He couldn't let them kill her.

"Drop it!"

The gun felt heavy and alien in his hand. And still Billie stared at him, her eyes challenging, fearless.

"I'll count to three," Phin said calmly. His gun muzzle was pressed into Billie's ear.

There was no choice. Phin couldn't miss at that distance. Even if Sam was able to shoot him, even if Phin died instantly, the man's reflexes would probably send a bullet into Billie's brain. Sam opened his fingers and the gun slid from his hand.

Billie's eyes turned bleak. But he couldn't let Phin kill her. He could do anything in this world but that.

Phin laughed. "Dwight, the ranger's kind enough to bring along handcuffs. Get his hands and feet."

"What about Stevenson?" Dwight's voice was agitated.

"First things first. Let's take care of the ranger."

"But he'll get away!"

Phin waved his arm. "Where's he gonna go? The way that horse was bucking, it probably dumped him by now. We'll get him."

Billie felt the gun muzzle withdraw from her ear, and nearly toppled into a heap. But she closed her eyes and willed her rubbery legs to stiffen, hold her up. Even though her first instinct had warned against Sam giving up his gun so easily—they were both captive now—she was relieved and grateful that he had. She was still alive!

Phin had thrust her away from him, and stood, legs slightly splayed as he watched the ranger.

267

Billie breathed in the dry air, and it tasted as sweet as honey. The blood in her veins, which had seemed to freeze while Phin held her, now exploded like rivers undammed through her limbs, causing her to shake uncontrollably. Her heart pounded in her ears and throbbed at the pulse of her throat.

Dwight manacled the ranger hand and foot. Sam stood very still, and again Billie was aware of how strong he was. Another man would be reduced by such an ignominious position, made to look smaller and weaker. But the ranger still looked as dangerous as he had when Mac Monroe had gotten the drop on him the other day.

He'd escaped that time.

"Well, well," said Phin. "Look what we bagged."

The ranger said nothing.

Phin pressed the muzzle of his gun against Sam's chin. "I know you. You delivered our brother to the executioner. You killed Howard. What do you think we should do with him, Dwight?"

"Do him like he did Howard."

Phin laughed shortly. "You know, sometimes you make a lot of sense," he told Dwight. "How long did Howard have to rot in that stinking jail before he was hanged? Do you know, Ranger?"

Sam didn't reply. Billie felt fear take her, kiting through her extremities. She had brought Sam to this. He would die because of her.

"You know, at the courthouse in Tombstone you can see the gallows. I can't stand the thought of my brother sitting there in that jail, waiting to die, and looking out at the gallows and knowin' they were meant for him. How long did Howard wait?"

"A day and a night," Sam said calmly. "You know that as well as I do."

Phin nodded. "I was there. We were waiting, too. They hanged him at eleven o'clock in the morning on the next day, and people bought tickets to see him die. Only you must've got one of them engraved invitations. You weren't satisfied just to bring him in. You had to watch him die."

"He was the marshal's guest!" put in Dwight.

"Did you like what you saw?" demanded Phin. "Did you like seeing our brother die? He didn't even go quick. The fall didn't break his neck, so he swung there for a while, choking to death. Bet you enjoyed that, didn't you, Ranger?"

"No."

"Maybe you had a hand in it. What do you think, Dwight? Maybe the ranger here talked the executioner into giving Howard a slow death."

"He would never do anything like that!" Billie shouted.

Phin ignored her. "What do you say, Dwight? Why don't we make the punishment fit the crime?"

"You mean hang him?"

"I mean execute him." Phin warmed to his subject. "We'll have our own hanging tomorrow, at eleven o'clock. That way you can spend the night thinkin' about it, just the way Howard did. What do you say to that, Ranger?"

Sam said nothing.

"I saw a cottonwood tree in a canyon not a mile from here," volunteered Dwight. "We could hang him there. We could do it slow, too, just like they did to Howard."

"He was just doing his job," Billie cried. "He didn't hang your brother; he just arrested him. The court sentenced him!"

"Shut up!" Phin smacked her, sending her reeling.

Sam straightened, his eyes glittering with hatred. His knuckles turned white as he strained against his bonds.

"No call to hit her," Dwight said.

"Dwight, shut your damned mouth!"

"I'm sorry," Dwight replied in an injured tone. "What about Stevenson?"

"You better go get him."

Dwight mounted his bay and kicked it into a gallop.

Sam spoke up. "You want revenge, you've got it. But the lady shouldn't have to see it. Why don't you let her go?"

"Now why should I do that?"

"You wanted me. Make it a trade."

"A trade?" Phin laughed. "What do you have to trade? We already got you, lawman. Besides, Dwight is sweet on her. I promised him he could have her, once Elliot found the mine."

Billie felt sick. She couldn't imagine having Dwight's hands on her, his body—it was unthinkable. But the revulsion she felt was eclipsed by her fear for Sam. He had put himself into this situation for her, and now he would die a horrible death. "Please!" she cried. "Do anything you want to me, but don't kill him. He was just the arresting officer—"

"Don't listen to her," Sam interrupted, and for the first time a crack showed in his remarkable composure. "Let her go. You'll have Elliot; you'll have me."

Phin strolled over to Billie and brushed her cheek with his gun. Billie shuddered, despite herself.

Phin laughed at her distaste. "It's been a long time since I had a woman. An' I told you, Dwight wants her. You don't have any cards left to deal, Ranger."

When Phin touched Billie, Sam's eyes narrowed with fury. "Let her be." His voice was soft but deadly.

"Sounds to me like there's more than Dwight that's sweet on this young lady. Is that it, Ranger? You in love, are you?"

Again Sam refused to answer.

"This could make it even more interesting. How'd you like it if Dwight and I showed you a thing or two about loving, right before we hang you. That would be torture, wouldn't it?"

Sam stepped toward Phin, his jaw muscles clenched, and lifted his manacled hands.

Phin hit him a blow to the jaw, and Sam crashed to his knees.

"That riles you, don't it? Dwight's gonna like this. We can put on quite a show."

Sam rose unsteadily to his feet. Blood dripped from his jaw and down his shirtfront. He glanced at Billie and his eyes seemed to lose their color, as if he were stepping back from the situation and looking at it from far away. "You could do that," he said at last, his tone detached. "But it wouldn't be wise."

"And just why is that?"

"You don't strike me as the kind of man who'd throw money away with both hands on petty revenge. Especially since you're already going to kill me."

"What do you mean by that? What money?"

"You don't know who she is, do you?"

"She's Stevenson's slut."

"She's Colonel Roland Bahill's daughter. Elizabeth Bahill. She ran away from home. Her father put out a big reward for her safe return."

"You're lying."

"Why should I lie to you? I'm already a dead man."

"You're in love with her."

Phin's words bolted through Billie, a brilliant explosion of joy. In love with her!

Sam laughed. "Not on your life. She's been nothing but trouble ever since I met her."

"What are you tryin' to pull?" demanded Phin.

Sam spoke with casual indifference. "I was taking her to her fiancé when you caught her. Would a man who loved her do that?"

Billie stared at him, trying to decide if he was

telling the truth. The way he looked just now, the tone of his voice—it had such a cold finality to it. He must mean it. She had thought he liked her, was even attracted to her. But maybe all she represented to him was an unpleasant duty he must fulfill.

"You sure seemed riled a minute ago. She's nobody's daughter—she wouldn't come out here dressed like that—"

"I can prove it. My horse is just over the hill. In my saddlebags you'll find a whole stack of reward posters. They have her picture on it, and the amount of the reward."

"We'll just wait till Dwight gets back."

"Five thousand dollars," Sam said. "More than you would have gotten in the payroll robbery."

"Shut up!"

"Five thousand dollars for the return of Elizabeth Bahill, in the same condition as she started out. Bahill's a real stickler about that kind of thing. Wants his daughter to remain a virgin until she's married—"

"Shut your trap!"

Sam ignored him and kept on talking. "Colonel Bahill's an important man. He has high hopes for a good marriage for his daughter, and he wants a virgin," he said flatly.

Billie listened with amazement. He was protecting her.

Sam grinned. "Can you control yourself for five thousand dollars? You can go right into Phoenix and have your fun with any whore you want—you'll be able to afford the best—but can you keep your hands off Bahill's daughter?"

"Shut up!"

"Can you control Dwight?"

This time Phin hit Sam again. But Sam simply smiled, his mouth bloody. "Think about it," he said.

Phin took a rope and secured Billie and Sam to a couple of paloverde trees, about ten feet apart, then went over the hill to bring back Sam's horse. He clutched the reward poster in one hand, grinning. "Looks like you weren't kidding me, Ranger. This girl here's worth a lot of money."

"Unharmed," Sam said.

"She's his daughter, ain't she? He'll take her in any condition we deem fit, as long as she ain't dead."

Billie spoke up. "You don't know my father. He won't pay you a penny if you touch me."

"He will if we threaten to kill you."

"No, he won't."

Phin's mouth dropped open. "He's your father."

"He doesn't care about me, just the kind of marriage I'll make." Billie tried to sound convincing. She had once thought that way, when the colonel had tried to keep her and Elliot apart. Now she knew it wasn't true. Now she knew he loved her so much that he wanted to prevent her from being hurt.

"You expect me to believe that bull?"

She shrugged. "Try him and see."

"You can have *any* woman," Sam said. "Is she

worth the gamble? Look at her. She's not much, is she? Tanned like an Indian. She's even got muscles like a man."

Billie would have kicked Sam if he were any closer. Then she thought about what he faced, and wondered how he could act on her behalf at all. If she were in his shoes, she wouldn't have been so generous.

Phin stared down at her, his mind obviously working. She knew he didn't quite believe her about her father, but he didn't completely disbelieve her, either.

"You're right," Phin said, and spat. "She's not worth losing money over."

Dwight returned around noon, alone, on foot. His saddle was slung over his shoulder. He was scraped and bleeding.

"What happened to you?" asked Phin.

"Horse put his foot in a hole. Had to shoot him."

"Stevenson got away?" Phin demanded, although the answer was obvious.

"I think the buckskin was running away with him. That pony can sure run over rocks. Neat as you please."

"Damn it!" Phin kicked at a rock.

"I can go after him again."

"Never mind. He's probably halfway out of the mountains by now."

"But now we won't find the damn mine!"

"He probably couldn't find it anyway. Maybe there wasn't any mine. Maybe he high-graded that stuff from Goldfield." He glanced at Billie. "We have bigger fish to fry. A sure thing."

Dwight followed Phin's gaze. "What do you mean?"

Phin told him.

"But that ain't fair! You promised me I could have her! We were going to get married!"

"That was before I learned how valuable she was."

"You can't believe that cock-and-bull story. Bahill will pay to get her back. I'll take her in myself, right after the honeymoon. He won't fuss if she's married."

"Dwight, are you as pigeon-headed as you look? Do you think Colonel Bahill is going to welcome you with open arms? He owns half of Santa Cruz County! People like that have no truck with people like us."

Dwight's face had set in stubborn lines. "I want her."

"You want her. Are you willing to let five thousand dollars go? What do you think Ma will say when we turn up empty-handed?" demanded Phin in a good imitation of Sam's own argument. "She ain't worth losing five thousand dollars for!"

Dwight cursed and threw his hat on the ground.

"What I say goes. You want to argue with that?"

"No," Dwight replied, his voice sullen.

"You've got to learn patience, boy. We hold

her for ransom, get the money first, then you can do what you want with her."

Billie's heart lurched.

"We just have to wait a little longer, is all," Phin continued.

It was too much for Dwight's temper. He stomped through the camp, over the already trampled campfire, kicking plates and empty cans and divots of dirt.

Billie felt cold. These were violent men, cruel men. She had no doubt that what they would do to her would make her wish for death. But first, she knew, she'd have to witness Sam's death. She'd have to see him hang.

She couldn't imagine anything worse than that.

Suddenly Billie realized she loved Sam Gray. She had loved him from the moment they had sought refuge from the storm.

Her heart twisted. He was going to die, and it was all her fault. She'd plotted against him with Mac Monroe. She'd thrown herself at him in the mountain pool, then pulled back at the last moment, knowing full well what she was doing to him. She'd begged him to look for Elliot, distracting him from his true purpose and putting him in greater danger. And when Phin had put the gun to her head, the ranger had chosen her life over his own.

He should have let Phin shoot her.

I love him, she thought wretchedly, *and look what I've done. I've embroiled him in this mess, lured him to his death as surely as if I planned it.*

Obviously he'd pitied her. How could he not? Without pride, without a care for his feelings, she'd exposed him to her sordid little predicament, shamelessly begging him to bring back the fiancé who had run away from her. She'd played upon his sense of honor and duty, using the basest excuse—her delicate condition—to enlist his aid.

How could a man like Sam Gray love a woman so depraved, so foolish, so . . . pathetic?

The truth was, he couldn't. He had risked his own life for her out of duty, not love.

And now he would pay for his kindness to her.

"Let's move our camp over to the hanging tree," Phin said. He looped his rope around Sam's shoulders and pulled it tight. "The ranger can walk. I think I'll take his horse, since he won't need it anymore. Mighty fine animal," he added, stroking Panther's dark neck. "Put the girl on Dink," he added, motioning to his own horse.

"What about me?"

"You lost your horse. You can walk."

"Shoot," Dwight said, but he did as he was told. As he set Billie on Phin's horse he whispered to her, "Don't worry; I won't let Phin touch you. You and me'll be long gone, just as soon as I get the chance. Of course, I want to see the ranger hang first."

Billie shuddered.

His hands lingered on her waist. "You feelin' low? I'll bet you feel right bad about Elliot taking off. You don't need him. I'll take care of you from now on."

So much had happened in the last hour that Billie hadn't spared Elliot a thought. But now his betrayal sank in. He had shown his stripes again. Had he meant anything he'd told her this morning, or had it been just another act? She wondered if he even cared what had happened to them after he'd seized his opportunity to escape. She sincerely hoped that Buttermilk had pounded him into dust.

She and Elliot were responsible for Sam's death. There was no way around it. If she lived, she'd have to carry that around with her for the rest of her life. She was no better than Elliot; they deserved each other.

The outlaws walked the horses the short distance to the canyon where the cottonwood tree grew. Phin jerked Sam along behind him. Sam could only shuffle in his leg irons, and fell twice. He was dragged until he could get to his feet again. Billie's heart went out to him, and she hated herself even more.

The cottonwood tree was very old. Its trunk was as wide around as two pickle barrels, and half of it was dead, blackened by a lightning strike. The other half reared against the sky, its leaves shivering restlessly. One thick bough spanned the trail, high enough to hang a man, as if it had been made for that purpose.

Phin pulled up. "Dwight, throw a rope over. Might as well let the ranger see what he's getting, just the way our Howard did."

Billie felt the rising tide of terror in her chest. It felt just like water, threatening to choke her. She could not even look at Sam. The thought of him dying like this—and having to wait the whole night—couldn't be borne. Tears sprang to her eyes. She squeezed her eyelashes tightly together, tried to swallow the tears back into herself. Phin would like to see her cry for the ranger. He already suspected that they cared more about each other than they'd let on. No doubt he would taunt Sam about it, make him suffer even more.

There had to be some way to escape. But she could see none.

Dwight fashioned a rough noose, then threw the rope over the bough, made it fast. The noose swayed in the hot breeze, malignant, evil. Billie could see the filaments of the rope catching the sunlight on the deadly coil above the knot. She swallowed as she imagined that rough rope pulled tight against the tender skin of her own neck. Pulling tighter, cutting off air.

Her heart pumped wildly. At last she couldn't stand it anymore. She looked at Sam.

He stood in the shadow of the tree, covered with dust from head to toe. His face and hands were scraped raw, and blood ran down over one eye. But he stood straight, his head held high. His mouth was grim but he didn't look particularly afraid. Perhaps he was hiding his fear. Again she realized how much she loved him, and the pain in her heart was almost physical.

She had to do something. She could not let this happen.

Dwight had already made it clear he was willing to double-cross his brother for her.

He was her only chance.

Chapter Sixteen

Elliot clung to Buttermilk's neck. The horse was finally slowing down, his breath coming in loud snorts. He began stumbling over the rocks in his path, sometimes sending Elliot's heart into his mouth.

Elliot sawed on the halter rope. This time Buttermilk obeyed, dropping down into a trot and then a walk, blowing through his nostrils. At last he stood still, head down, sides quivering. Foam lathered his neck, and sweat dripped from his heaving chest and belly, turning his hide slick brown.

Almost unable to comprehend his good fortune, Elliot slid from the horse's steaming back. His legs shook like jelly. He toppled into a heap as soon as his boots hit the ground.

He held on to the halter rope as he scuttled

backward under a creosote's sparse shade. He still couldn't believe he'd escaped.

Even Dwight Daw couldn't catch him. There was something to be said for Billie's horse. He could really run over rocks. But it had been a narrow escape. A couple of shots had come damn close, and it was only luck that Dwight's pony had fallen and broken its leg.

Elliot giggled. Luck had sure been on his side. He was glad he made a break for it when he did. Obviously, if Dwight had come after him, the Arizona Ranger's attempt at rescue had failed.

Too bad about Billie. But he doubted the Daws would hurt her. Dwight was smitten with her; she'd be all right.

He wiped his face. It was as wet as if he'd put his head underwater. He still didn't know how he'd managed to stay with Buttermilk, and bareback, too. He'd clamped his legs around the pony's barrel, as tight as pincers, and grabbed onto Buttermilk's mane, leaning close. The sight of the rocks skimming by underneath had forced him to keep his grip tight. Maybe he'd make a horseman after all.

Well, Billie was right, Elliot thought with a self-congratulatory sigh. Buttermilk sure liked to buck in the morning. When Elliot had seen his chance and pulled himself up, the horse had given a startled crowhop. Buttermilk, sensing a different rider, must have decided to take advantage of the situation. All of a sudden he'd exploded into a pitching, squealing dynamo.

But he had saved Elliot's life.

"If you didn't smell so bad I'd kiss you," Elliot told him.

His elation was short-lived, however. He had no water, no food, and still didn't know where he was. He would try to find his way back to the canyon where they'd first found Billie. There was a pack burro there, and plenty of water.

He stood up and reached for Buttermilk. Somehow he managed to pull himself back aboard. Which way to go?

He thought the ridge to his left looked familiar. As he walked Buttermilk in that direction, Elliot felt a tug of guilt. Billie had risked her life for him, and how did he repay her? He told himself that he'd had no other choice; there had been only one free horse.

Sam Gray should have been able to protect her. He was an Arizona Ranger, wasn't he?

The more Elliot thought about it, the more the blame rested squarely on Sam Gray's shoulders. What kind of lawman would get the drop on the bad guys and then bungle it?

The man was inept.

"I'm sorry, Billie," he muttered as he rode along. "You know I would have taken you along if I could."

He owed her. She had been good to him. He cared about Billie, cared a lot. But she'd be all right. She might spend some uncomfortable moments with the Daw brothers, but he had no doubt they would treat her just fine.

She already had Dwight eating out of her hand. All she had to do was tell that dimwit she was pregnant and he wouldn't lay a hand on her.

Elliot felt better after thinking it out. Good thing for Billie he had managed to escape, no thanks to Ranger Gray's ineptitude.

He'd tell the authorities where to find her as soon as he made it out of this godforsaken desert. First thing.

"Since this is my last night on earth," Sam said to Phin Daw, "I can request anything I want for a last meal. Your brother got that."

"Don't you even mention my brother!" shouted Dwight.

"Dwight, shut up." Phin eyed Sam speculatively. "That's reasonable. We've got makings for a good last meal."

"I want Billie to serve it to me. Alone."

"Have you been eatin' loco weed? What do you take us for?"

"It's my last request."

"Your last *meal*," Phin corrected. "You can choose what you want to eat, but you can't choose who you want to eat it with."

"Who made up that rule?"

"I did!" shouted Phin. "Ranger, you're strainin' my patience."

Unruffled, Sam just stared at him. At last he shrugged. "I'll be dead tomorrow anyway. I don't see what difference it makes."

"Then don't talk about it again."

"I just thought I could leave a will for my wife."

The words bludgeoned Billie's consciousness. His wife? Sam was still married?

"She'll want to know how I faced my death, what my last hours were like. I never left a will. Can either of you boys write?"

"Don't read, don't write," Phin said proudly. "On'y thing worth readin' is the Bible, and our ma can read me that."

"Billie can. I'd like her to write down my last will and testament." Sam glanced at Billie. "Would you do that for me?"

She nodded. Her heart felt like a rag, wrung out of all emotion.

Phin's face turned red. "Now see here just a minute—"

"That's my request. I want a last meal, and some time alone with Billie to take down my last wishes."

"Phin, he's tryin' something," Dwight warned.

"Aim your rifle at my head if you want. I just want to be able to say my words in private." Sam held up his hands. "I can't get away the way I'm chained, and you already said Billie will go free when the ransom money comes."

"You never mind about that. That transaction will happen long after the buzzards get you. It won't concern you."

Billie couldn't bear it if she couldn't spend some time alone with Sam. Even if he was married, even if he didn't love her. She loved him. That was enough. Just to be in his proximity, to hear that calm voice of his telling her stories . . .

Billie realized that even now she was seeking

comfort from him, thinking only of *her* pain, not his. It didn't make her feel any better to know that Sam would offer her that comfort freely. He was the finest person she had ever known.

At least he didn't know how truly base and cowardly she was, the selfishness with which she clung to him, hoping for solace for herself when he was the one who faced death.

"What do you think, Billie?" Dwight asked. "You're the one who'd have to do it." He rested his hand on her arm and she suppressed the urge to flinch.

"I—I think I should. When you let me go, I can take the will to his wife personally."

Dwight looked stricken. "When you go?"

She realized she'd made a mistake. "When *we* go," she added quickly. "To the ranch. To La Zanja. You'll love the ranch—"

"She's teasin' you, Dwight!" Phin said. "Cain't you see that? I told you, girl, leave my brother alone—"

"You leave *her* alone!" Dwight shouted. "You don't know anything!"

Billie thought they'd start fighting right there, but Phin seemed to get a grip on himself. He glared at Billie, and she felt his gaze like ice picks stabbing into her own. "Ranger, you get your wish. I don't think the girl and Dwight ought to spend much time together, anyway. She has an effect on him."

Billie breathed a sigh of relief. Dwight, impotently angry, stomped off, muttering to himself.

They chained Sam Gray to the tree, in the shadow of the noose. As the sun set, Phin prepared son-of-a-bitch stew, bacon, biscuits, and peaches for dessert. Billie carried it over to Sam, a towel draped over the plate and her bound hands.

"Thanks, Billie." Sam tucked into his dinner with fervor.

Billie glanced back at their captors. They had situated themselves beside a huge boulder, and Dwight's rifle was aimed at Sam. "One wrong move and I'll blow your head off!" he shouted.

Sam grinned and held up his hands in acknowledgment. The chains clanked. He started to eat. "Mmmm. This bacon is—"

"How can you talk about bacon when they're going to kill you tomorrow?" Billie said in a hiss.

Sam grinned. "I'd best enjoy it. It's the last bacon I'm likely to get."

"I know we can escape. I can talk to Dwight, talk him into helping us."

"Dwight won't help us."

"He'll help me. I won't leave without you."

Sam set his plate down on the ground. "Billie, Dwight's not right in the head. Can't you see that? One minute he's pining for you like a shy suitor, and the next he's throwing a tantrum because he can't have you while I watch. You can't count on him. Besides, no woman on earth can keep those two from hanging me. I was responsible for their brother's death."

In her heart, Billie knew what Sam said was true, but she was reluctant to give Dwight up.

He was the weak link. He could be manipulated. But how much? "Let me try, Sam."

"No. He's too dangerous. You don't know what he'll do."

"But I—"

Sam looked at her, his face stern. "If you're doing this for me, Billie, and not yourself, I'm asking you not to. Remember Mac Monroe."

"But I can't stand by and watch them kill you! I just can't!" she whispered savagely. Tears brimmed over her lashes, and at that moment she realized that if she could not stop them now, she would cry herself to death.

"Stop it!" His hands grabbed hers, strong and unyielding. "Don't let them see you cry. Phin will only use it against both of us."

She nodded, choking back the whimper that came to her throat. She had to be strong, for him.

"I've made my peace with God," Sam said gently. "I've had a good life. A full life. I knew when I hired on with the Arizona Rangers that it was likely to kill me."

"Don't talk that way!"

"We have to face facts, Billie." He held her gaze, his own eyes dark. She couldn't read what emotion lay behind them. "There's no way out of this."

"I could offer them money. I still have the money I offered Mac Monroe—"

"They don't want money. They want my death. You have to think of the future, Billie. Your future. All your energy should be spent on saving yourself. You know they'll try to get the ransom and keep you, too. I want you to take my horse, if you can. He's a good one. Run for it if you get the chance."

"Like Elliot? Just ride off and leave you here to die?"

"That's what I want," Sam said solemnly. "A condemned man gets a request. That's mine."

She felt as if a cold hand had clamped down on her heart. Looking at the way he was manacled, hand and foot, and tied to the tree, she realized that he was right. There was no way out, unless she could get one of the outlaws' guns.

There wasn't much chance of that. Phin was too smart.

"I'd better write down your will, then," she said, trying to keep the grief out of her voice.

"I expect you'd better. There's a pen and a ledger for writing in my saddlebags. Cap'n Mossman likes us to write reports on our arrests."

She walked over to Phin and directed him to give her the pen, inkwell and ledger. Soon she was before Sam again, sitting on a rock, her bound hands poised over the pad on her knee. Her writing would be painstakingly slow, because of the awkwardness of her hands.

"Ready?" he asked.

She swallowed hard. "Yes."

"Being of sound mind and body, I give this as my last will and testament. I bequeath all my possessions to my wife, Marisa, location unknown, and my son, Joe."

Billie started. "You have a son?"

Sam nodded and continued, "My wife and son are in a location unknown to me, but if it is possible to give them my possessions, I hope it can be done. My worldly goods include one bay horse, Panther; one saddle; a Winchester repeater rifle; a Colt forty-five revolver. I have a month's salary of fifty-five dollars coming to me for my duties as an Arizona Ranger. Billie, there's a badge pinned on the inside of the vest in my saddlebags. The captain likes us to work undercover—we never show our badges until we make an arrest. It means a lot to me. I want you to have it." He thought for another minute. "I have a savings account at the Bank of Bisbee. There's about five hundred dollars in it. If you can get this will to Arizona Ranger headquarters, maybe they'll be able to find my wife and give it to her. The only other thing I own in this world are my law books—"

"Law books?"

He grinned. "Too bad Dwight and Phin couldn't give me a trial. I was a pretty good criminal lawyer at one time."

"You were a lawyer?"

"I hope that doesn't lessen your opinion of me."

"I just realized I know almost nothing about you. I didn't know you had a child."

"Joey . . ." He shook his head as if to clear it. "I doubt he remembers me at all. He's only four."

Billie couldn't help asking, even though the question tore her apart. "When did you see him last?"

"When he was a baby. Marisa took off a few months after he was born."

"Why?" She couldn't imagine anyone leaving a man like Sam.

"Fell for a piano player while I was in Cuba. I remember coming back on the same train they sent us out in a few months before. Then, there were patriots at every stop, waving flags, offering us food and gifts." His mouth turned up at the corners, but Billie wouldn't call it a smile. "No one wanted to look at us on the way back. We were a sorry bunch. Emaciated, sick—a lot of the men had yellow fever, dysentery. . . . I fared better than most, but I was sick for a long time. I had this locket with Marisa's picture in it, and the baby's. It was the only thing that kept me going. I thought she'd be there at the station waiting for me, as pretty as the day I left."

"She wasn't," Billie said.

"No. She wasn't. A couple of months after I came back, she wrote me a letter, pleading for me to come and get her. The piano player left her in New Mexico. I was too sick to travel. By the time I got to Silver City—that's where she was—she'd gone. Heard she'd been working in a brothel there."

Billie flinched. How could any woman choose such a degrading life over this man?

As if reading her thoughts, Sam said, "She hated herself, I guess. Finally I caught up with her in Colorado. She'd come down in the world. Worked in a crib—a shack that wasn't big enough to turn around in. I insisted she come back with me, but she fought me like a wildcat. She told me she hated me."

The anguish in his voice resonated in Billie's heart. "She hated you? After what she'd done? She had no right!"

"Maybe it was because I didn't come right away. Maybe because I saw, as no one else had, how far she'd fallen. She'd been brought up by genteel, elderly parents. She'd had a good education. But there was always that wild thing in her that made her look for trouble. She thought I'd be exciting, since I'd done so many things, but I wasn't exciting the way she wanted."

He paused, looking inward. "I told her she was coming back with me. I was working with a law firm in Tucson, I could support her very well. She told me to come back the next day. I shouldn't have trusted her. When I went back, she'd cleared out. It kills me to know how I just missed my boy, and now he's disappeared. Imagine the kind of life he's living."

"Sam, I'm so sorry."

"They vanished. I spent a year looking for them, but it was as if they never existed."

Billie didn't know what else to say. She wanted to hug him, soothe him, but it was obvious his heart still belonged to his wife. He would find Billie's touch cold comfort indeed.

"I spent every penny I had. Every once in a while I'd try looking for them again. I'd get some kind of a job—hunter's guide, cowboy, anything to keep me going for a while, and when I saved enough I'd go looking again. That's one reason I took the job of Arizona Ranger. We're on the move a lot, going wherever there's trouble. I kept hoping that she'd return to Arizona, and on one of my missions I'd find her." He laughed softly. "Spent a lot of time in the tenderloin district of just about every city in Arizona. Word got around. Everyone knew about the Arizona Ranger who would pay a girl for information. It was easier work than they were used to. I got a lot of false leads, but I felt I had to follow every one. Not for Marisa. She's too far gone. For the boy." Sam lapsed into silence.

But she's still your wife, Billie thought bleakly. Even though there was a finality in Sam's tone when he talked of Marisa, he must still care about her. Sam was the kind of man who would do his duty, even if that duty entailed taking back his prodigal wife—a woman who had hurt him beyond measure. He would do it for his son, if for no other reason. Because a child needed its mother.

Even now, as he faced death, his last thoughts were for her and the child he hardly knew.

It was funny. She and Sam were in the same sort of quandary. Sam would take back his wife for the sake of his son. Billie had entertained the idea of marrying Elliot, even though she didn't love him, to give her child a name.

She closed her eyes. She couldn't think about the future. It was unbearable. She could only try to take what was good from the moment.

Sam was looking at her. His eyes caught the firelight, dark as the ocean. Billie wanted to memorize every line of his strong face, the ironic smile stamped on his lips, the tiny web of lines around his eyes. He'd told her he was thirty years old. In those thirty years he had done so many things. *Don't cry for me, Billie*, he'd said earlier tonight. *I've had a full life. I've done everything I wanted to do*. Except, of course, find his son. That, he still had left to do.

She still could not fathom what life would be like when he was gone. It seemed impossible that this vital, strong life could be snuffed out so quickly, so pointlessly.

I love you, she thought. *I love you, and I can't even tell you*. But what good would it do? It would only serve to make him feel guilty.

"I never expected Elliot to be able to ride a bucking horse," Sam said.

"I guess you can do anything when you're in danger of losing your hide," she replied bitterly.

Sam shrugged. "You can't blame him. He did what I pretty much expected he would do under the circumstances."

"How can you be philosophical about it? It's because of him that we're in this mess."

"I should have watched him closer."

"When will you realize that other people have failings?" demanded Billie. "That it's not always your fault? Elliot is a spineless coward who put both our lives in jeopardy. Your wife is—" She broke off, horrified at her own words.

"You're right, of course."

"You act like . . . Atlas. Taking the whole world on your shoulders. If you hadn't been trying to save me, you'd have both those outlaws trussed up and be on your way out of here. I got you into this," she added sadly.

He smiled. "I won't blame myself, if you'll do the same."

"Oh, Sam, I'm sorry. But I can't stand the thought of . . . I can't think of it!"

"Then don't." He leaned closer, took her hands in his. She heard the chains rattle, felt their coldness against her skin. But his hands were warm, and she memorized the imprint of his fingers against hers. Oh, how she wanted this man!

His gaze lingering on hers, Sam smoothed his thumb over the back of her hand. His touch still caused goose bumps, and Billie was surprised at the sensual thrill that leaped up inside her. His eyes took on that lazy, shuttered look that meant he knew what she was thinking, and he grinned. "Did I ever tell you the story of the Grulla? He was a little Spanish horse that beat Wyatt Earp's Thoroughbred in a match race, back in the eighties."

"Sam, how can you tell stories when we're facing death?"

"What else is there to do? This is a good story. You'll like it." And so, his hands wrapped around her own, he started to talk, his steady voice soothing. Billie clung to the sensation of his skin against hers, memorizing it. She realized again that he was doing much more in the way of calming her than she could do to comfort him. But maybe telling stories did help him. She listened, becoming involved in the story despite herself.

Sam told stories all night. Dawn was shell pink on the horizon, bringing with it a deep, tearing fear in Billie. She held on to Sam as if he were a ship's spar after a wreck.

His voice had grown hoarse, but he never skipped a beat between stories. He told her about his father, who sounded just like Colonel Bahill. The man had high expectations of his son, was a tough taskmaster, but worse; he used his belt liberally and often.

"I would never do that with my son," Sam said. Then Billie saw the sadness in his eyes. She squeezed his hand.

"Remember, take my horse if you can. He's fast."

"I will," she promised.

Billie couldn't stand it anymore. She wanted to tell him she loved him, even if it was selfish. She had to let the words into the air. "Sam, I—"

"Dwight! Wake up. I'm falling asleep," Phin said from across the clearing. He kicked his brother. Dwight stirred in his bedroll. Phin had stayed up most of the night, his gun trained on Billie and Sam.

Dutifully, Dwight got up. Phin crawled into his bedroll. "Wake me around ten o'clock," he instructed his brother. "I've got to get some sleep." He called over to Sam. "Enjoy the dawn, Ranger. It's the last one you'll ever see."

The moment was lost. Billie couldn't tell Sam

how much she loved him now. She knew that Sam would not want to hear the words she had to say. It would only add to his burden.

As the morning wore on, Billie's dread grew. Her mouth was dry, and her heart hammered hard against her rib cage. She couldn't keep still. Sam, remarkably, dozed a little. Could he really be that unconcerned?

She had to try to save him. Phin was asleep; his snoring droned across the campsite. Dwight yawned, training his gun on them as he made himself some coffee.

Billie thought of Sam's request. He didn't want her to try anything with Dwight. He thought she'd have a better chance to save herself during the exchange for the ransom. But she could not stand to sit here and wait helplessly for the Daw brothers to hang the man she loved.

She couldn't. That was all.

Rising stiffly, Billie walked toward Dwight. She had no real plan, other than getting his gun away from him and making him unchain Sam. But she would fight with her last breath to achieve that aim.

Chapter Seventeen

Elliot did find the place where Billie and the ranger had camped. Or rather, Buttermilk did. Elliot had heard that if you gave a horse its head, it would go back home. Or someplace it perceived as home. Buttermilk made for the canyon with unerring accuracy.

As they rounded the bend, Elliot felt a quick elation. There was the cottonwood tree, the stream. . . .

And people. He was safe!

There were four or five horses he didn't recognize, and several men sitting in the shade of the cottonwood, eating lunch. The first thing Elliot recognized was that white son of a bitch that had thrown him. Pegasus!

He booted the buckskin into a trot. Everything would be all right now. He had made it!

A man detached himself from the shade of the cottonwood tree and walked toward him.

It was Roland Bahill.

Elliot swallowed. Of all the people he could run into in this godforsaken wilderness, he had to run into Billie's father!

For a split second, he debated turning Buttermilk around and making a run for it. He had absolutely no doubt that Colonel Bahill would shoot him on the spot if he knew Elliot had deserted his daughter.

Unless . . . unless Elliot told him he had managed to escape, and had ridden for help. He *had* meant to find help, anyway. It had just come sooner than he'd expected.

Yes, that was what he'd do. And while he was at it, he might as well tell Bahill about the child. The colonel would be spitting mad at first, but once he calmed down, he would realize that it would be best for all concerned if Billie's child had a father.

The next few minutes would be unpleasant— downright dangerous—but think of the results!

Squaring his shoulders and fixing a smile on his face, Elliot rode into camp.

· The cool breath of morning was redolent with the dry, dusty scent of desert sunflowers, which grew in profusion under the mesquite trees. The cottonwood boughs clattered and rustled, their bright green leaves translucent where the sun touched them. The dark shadow of the cliff above sheathed Billie's skin like cool velvet. She couldn't fathom missing another morning like this.

The fear that gripped her was like none she'd known before. Her fear was for Sam, not herself. She would give anything for things to be different.

Love, she realized, was an unselfish thing. With Elliot she had been possessive. He had run away, and she had come after him, determined to make things right between them. She had *willed* him to love her. Her search for him was driven by her own needs, her own desires. She had even fantasized that if Elliot died in these mountains, his last words would be for her. She had pictured him, his Byronic face suffused with agony, proclaiming his undying devotion. This was the "timeless" love she'd read about in women's magazines, a spiritual love that bridged the chasm of death. The same mentality that put forth the notion that it was far better to be a widow, beloved up to the moment of one's husband's death, than to be a divorcée. It would be better, she'd thought, for the man she loved to die with her name on his lips, than for him to reject her in some sordid manner.

How wrong she'd been!

I would gladly suffer unrequited love, joyfully give Sam up, if only he could see another morning like this one. Just to know that he was alive and happy . . . that would be enough.

It was this determination that made her flirtation with Dwight Daw palatable.

Dwight sat cross-legged on the ground, rifle

bridging his lap, a tin coffee cup at his side. At Billie's approach, he stood up, his expression sullen.

"I finished writing his will," she told him.

"You and the ranger are pretty chummy."

"It's not that. He had a lot to say."

Dwight turned his malevolent gaze in Sam's direction. "I hope he dies real slow. I hope he's just as scared as Howard was."

"You loved your brother a lot," Billie said. She stood near him, hands clasped in front of her. "I can understand that."

"You don't have to watch. I know how that kind of thing affects a woman, bein' so delicate an' all."

"That's very kind of you." She tilted her chin up and looked him in the eyes. "You've treated me very well, Dwight. Not like Phin."

"He don't mean nothin'. He's mad at everybody. Ever since Pa died he's had a chip on his shoulder."

"I can't believe that you and Phin are brothers," Billie continued. "I hope he'll let us be, once this is all behind us. Do you think he will, Dwight?"

Dwight glowered, and his eyes were so little and mean that Billie caught her breath in her throat and had to look away. "He'd better leave us alone. He'd just better."

"I don't want to come between you and your brother."

"He's not telling me who I can marry and who I can't."

Billie eyed the gun in his hand. He'd lowered it so that it was pointing at the ground. Her fingers were only about four inches away, and she could almost feel the ghost of the gun's stock in her palm. She leaned closer to him. "It will be hard at first," she said huskily. Having never played the femme fatale role before, she wondered if she was overdoing it. But Dwight didn't look like the kind of man who would know the difference. She puffed her lips into what she imagined was a bee-sting pout and slanted him a smoky look from under her lashes. "My father won't approve, but he'll come around. He'll have to, won't he?"

"I knew you loved me!" Dwight suddenly caught her in one big paw and pulled her toward him, kissing her hard on the lips. Billie stemmed the revulsion that rose in her and burrowed her fists against his chest, rubbing her fingers along his grimy shirt. His bulk pressed against her, almost suffocating her, and she tried not to flinch away from the jutting crudeness at the hollow of her hip. Unfortunately, he held her with his gun arm. The gun hovered uselessly near her ear. It would be impossible to get hold of it—

"Dwight! Let go of her!" shouted Phin. Wide-awake and red-eyed with anger, Phin Daw exploded out of his bedroll.

"No!"

"Dwight. You'd better do as I say. Now!"

Disgusted, Dwight let Billie go.

"You're as stupid as a cockroach," Phin said. "Can't you see what she's trying to do?"

"I'm tellin' you, Phin, I'm not gonna put up with your meddling in my affairs much more," Dwight shouted, but he put another foot between himself and Billie.

"Go get some firewood."

Slapping his hat on his head, Dwight obeyed, grumbling.

Phin towered over Billie, his face contorted with rage. "I'm only gonna tell you one more time. You leave that boy alone. Next time—"

"Next time you'll what?" she replied, glaring at him in defiance. "Kill me? Then where would you be? I'm worth a lot of money."

"There are ways to make you toe the line, ways you won't like." Phin motioned with his chin to Sam. "You know what the Apaches used to do? Strip a man naked, tie him up, then roll him in cholla. They'd take their lances, see, and roll 'em back and forth on the branches. It's a bad way to die. But no more than the ranger deserves!" He spat.

"You wouldn't!"

He leaned over her, his eyes like blue marbles. "I'll kill him by inches unless you do as I say. Stay away from Dwight!"

Fearfully, Billie glanced at Sam. He sat at the base of the tree, his face impassive but his eyes smoldering. He had seen her accepting Dwight's kiss. She could tell he was very, very angry with her. Did he think that she was flirting with Dwight because she wanted to save herself? After all, she had given in to Elliot, and thrown herself at Sam.

No, he wouldn't think that. He would know that she was trying to save him, and he didn't want her to take such a risk.

For the first time, despair overwhelmed her. Billie had always believed in the words "Where there's life, there's hope," but she was beginning to realize that escape was futile.

"Keep away from Dwight!" Phin said again.

"Don't worry," she replied. "I'll be happy to oblige." Wiping her mouth and spitting out the scent and taste of Dwight Daw, she walked unsteadily over to Sam and sat beside him.

He didn't say a word. She didn't feel much like talking, herself. Drained of energy, even fear, she sat beside him, her back against the big tree. Just being with him soothed her. After a while his anger seemed to vanish; his eyes were kind and—she could hardly believe it—pitying.

They remained in companionable silence, soaking in the morning. Billie listened to the breathy, womanly moan of a mourning dove from somewhere in the brush nearby. The awareness of Sam beside her sang in her veins. His chest rising and falling in even breaths, the tingling feeling where his clothes adjoined hers. She stared at the ridge opposite, rearing up like a bar of carved pink soap, polished by the sun.

Billie had finally admitted defeat, and that was somehow comforting. She didn't have to fight the current anymore. Whatever happened after Sam died, she was with him now, and she would take what she could from it.

Annie McKnight

That was all life really offered, anyway: the present. Everything else was either regret, anticipation or dread—and none of it was as real as this moment.

Chapter Eighteen

Roland Bahill stared at the wild man riding his daughter's buckskin horse. He shouldered his rifle, hot tentacles of anger and fear writhing in his gut. "Hold it right there!"

The man drew rein and put his hands up.

"What did you do with my daughter?" the colonel demanded.

"Nothing, I swear it! Don't you recognize me? It's me! Elliot!"

Bahill felt his finger involuntarily tighten on the trigger. It took a conscious effort to ease his grip. Although he would dearly love to shoot Elliot Stevenson right now, it wouldn't be wise. "Where is she?"

Elliot's eyes were wild with fright as he stared at the rifle still pointed at him. "I was riding for help when I saw you—"

"Make sense, man!"

"She's a hostage," Stevenson said. "Two men are holding her—they had me, too, but I saw a chance to get away and save us both."

Rage blinded the colonel. He grasped Elliot's arm and pulled him off the buckskin, surprised at his own strength. "Have they hurt her? If they've hurt her I'll kill you!"

Stevenson's voice went up an octave. "She's all right—they haven't touched her—I wouldn't let them."

"*You* wouldn't let them?"

Elliot shook Bahill's hand away, shrugged his shoulders and adjusted his shirtsleeves. He smelled as rank as a javelina. "I made sure no one so much as touched a hair on her head. I did what I had to do, as any future husband would."

Bahill couldn't believe the gall of this man. "What did you say?" He took a step toward Stevenson, pushing the rifle's muzzle into the soft flesh of the man's throat.

Elliot Stevenson cowered, but to his credit he did not back down. "Sir, I know how you are against our marriage, but we love each other—"

"That's not what you told me less than a month ago!"

"I was angry. I said things I shouldn't, just to spite you. But the truth is, I love Billie. And I want to do right by her."

Stevenson's words hit home. "Do right by her? What do you mean by that?"

"It was a mistake, but we were so in love—you know how it is when you're young, in love—it wasn't her fault, not at all; I take complete responsibility. . . ."

"What are you babbling about?"

Stevenson gulped. "Billie's going to have a baby. My baby."

Bahill felt as if a bull had knocked him to the ground and gored him of all feeling. "You're lying."

"No. No, sir, I'm not. I know it will take some time to get used to—it was a shock to me, too—but it's really very good news, isn't it? I mean if you look at it another way. Think of it. You'll be a grandfather!"

Feeling suddenly empty, Colonel Bahill had to lean against something. He grabbed hold of Buttermilk's neck and closed his eyes, his head throbbing. How could he have been betrayed like this? How could she have done it? But another realization, bigger, stronger, pushed into his consciousness. Billie was still alive.

He would sort out this mess later. "Boys! Saddle up!" he shouted. "This man knows where Billie is."

As the riders mounted up, Bahill looked down at Elliot, who stood uncertainly beside Billie's horse.

"What's wrong?" Bahill asked sarcastically. "You afraid to go back?"

"I—I could use a saddle."

"We don't have another. Roy!"

The top hand at La Zanja rode up to them. "Yes, sir?"

"Give Stevenson your horse. You ride the buckskin."

They traded horses. Roy was agile as an Apache—one of the best horsemen in Arizona; he'd have no trouble riding bareback.

"Lead the way, then," Bahill said. "You'd better hope for your sake she's all right."

But the fear in his gut told him they were probably too late. If that was true, he'd take Elliot Stevenson apart with his own two hands.

"Say your prayers," Phin announced. "You're about to pay for your many sins."

The cold wind of fear tore through Billie's throat. It couldn't happen, not so soon! Tears filled her eyes, choked her.

Sam rose to his feet. The noose hung near him, deathly still in the hot morning.

"Get his horse."

Dwight lifted Panther's saddle and walked toward the horse.

"Don't bother with the saddle," Phin shouted. "He won't need it."

Billie couldn't get her breath. Her heart pounded in her chest, in her veins, ears and throat. She couldn't focus. A black swarm of bees seemed to fill her head. It lowered in a cloud over her eyes, obscuring her vision. Her stomach tightened, and she leaned against the cottonwood tree for support. She felt as if she were the one about to die. Needles of pain bris-

tled along her skin. Her hands and legs had gone
to sleep. She honestly didn't know if she could
walk.

*Lord, please help me. Please help me to get
through this. If he has to die, let it be quickly.*

The black veil lifted, and Billie watched as
Dwight led the horse under the tree.

"Put him on his horse." Phin's voice seemed
to come from underwater, distant and distorted.
But there was no mistaking the righteous anger
in his eyes. He looked like an old-time preacher
at his pulpit.

"His leg irons are in the way."

"Damn it, Dwight! Do I have to do everything?" Phin took the key to the manacles and
strode over to the ranger.

Abruptly, Billie felt as if she were being pulled
away from the scene. As if this were a play, and
she the trapped audience of one. She saw Phin
hunker down to put the key in the manacle lock.
Dwight looked on, one hand casually stretched
out to hold the horse at his bridle. Phin put his
key into the lock, his head bent in concentration.
The ranger shifted his feet.

"Keep still, damn you!"

The lock clicked.

It happened so quickly that Billie wondered if
it were just wishful thinking on her part. Sam
kicked his foot up and into Phin's head, the toe
of his boot cracking the outlaw's skull. With
lightning quickness, the ranger's handcuffed
hands shot up and then down again on Dwight's
outstretched arm.

311

Annie McKnight

Dwight screamed in agony. "Dammit! You broke my arm!" he shouted, his eyes wide with disbelief. "You broke it! Phin, he broke my arm!"

Phin lay in the dirt heedless of his brother, blood seeping from the gash in his skull. Billie thought he must be dead.

"Damn you!" Dwight's good hand snaked for the gun in his pants, but the ranger was quicker, even with his manacled hands.

When the dust cleared, Sam Gray had the gun pointed at Dwight's chest. "Billie! Get me out of these things."

Billie shook herself from her reverie. She did as she was told, no easy feat with her own hands still manacled. When she had freed him, he returned the favor, his eyes never leaving Dwight's face.

She rubbed her hands, trying to get more feeling into them. He must have planned this all along. Why didn't he tell her? She could have helped him!

At any rate, they were safe now. That was all that counted. He had saved them both.

Cradling his arm, Dwight looked down at his brother. "What did you do to him?"

"No more than he would have done to me," Sam replied, his voice even.

Dwight seemed to shrink before Billie's eyes. He dropped to his knees, sobbing, and grasped his brother's body with his left hand. "Oh, Phin! What'll I tell Ma?"

Despite herself, Billie felt sorry for him.

Sam did not let down his guard, but even he

was surprised when the crying man launched himself forward, hurtling into the ranger's mid-section. The gun flew out of his hand.

"You killed my brother!" shrieked Dwight, his fingers clutched around Sam's throat.

Stunned, Billie felt unable to move. How could he do that with a broken arm? But his fingers held on, shutting off Sam's air, his strength inhuman.

He was killing Sam.

The realization knocked her into action. She scrambled for the gun, just as another gun went off.

"Let him go."

The voice was stern, masculine, angry.

Billie looked in the direction of the speaker. Her father sat his horse not fifteen feet from them, and ranged around him were five other horsemen. One of them was Elliot.

She glanced at Dwight, and saw that he had been shot again. One bloody ear hung by its skin from the side of his head. His face was drawn with shock. The gunshot wound had been enough to stop his murderous rage.

Sam struggled to rise. He sucked air into his lungs in huge gasps. Billie ran to him. "Water!" she shouted. "He needs water. Hurry."

Someone pressed the canteen into her hands. She ministered to him, her gaze never leaving his face. *I love you*, she thought, but did not say. *I'll love you as long as I live*. She dared not tell him. He had a wife and child; there could be no room in his life for her.

313

When he could breathe again, his arm came around her in a heavy hug. "Thank you for being so brave."

He admired her bravery. Was that all? The disappointment she experienced was nothing compared to her joy that he was still alive.

Tears of joy and relief ran down her face. She was oblivious to everyone else. It didn't matter that her father was there, or Elliot. Her eyes were only for Sam. She rejoiced in the feeling of Sam's arm around her, and wanted to remain with him forever. Even if he didn't love her, just being with him was enough.

"Billie." Colonel Bahill cleared his throat. "Are you all right?"

"I'm fine."

The colonel stared at her, a puzzled expression on his face, as if he'd seen something he hadn't expected. Could he tell how she felt about Sam? Did it show on her face?

And if her father, who had never been sensitive to the vagaries of human nature, saw through her, did Sam?

Elliot placed his arm on hers. "Billie, thank God we got here in time!"

Billie paid him scant attention. Sam had caught her gaze again, and they stared into each other's eyes. What was he trying to tell her? She allowed Elliot to help her up, her eyes never leaving Sam's face.

"I thought I'd lost you," Elliot said. "I have wonderful news! Your father has given us his blessing."

"What?" Her ears were ringing. Sam's eyes sparkled, but like the ocean under a mist. They seemed more distant now, less compelling. Elliot was babbling something but she could not understand his words. She only knew that if she drew her gaze from the ranger's, the last tenuous thread between them would break.

"Did you hear me? We can get married after all, and your father will give you away!"

Shocked, bruised, Billie at last understood the words filtering into her brain. She glanced at her father, who still sat his horse at the edge of the clearing. "Is it true?" she whispered.

The effort pained him; that was obvious. "Yes, it's true. You have my blessing."

After all this, her father finally had given her what she wanted. And now she didn't want it at all. She looked back at Sam.

He would not meet her eyes. The moment was gone. Whatever he had been about to say, he would not say it now. The gap between them had grown in the space of a few seconds.

Maybe he'd never wanted her at all. Even if he wasn't bound by duty to his wife.

Elliot took her hand in his, linking fingers. "I told him, Billie. All about—" His gaze swerved to the other riders. "About . . . everything. We shall be married as soon as we get back to La Zanja."

Billie opened her mouth to object, then closed it again. She couldn't think about it right now. After coming so close to death, it was too soon to think about the future. She allowed herself to be led over to her father.

His face was stern, as unyielding as she remembered. And then she saw the tears at the corners of his eyes. In one movement he swung down from his horse and hugged her to him. His hold almost smothered her, and she felt his tears wet against the nape of her neck. He said nothing, but that one action spoke volumes. She realized then that he loved her, and always had.

He pulled back, suddenly embarrassed. "Welcome home, girl," he said gruffly, and patted her gently on the back.

Elliot glowed. "We're reunited," he said. "A family again."

Billie didn't see Sam turn away, pushing Dwight Daw, now wearing the ranger's chains, before him. She did not see the bleakness on his face that had settled there when Colonel Bahill gave Elliot and Billie his blessing.

They rode toward the other camp to pick up Elliot's horse and the other pack animals. Billie had not had a chance to talk to Sam, who rode at the front of the party with his prisoner. Dwight Daw, greatly subdued, rode before him, a mule snubbed to his horse. Phin Daw's body was slung over the mule.

Billie should have been happy. Sam would live to see other beautiful mornings; he would have the chance to look for his son again. Her father had given her his blessing to marry Elliot.

The fear that she had nursed in her heart for

the last couple of months vanished like melting snow. Her father did not hate her for what she'd done. Whenever he glanced at her, his gaze was not accusing, but joyful. He looked like a man who had won a million dollars. She could tell he still didn't approve of Elliot, but his joy over finding his daughter safe and sound was apparently enough.

Elliot rode beside her. It was difficult for her to sort out her feelings regarding him. What had been his intentions when he took off on Buttermilk yesterday? To save his own skin, or to run for help?

Elliot, of course, told her that all along he had been planning to save them. He saw his opportunity, and took it, racing hell-for-leather for the nearest aid. Hadn't he brought back help? Hadn't his actions saved the ranger's life?

It was a puzzle. She could have sworn that he was just trying to save himself, but if so, why did he go to the one man who would have liked to shoot him on sight? Elliot could have kept on running. It had to take some courage to face her father.

Elliot spoke as if their marriage were a foregone conclusion. Billie kept her own counsel. Perhaps it would be the wisest thing to marry him.

"It will be so wonderful. Imagine, Billie. The three of us, a family! Your father has agreed to teach me about the running of the ranch. . . ."

Billie allowed his words to wash over her. She couldn't absorb it all now.

Up ahead, the ranger rode straight-backed, and never once turned around in his saddle. Just looking at him filled Billie's heart with an aching loss.

And later that day when the trail forked, and Sam Gray split off from the party to take his prisoner back to Globe, they said hardly a word to each other, just polite good-byes.

Chapter Nineteen

Elliot was awakened by a noise.

He lay in his bedroll, trying to orient himself. He had lived in abject fear for so long that it took a moment to adjust to his good fortune.

Everything had worked out perfectly. He and Billie would be married the moment they reached La Zanja. The gold he'd discovered was safely stowed away in the packsaddle. Perhaps later, after the baton was passed from the colonel to himself and he had mastered the running of La Zanja, he could delegate his duties for a short time and return to the Lost Dutchman Mine. Of course he would need a tremendous amount of equipment to retrieve the ore. And miners, at three dollars a day. And of course he would have to find the mine again. Well, he'd found it once. He would work all that out later.

Elliot grinned. Not only would he be a wealthy landowner, but a mining magnate as well. All his dreams had been realized. And through it all, beautiful, courageous Billie would stand by his side as his helpmeet.

Sweetness pervaded his body. Soon he would have her again, and this time it would not be rushed, in secret. He would teach her the tricks of his French mistress. And when their son came along . . .

It would be a Stevenson dynasty.

The noise again. It must be a rock, trickling down the slope above them. They had camped at the cottonwoods where he'd first seen Billie, mainly to rest the horses. This ungodly heat had taken its toll on everyone, man and beast alike.

Elliot caught a movement out of the corner of his eye. He glanced up at the ridge.

Unbelievable! Above him, washed in the moonlight, stood an old man and a burro. Stooped with age, the prospector sported a long white beard and a hangdog expression. The man stared directly at Elliot and lifted a finger to his lips.

Elliot glanced around him. Everyone was fast asleep.

The old man turned away, but not before he lifted one hand and motioned Elliot to follow him.

Stealthily, Elliot pushed back the blankets and struggled into his boots. Excitement prickled the hairs on the back of his neck. Was this a dream? Whatever it was, curiosity got the better of him.

He started up the ridge. The ancient prospector moved quickly, easily, over the rough landscape, always keeping himself a certain distance ahead. He was pretty agile for his years.

Elliot followed the old man and burro for what seemed like hours across the desert, through the canyon and over several hills. He didn't know why it was so important to keep the prospector in sight, but the urge was irresistible. The moonlight blanched the sand and turned the desert into a blighted, alien landscape, but Elliot didn't think about turning back.

At last the prospector stopped on a hill overlooking a steep canyon. Even at night, the area looked familiar.

Elliot's breath caught in his throat as he saw the rock house at the mouth of the canyon. This had to be the canyon that guarded the Lost Dutchman Mine!

He glanced over at the prospector, who had started down the hill, leading his burro. Hastily, Elliot followed. Yes! He could see the hole gouged into the cliff face. The prospector had led him here on purpose.

Below him, the old man disappeared behind an outcropping of rock. Elliot picked up his pace, half running and half sliding down the slippery scree.

When he reached the outcropping and looked beyond it, he could not see the prospector or his burro. Where had they gone?

He sat down, his heart pumping wildly. What did it mean? He could have sworn that the prospector would come out the other side in a couple of seconds.

There was no sound. A light breeze teased his hair, ruffled his clothing. Elliot suddenly realized he was utterly, completely alone. Had the bent old man been some kind of ghost? He shivered. Maybe it was the old Dutchman himself, Jacob Waltz. Maybe Jacob Waltz wanted him to have the mine.

Now that he had stopped walking, the air was suddenly cool. Elliot stuck his hands in his pockets and discovered the crumpled-up page from his sketchbook. He had tried to draw Billie earlier this evening, by the campfire, but hadn't been able to concentrate.

Suddenly he had an idea. He could draw the canyon, so he would recognize it again. At last he could do something useful with his artistic ability. That was, if he had kept the charcoal he'd used earlier.

Elliot's fingers closed around a soft squarish lump. Ah, there it was, the charcoal. He couldn't believe his good fortune. I must be meant to have this mine, he thought.

He spent the rest of the night making sketches, first of the canyon and its stone house, and then, as he followed his own tracks back toward camp, drawing a map liberally sprinkled with landmarks; a many-armed saguaro here, a rock formation there. Thank God the moon was up.

He reached the camp by morning, just as the others were stirring. After hiding the page in his pack, Elliot lit the fire and cooked coffee for his rescuers.

Later that day, the party left the Superstition Mountains for good. They stayed a couple of days at Bark's Ranch, and when the horses were rested, went on to Phoenix. Within a week's time, Billie, Elliot and the colonel had returned to La Zanja.

"Can we slow down a little? I got a stitch in my side!" complained Dwight.

Sam stifled an angry retort, and slowed his horse. It wasn't Dwight's fault he was in such a foul mood. And yet anything Dwight said, Sam nearly bit his head off. The ride back to Globe was long and arduous, made even more difficult by the depression that weighed the ranger down.

He missed Billie. It felt as if an essential piece had been ripped from his heart. To think that they would never again play cards on a stormy day, exchanging lively banter. Never again would he hold her against him, feel the softness of her lips on his.

He wished he had taken her there in the pool, and damn the consequences. At least he'd have the memory.

Sam tried to block her out of his mind, but couldn't. His mind kept replaying the last several days.

Was it his imagination, or did she really care about him?

For a moment, when she'd run into his arms after Dwight had tried to kill him, Sam had thought so. But when Colonel Bahill agreed to her marriage to Elliot, she had pulled away as if they'd never been close.

"Is it true?" she'd demanded of her father. Had that been confusion in her voice? Or wonder? He didn't know.

Since then, she and Elliot had ridden and talked together, looking very much like an affianced couple. Sam had wanted to talk some sense into her, remind her just how bad Stevenson was, but in the end, realized he couldn't interfere. Billie must sort it out for herself.

Sam couldn't marry her. He was already married. If he could find his wife, obtain a divorce . . .

But what about Joey? Would Billie want to raise another woman's four-year-old boy when she had her own pregnancy to deal with? Was he so arrogant to think she would do anything, grasp at any straw, to give her child a name? That he was the answer to all her problems?

Billie had more guts than that.

No, it was obvious that Billie loved Elliot, despite his failings.

And so Sam had left them at the first opportunity, and although his soul ached for her, he never looked back.

Chapter Twenty

"We have to set a date," Elliot told Billie. "It's already the first of May and pretty soon people will know."

Billie bit her lip. What Elliot said was true. Any further delay would lead to embarrassment for them all.

Elliot took her hand in his. The sun streaming through the lace curtains of the morning room glowed on his hair. It was as smooth and black as a raven's wing. He had recovered completely from his harrowing adventure in the Superstitions, and was more handsome than ever. He had bought new clothes with the gold he'd brought back, and they suited him to perfection. "I don't want to press you, but you have to make up your mind. Your father is an important man.

He'll want to invite most of the county. Arrangements must be made."

Billie sighed. "I suppose you're right." But it was hard to overcome the apathy she felt. Marrying Elliot was the right thing to do. She was convinced of that. Her father would certainly breathe easier once the deed was done. And Elliot's experience had changed him for the better. Oh, there would always be a certain amount of enlightened self-interest in Elliot—she couldn't expect him to change the habits of a lifetime— but Billie began to realize that there was some good in him.

She sensed that he knew he had lost part of her forever. This had a humbling effect on him. In the past few weeks he had wooed her with an ardor that had to be genuine. She could almost feel sorry for him.

Billie knew she could raise this baby alone, if she had to. But did she want to cut Elliot off from the chance to know his own child?

Now he caught her gaze, and his eyes reflected his disappointment. "I know what you're thinking, Billie. You're thinking that I would make a very bad husband. A month ago, that would have been true. But I promise you I'll never betray you again. I mean it."

"I know you do."

"Then please, let's act before it's too late. I know it's what your father wants."

"I'll think about it," Billie said listlessly. "I'll let you know tomorrow."

*   *   *

Colonel Bahill watched his daughter as she walked down to the corrals. She was still dressed in her morning gown, a salmon-colored confection that seemed to float around her as she walked. He could never recall her looking so completely feminine.

She looked so beautiful, and the sight of her made him proud, but he couldn't help feeling ambivalent about the change in her.

He had always urged his daughter to be strong, to ignore her feminine side. He realized now that he had encouraged the tomboy in her out of fear. Emily had been feminine, fragile, and look what had happened to her. He couldn't stand the thought of losing Billie, too. That was why he had tried to toughen her up, make her self-reliant and strong: fear, plain and simple. Fear that a delicate flower could not grow in this rugged country and survive.

Billie used to spend a lot of time with the cowhands, but in the last two weeks she had been down to the corrals only once to feed Buttermilk his carrots. It was as if she had turned her back completely on the life she had led before her experience in the Superstition Mountains.

The colonel stood at the window, watching as Billie leaned against the fence. Buttermilk ambled toward her with a nickered greeting. Billie stretched out her hand and fed him his treat.

Her figure was as slim as ever, but that would change soon. And yet she still hadn't discussed her wedding plans. Not once.

Billie patted the horse's neck absently. The

colonel didn't like the way she looked. Her complexion was too pale. Her shoulders seemed to droop. Olivia had mentioned more than once that since her return Billie seemed listless, uninterested in life around her.

Was that the way for a future bride to act? Hadn't he made the greatest sacrifice a father could make? He loathed Stevenson, but he had given her his blessing to marry him.

What was wrong with her?

He watched as she started back toward the house, sadness palpable in every line of her body, and decided he couldn't stand it any longer. She needed a good talking-to. And he was going to give it to her.

He intercepted her by the washhouse. "How are you today?" he said as cheerfully as he could.

"Just fine, Father."

What a simpering reply! He clamped down on his anger and frustration. "Have you two decided on a date yet?"

She paused. Her eyes looked shadowed in her drawn face. "Elliot likes the idea of a June wedding, but that might be . . . a little late."

Embarrassed, he cleared his throat and pressed on. "What do *you* want?"

She shrugged. "I suppose mid-May would be best."

"That's only two weeks away. We'd better get a move on if we're going to do it up right."

"I suppose so."

"You aren't exactly doing handsprings. I thought this was what you wanted."

She looked at him. "Thank you, Father. I know how hard it is for you to accept Elliot, and I really appreciate it." Her voice had the mechanical sameness to it of a machine.

"You don't sound like you appreciate it."

She turned away. When had she become so delicate? She wasn't his Billie at all. The sight of the haunted sadness in her eyes caused a sinking sensation in the pit of his stomach. How could he make her happy again? "You don't have to marry Elliot."

She looked up quickly, and he caught a fleeting light of hope in her eyes, soon extinguished. "I couldn't do that to him, Father."

"If you don't love him, don't marry him. You don't love him, do you?"

"It doesn't matter."

"Where's your spunk, girl? What kind of vaporish little idiot have I raised? You don't have to marry a man you don't love!"

"I've already committed myself to him. What would people say?"

"To hell with what people say! They wouldn't dare say anything. Not around me. What good is being the most powerful man in southern Arizona if you can't do what you want? If anybody so much as hints that it isn't right, I'll knock his words right down his throat!"

"I couldn't do that to Elliot, don't you see? I couldn't do that to you!"

"You can't do it to us, or you can't do it to yourself?" He grasped her arm. "Maybe Elliot's a safe bet. Maybe you're afraid that you won't be able to face the gossip. That's your affair. But if you're marrying this man for my sake, don't. We'll get by; we'll do just fine. No one will dare say a word about you; I can promise you that!"

Her mouth had a stubborn set. It was obvious she didn't believe him.

"Look, girl, you're a fool if you give up your life for someone else's happiness. Elliot won't be happy married to you. Even if he loves you— which I doubt—he'll know how you feel. You won't spare his feelings, only hurt him more."

"He has a right to know his own child."

"He can visit his child anytime! I won't stand in his way! But you're not doing him any favor by marrying him!" Suddenly the memory of Sam Gray loomed in his mind. He remembered the way she had run to him after Dwight Daw tried to strangle him, remembered the look in her eyes. "It's that ranger. You're in love with him, aren't you? What did he do, turn you down? If he did, I'll give him something to think about!"

Horror suffused his daughter's face. "He has nothing to do with this! Leave him alone!" She turned on her heel and ran for the house.

The colonel watched her go, berating himself for acting like a meddling old fool.

But later that day, he sent a telegram to Ranger Gray. He'd find out once and for all if he'd hit upon the truth.

Chapter Twenty-one

Sam sat near the second-floor window of Barris McCracken's law office in Bisbee, staring at the newly constructed Copper Queen Hotel, whose regal beauty dominated the busy mining metropolis. The Copper Queen was painted yellow, a border of red-brown bricks running along her corners like the pattern on a Navajo blanket. Her windows and portico were painted forest green, and her many red-tiled roofs were flung out to the sky in the modern architectural style that reminded Sam of Japanese pagodas.

It was better to occupy his mind with the view than to think about what McCracken had just told him.

Sam had returned to Bisbee this morning, after taking his prisoner to Globe and remaining there a week to testify at the trial. Because

Dwight Daw had been under the influence of his brother and had not actually shot any of the victims in the payroll robbery in Globe, he was sentenced to twenty years in Yuma Prison. The sentence was not a lenient one, since most criminals would choose death over sweltering behind the iron doors of the most inhumane prison in the West.

The letter from McCracken's office had been waiting for him at Arizona Ranger headquarters.

Sam passed a hand over his eyes. "There can be no mistake?"

The lawyer shook his head. Barris was an impossibly tall young man, thin and stooped like a string bean, his chestnut hair parted in the middle and smoothed flat. He wore wire-rimmed spectacles and a standup collar that had to be constricting on this hot, still day. Sam had known him in Tucson; they had practiced law in the same firm.

"The woman who owned the"—Barris paused delicately—"boardinghouse, found a copy of the wedding license in your wife's personal effects. Otherwise we might never have known. She sent the letter to our law firm in Tucson, and they forwarded it on to me. Damn it, Sam. I'm sorry to be the bearer of bad news."

In a way, Sam had been expecting this. Prostitutes did not last long in the West. "Did this woman say how they died?"

"Cholera."

Cholera. The word stuck in his head, large and

outsized like the black disaster headlines in a newspaper. It was a horrible way to die. He closed his eyes, as if by doing so he could squeeze out the thought of his son dying in agony. But the crushing pain obliterated every other sensation, grinding his emotions into dust. Imagine Joe dying without the comfort his own father could offer him, without knowing how much he was loved. Somewhere in a mining town in Montana, a little boy had suffered and died, and his own father had not even known it.

It took a moment for Sam's voice to gain purchase on vocal cords slippery with pain. "How long ago did it happen?"

He winced at the pity in Barris's eyes. "Almost a year."

He'd been searching all this time, and all along his son was dead. And his wife . . .

Both their deaths had been senseless, unnecessary. Sam would never have forced her to stay with him if she didn't want to. But he could have seen to it that they had money and lived in a decent place!

Rage possessed him. He stood abruptly, almost knocking his chair over. "I've got to go," he said, and headed for the door.

That night, he got drunker than he'd ever been in his life, and when the bars closed, ended up sleeping outside the Calumet Saloon on Brewery Gulch.

His sleep was filled with dreams: a little boy lying in a pine coffin, Marisa as he last saw her in a pink wrapper, her eyes cold and distant. He dreamed he and Billie and Joe were on a picnic, and Joe was saying that he was so glad he hadn't died after all. It was good that they were a family, the boy said. Billie had laughed and kissed Sam, and they had all gone for a swim in the stream nearby.

When the constables of Bisbee rousted Sam at dawn, they paid little attention to his ravings, or the fact that he called out one name in despair. The name he called was "Billie."

Bert Mossman, captain of the Arizona Rangers, sat across the desk from Sam. "You have a bad night?"

"It won't happen again."

"Damn right it won't. We're supposed to represent law and order in this city. If you go on a drunken spree, do it somewhere else. The constables in this town don't appreciate scraping Arizona Rangers off their streets."

"I'm resigning my commission." Sam reached under his vest and unpinned his badge.

Mossman accepted the tin star and leaned back in his chair. It squeaked under his weight. "Now why do you want to do that?"

Sam felt as if someone had taken to bashing his brain with a miner's pick. "It's time to move on."

Mossman's heavy face did not betray his emotions, but his eyes were calculating. "I'll accept your resignation after your last assignment."

"But—"

"I don't have anyone else to spare. It shouldn't take too much time. Just nab a few rustlers, not a day's ride from here. The rancher is one of the most important men in the territory. He has a lot of influence with the legislature and the governor, and we can't afford to turn him down. Besides that, you've already had dealings with him. He requested you specifically."

Feeling as punk as he did, Sam didn't attach any significance to the captain's words. "I can leave now."

"I'd sober up a little more first. I want you to be on your best behavior. Colonel Bahill is a good friend of the governor's."

"Colonel Bahill? Of La Zanja?"

"That's right."

"Get someone else."

Mossman threw the badge onto the table. "These are orders."

"And I'm resigning my commission."

"The month's not up yet. I don't accept your resignation."

Sam thought of Billie and Elliot, and his heart twisted. It had been two weeks since they'd parted company in the Superstitions; no doubt the two of them were married by now.

Well, maybe he should go. He'd have to face it sooner or later, and seeing them together would scotch his feelings for her once and for all. "All right," he said. "I'll go."

"Good. Clean yourself up first. You smell like a brewery."

* * *

Sam arrived at La Zanja on the eve of the biggest wedding in the history of Santa Cruz County.

He wanted to turn around and ride out again, but pride made him stay. Outside the house, in the shade of a cluster of black oaks, chairs had been set up on the lawn. White ribbons fluttered in the breeze, trailing from rosettes that lined the rail of a hastily built bandstand.

He did not see Billie. He was summoned immediately to Colonel Bahill's study. As Olivia led him up the hallway, she told him about tomorrow's wedding, which would take place around dusk. "Half the county will be here. Jim Bark and a lot of those high-toned politicians from Phoenix!"

Sam didn't reply. She left him and he knocked on the door of the study.

"Enter," came the imperious voice.

As Sam walked into the room, Colonel Bahill motioned for him to sit on the jade green horsehair sofa across from his desk.

"I understand you still have a rustler problem." Sam remained standing by the door.

"We caught 'em yesterday," Bahill replied. "They're in the hoosegow in Nogales already."

"Then you don't need me."

"Just a minute. You came all this way. Why don't you stay for the wedding?"

At the mention of the wedding, Sam felt as if a noose had tightened around his neck. He didn't trust himself to talk. Up until this moment, he'd thought he could handle this, but now he wasn't so sure. The despair that clawed at his throat was palpable. He never realized just how much he wanted Billie until now.

"You never gave me a chance to thank you for taking such good care of Billie. You saved her life a couple of times."

"She's a brave girl."

"I was under the impression that you were a brave man."

The censure in Bahill's voice made Sam look up. The room was submersed in gloom except for the light from a small lamp, which was covered by a dark green lampshade, but Sam could see the colonel's features clearly enough. There was a challenge in his eyes.

"Don't you feel the least bit guilty about all this?" the colonel asked.

"Guilty?"

"You trifled with my daughter's affections."

Sam remembered the day at the pool.

"Isn't that true?" Bahill demanded.

There was no excuse. He had indeed trifled with Billie's affections. "Yes. It's true."

Colonel Bahill pounced on the admission. "I knew it!" he thundered, his face alight with menacing glee. "What do you propose to do now? Now that you have compromised my daughter?"

Sam was stunned. So Billie had recounted the incident at the pool. What had she told him?

What did this man want from him? Confused, Sam glanced out the window at the chairs, the ribbons, the tables being set up under the oaks.

"I don't understand," he said slowly. "What do you want me to do?"

"My daughter is good enough to trifle with, but not good enough to marry. Is that it?"

Why was the colonel baiting him? Angry now, Sam didn't bother to control the curtness of his voice. "If you're implying that I would think such a thing, you are fatally wrong."

Bahill slammed his fist on the desk. "I want satisfaction! Do you or do you not care about my daughter?"

Goaded beyond all reason, Sam shouted back, "Of course I care about your damn daughter! I'm sorry I ever laid eyes on her, but now that I have, I think about her every minute of the day. But in case you haven't noticed, she's getting married tomorrow. So you'll receive no satisfaction from me!"

Colonel Bahill was grinning. As Sam watched, the colonel took a cigar from his humidor, put it in his mouth, lit it and blew smoke lazily into the air. "You mean that?"

"Yes. Of course I mean it. What does that have to do with anything?"

"Have you told her?"

"She's marrying Elliot Stevenson."

"Have you told her?" repeated Bahill.

"No."

"Well then, why don't you?"

Again, as if to a child, Sam explained, "Billie is marrying Elliot Stevenson tomorrow. Whatever you may think of him, it's obvious that she loves him, and—"

"It's obvious, is it?"

"What do you mean?"

Bahill stood up and walked to the window. He pulled aside the heavy velvet drapes. Outside, the afternoon sun burnished the dry, brittle grass. Billie stood in the field out beyond the lawn, staring out at the mountains. Even from here, Sam could tell that her expression was bleak. "What's wrong with her?" he asked.

"She's unhappy."

"Why?"

"I think it's because she's marrying the wrong man."

Sam shook his head. He couldn't take it all in.

"She's changed since she's come back. Downright mournful most of the time. Kept putting off the wedding like it was something unpleasant. She doesn't even ride her horse anymore."

"What does that have to do with me?"

"I'm not blind, man. I saw the way she looked at you in the mountains." Suddenly a suspicious glint came to Bahill's eyes. "It's the baby, isn't it? You don't want her because of the baby."

"Of course I want her, baby and all!" Sam blurted out.

"Then why did you leave her to that vulture Stevenson?"

"Because," Sam said succinctly, "she loved him."

"Well, she doesn't love him anymore. And what I want to know is, what are you going to do about it? Turn tail and run back to Bisbee? Or are you going to tell her how you feel?"

It seemed as if a door had opened in Sam. He didn't bother to question how the colonel knew so much, or even think about what he would say to Billie, or where they would live or what they would do. The pain that had crushed him like a weight since he learned of Marisa's and Joey's deaths suddenly seemed bearable. Adrenaline flooded his limbs, and a great rushing feeling seemed to branch out from his heart. He reached for the door.

"What are you going to do?" Bahill shouted.

"I'm going to ask her to marry me."

Billie had been in her room when she noticed the dark horse in the corral. It looked like Panther.

She decided to walk down and take a look. Of course it wouldn't be Panther. It was probably one of the new cowboy's string.

As she crossed the space between the house and barn, she glanced at the area on the lawn where the wedding would be held tomorrow, and her stomach gave a little lurch. Tomorrow she would be Mrs. Elliot Stevenson. She and Elliot would sleep in the same room, in the same bed, and she would have to lie under him night after night, while her heart was filled with love for another man.

It was almost unbearable. Almost. The only comfort she could take from it was in knowing she had done the right thing, no matter how distasteful it appeared to be at the moment.

Olivia directed a couple of the Chinese gardeners as they dug holes for the barbecue pit. Billie had just come from trying on the French-made wedding dress that had belonged to her mother, which had been altered to appear more modern. Elliot had gone into town today for his own fitting. They had so little time to prepare. . . .

Least of all to prepare emotionally. Billie's gaze swung to the Huachuca Mountains, and the dry yellow grass that stood still and lifeless before them. Thunderheads boiled above the mountains like cauliflower tops, their hazy blue underbellies blending with the peaks they rested on. Somewhere east of there lived Sam Gray.

She stood a little straighter. It was better not to think about Sam Gray.

"Billie."

She closed her eyes. *Am I going crazy?* She could swear she heard his voice.

"Billie."

This time she could not ignore it. She spun around.

He stood before her, absolutely real. His strong face, teal blue eyes, the serious line of his mouth. The way his gray shirt hugged the broad shoulders she knew so well, the gleaming, sinewy muscles of his tanned arms. Tall and straight, capable and gentle.

Her mouth was dry. Her heart pounded. "What are you doing here?"

"Your father sent for me."

"My father? But what—"

He stepped closer, his very presence seeming

to cause the air to snap with energy, as if heralding a thunderstorm. "Billie, I have to ask you a question, and I want an honest answer. Do you remember the time at the pool?"

Did she remember? She thought about it day and night! How she wished he had made love to her, even if it was only that one time.

When she didn't reply, he spoke again. "That day, at the pool . . . I thought you felt something for me."

"That was a mistake." Why had he come here? To torture her with what might have been?

"Maybe it was a mistake. But I have to know. Do you love me?"

Her heart ached to give him the answer, but she'd already made her choice. "Please, Sam, don't ask me that."

"Why not?"

The look in his eyes made her want to fall into his arms, but Billie stiffened her spine. She had made a commitment to Elliot. She could not go back on her word now. "I'm sorry. You'd better go."

His left hand clasped hers, his touch sending a shock through her body. He tipped her chin up with the other cupped hand and stared into her eyes. "Look at me."

"It won't do any good to—"

"Look at me," he commanded.

She did. His eyes were level with hers, sparkling with some inner fire. "I love you," he said softly.

For one brief instant, joy burst like a shooting

star through her soul. It rang like bells in her ears, beat wildly in her heart, hummed along the flesh of her arms, made her limbs quake. It flowered behind her eyes like two brilliant blooms, obscuring her vision with tears of happiness, and flooded her whole being with golden light. She couldn't take it all in, couldn't seem to catch her breath.

But despair came quickly on the heels of elation. His revelation gave her momentary pleasure, but it couldn't change anything. Not now. Not after her father had spent all this money. Not when some of his most influential friends were coming from as far away as New York to see this wedding. How could she face anyone again if she pulled such a stunt? How would her father ever live it down? Through eyes blurred by tears she saw the bandstand, the white ribbons, the velvet ropes marking the aisle, and knew it was impossible. Her heart sank.

She had agreed to marry Elliot. A Bahill never went back on a promise. It was one of the things her father had drummed into her from an early age. "Sam, please leave me alone. I—I can't bear this—"

"Do you love me?"

"Please—"

"Do you?"

She felt like a bird shot out of the sky. Defeated, she nodded. "Yes."

"Then marry me."

"I can't!" The burden of that statement crushed her. "I've already made my decision."

343

"You've made your decision. So now you'll spend the rest of your life with a man you don't love because you're too stubborn to change your mind?"

"It's what I have to do."

"Why?"

"Because . . . because it's my duty."

"Your duty? To whom? Elliot?" He waved his arm, encompassing the clearing, the altar. "The wedding guests? Would you really go through with a wedding you don't want just to please people you don't even know?"

"My father—"

"Your father doesn't want you to marry Elliot."

"He may say that, but he doesn't really mean it. If I don't go through with this he won't be able to hold his head up in this community."

Sam's arms dropped to his sides and he strode in a brisk circle, staring at the sky. "I don't believe you! Has your father ever been the least bit subtle with his desires? Has he ever once beaten around the bush? No! He says what he feels. If he says he doesn't approve of your marriage to Elliot—no matter how much money he's spent— he means it!"

"This is really none of your business."

"Not my business? I love you, Billie. And you just admitted that you love me."

What could she do to convince him that her path was chosen? "What about your wife?"

Sam's jaw tightened, and she saw acute pain in his eyes. "She's dead."

"Dead," Billie repeated, stunned.

"The boy, too. They died of cholera."

"I'm so sorry."

He put his hands on her shoulders. His eyes had darkened to jade, hard and glittering in the harsh sunlight. "Billie, don't do this," he said, his tone urgent. "Postpone the wedding—at least give yourself some time to think."

His will was so strong that she almost melted into his arms, almost agreed. The force of his personality was like a magnetic field, pulling her toward him.

"Marry me. I want you. And the baby."

How she wanted to say yes! But wouldn't even a good man like Sam resent another man's child? Sooner or later wouldn't that resentment show? No, she had mapped out what to do. All she had to do was stick with the plan and do it.

"I love you, Billie."

"Billie," called Olivia. "Where do you want the *luminarias*?"

With an effort, Billie pulled her mind away from Sam. She glanced over to where Olivia stood. Beside Olivia, one of the hands was spacing the *luminarias*, bags of sand, along the drive to the house. Tomorrow night a candle would be set in each one and they would each throw off an orange glow.

Steeling herself, Billie let her gaze return to the ranger. The spell was broken. The die had been cast. There was absolutely no turning back now.

He reached for her hand. "Billie—"

345

"I—I can't." She jerked away from him, gathered her skirts and strode purposely toward Olivia.

He watched her go, but didn't follow.

Chapter Twenty-two

"Hold still," Olivia said through a mouthful of pins. "This material is so old it will tear if you pull."

Billie stood patiently. What else did she have to do? She *wanted* time to go by slowly. But already the shadows were stretching across the lawn. The musicians were tuning up.

"There! I can't believe this hem came down again. Remedios did a poor job."

"Thanks, Olivia." Billie glanced at her image in the mirror. She looked stately and tall in the silk dress. Her hair had been put up by Olivia, who had given her a beautiful comb and mantilla. The mantilla was Olivia's mother's, and the lace cascaded in a frothy foam down Billie's back.

Billie's heart thudded in her chest. In another half hour she'd be Mrs. Elliot Stevenson.

Sam decided to stay for the wedding. He didn't know what masochistic streak made him want to see the woman he loved marry someone else, but the urge was too great to deny.

He spent the early part of the day working cattle with Billie's father. It was good, hard exercise that cleared the mind and kept the body fit. As they rode back to the ranch house, Sam reflected that on another day, Billie might have been out there with them. He wondered how long it would be before she wanted out of the constricted lifestyle she had chosen. Apparently she was punishing herself, forcing herself to fit into the mold of a feminine, submissive wife.

Elliot seemed perfectly pleased with Billie the way she was now. He didn't miss the tomboy at all. But Sam did.

"What are you thinking?" Bahill asked.

"That Billie should be riding with us."

"She doesn't care about things like that anymore," Bahill said sadly. "She doesn't care about anything, far as I can see."

Sam nodded in agreement. He'd discovered that the autocratic colonel was pretty easy to get along with. Of course, they knew the same language.

"She refused you, I take it."

Sam's expression was answer enough.

"Of all the foolish women I've ever met in my

life, I raised the prize! Why do you think she's so set on marrying Stevenson?"

"She feels it's her duty."

"Her duty? What nonsense are you talking, man? That's the most ridiculous thing I've heard of in my life! Duty to whom?"

"To Elliot. To you. The wedding guests—"

"The wedding guests be damned! How can she be so pigheaded?"

"Well, sir, it seems to me that it's an inherited condition."

Bahill stared at him for a moment, then laughed heartily. "No backing down for you." His brow furrowed. "Doesn't she know I don't want her to marry Elliot?"

"You're paying for the wedding."

Bahill exploded. "She's my daughter! Of course I'm paying for it."

"She told me that a Bahill doesn't go back on her word."

"Hmm, she's right about that," Bahill admitted. "But she's carrying it too far. She's acting like a martyr, for God's sake! What do you think I should do about it?"

Sam had been pondering this very question all day, but could not come up with an answer. "I don't think there's anything you can do. It's her decision. Only she can make it."

He could only place his trust in the Billie he had gotten to know in the Superstitions. The woman who fought for her own life and the life of her child with such tenacity. *That* woman wouldn't care what people thought. That woman would choose happiness over martyrdom.

He only hoped she hadn't changed too much.

Devoid of all sensation, Billie didn't know how she made it up the aisle. She remembered to keep her head high, her eyes forward. Her father's presence was comforting beside her, and she leaned on his arm.

Elliot waited for her. He was very handsome in his black frock coat and gray and white cravat. His hair caught the sunlight, threads of sapphire against jet black.

"Sam's here," the colonel whispered to her as they walked in measured dignity between the rows of guests.

Billie swallowed. How had she gotten herself into this situation? Why was she marrying one man when she loved another? Sam had asked her to marry him. Could he really offer her marriage if he didn't mean it? And yet she hadn't even listened to what he had to say.

The colonel sighed. "It's your decision. If you want to stop this charade now, I'll back you."

"Elliot needs me."

"He doesn't need you. I think you know that, deep down."

"But all the money you've spent—"

"Hang the money! You're the only daughter I have. I want you to be happy, and you'll never be happy with Elliot. Forget marrying Sam, if that's what's bothering you. Just call it off."

They were almost to the altar. Beaming, Elliot turned to greet her. Her father let her go. She stood beside Elliot; his coat brushed against her arm.

And then she saw Sam. He was leaning against an oak tree off to the side. Billie couldn't see his expression.

Reverend Taylor was speaking now. Elliot grasped her hand in his. His palm was sweaty, his grip proprietary.

Call it off. I'll back you.

"Do you, Elliot, take this woman, Elizabeth, to be your lawfully wedded wife?" Reverend Taylor's voice was a monotone.

"I do."

So sure of himself. Almost smug.

What am I doing? I'm tying myself to a man I have no respect for, a man I don't love, for all eternity.

The preacher droned on. ". . . husband?"

Elliot nudged her.

Startled, Billie blinked her eyes. "I'm sorry?"

"I said, do you, Elizabeth, take this man, Elliot, to be your lawfully wedded husband?"

Her heart hammered in her chest. She opened her mouth. The words would not come. She glanced at Elliot, hoping for encouragement. He looked annoyed.

Billie swallowed again, looked directly into his eyes. Light reflected back at her as if off a hard surface. She couldn't see into those brittle, dark orbs; couldn't see through them to the man. There was nothing there except impatience.

It came home to her, suddenly, that Elliot didn't care at all about her, or his child. He hadn't changed at all; he'd just put on another mask—that of the chastened suitor and proud father. Elliot Stevenson cared only for himself.

"Now don't be nervous," the preacher said. "Would you like a drink of water before we continue?"

Billie shook her head. She looked over at Sam. He had straightened, his whole body at attention.

She looked at the ribbons, the musicians, the guests.

It was her decision. No one else could make it for her.

Billie didn't look back. She gathered her skirts and ran toward Sam, and didn't stop until she was clasped in his arms and he was lifting her in the air, spinning her about so that her white silk dress whirled about her like flower petals in a wind.

Chapter Twenty-three

The paperboy darted through the crowded lobby of the Hotel del Coronado, the gracious seaside resort situated on Coronado Island off San Diego, California. "Extra, extra!" the boy called, holding the paper aloft. "The search for the Lost Dutchman Mine claims another victim!"

A young gentleman in a white sweater and plus fours motioned to the boy, paid him for the paper and walked to the solarium to await his female companion for dinner. His name was James McCrae, and he had once ridden into the Superstition Mountains, just a day in and out from Bark's Ranch, during his visit there a year ago. He read the article with interest. Apparently, riders had come across the body of an artist named Elliot Stevenson, who had gone in search of the Lost Dutchman Mine. Although badly depredated upon by wild animals, Stevenson was positively identified through his possessions. Poor fellow. God only knew what fears he must have faced in his last hours.

McCrae gazed out the window at the boardwalk and the ocean beyond it, remembering the towering saguaros and brooding edifices of the Superstitions. He shivered, glad that he hadn't lingered after dark. Despite the vigor of this new century, there were still many uncivilized places left in the world.

Down on the boardwalk, a young woman walked with her husband. Even from here James could see she was exquisite; her fine carriage, the slender figure that so flattered the leg-o-mutton sleeves and form-fitting skirt, the glimpse of raven hair under her hat. The husband was a lucky man, James thought.

Mr. and Mrs. Sam Gray strolled arm in arm, enjoying the fresh air after dining in the Hotel del Coronado's world-famous Crown Room.

Rose pink and pearl gray clouds were scattered across the sky like the contents of a feather pillow, muting the setting sun. With a warning rumble, the ocean swelled and broke on the crescent of sand before them, its lacy hem surging forward, then receding with a sigh, spent.

Billie breathed in the tangy scent of the ocean, reveling in the presence of the man walking beside her. This was the happiest moment of her life. Even the faint nervousness tugging at her stomach like an unseen wire was due more to exhilaration than worry. She and Sam were on the brink of a happy future life together, and whatever happened tonight, she knew it was part and parcel of the love they shared.

Sam leaned close and whispered into her ear. "Shall we turn in?"

The words caused her to react with a pleasurable shudder. Suddenly she couldn't wait to get back to their room, couldn't wait to know the man she had married . . . know him completely. Last night had been their first as man and wife, but they had been on a crowded train. There had been no privacy then. But there was now.

Their return to the room held a greater urgency than the trip out. Billie was achingly aware of Sam's steady hand under her elbow, guiding her. The way the sleeve of his frock coat brushed against her arm, the goose bumps that fanned out over her skin. She glanced at him, noted the strong, lean line of his jaw, the eyes that were no longer guardedly watchful, but lazily observant. His sun-bronzed features glowed in the dying sun, suffused with contentment and joy. Billie had to lift her skirts to keep up with his quickening pace.

The oak-walled lobby was aglow with the frosty brilliance of myriad chandeliers. Sam and Billie stepped into the elevator cage and rode up to the second floor. Walking down the carpeted hall, Billie could still hear the sibilant hiss of the ocean outside.

At last they gained the room.

Suddenly Billie was more than nervous.

Would she be as unresponsive as she had been with Elliot? Would she disappoint him?

Heart pounding, Billie walked out onto the balcony of their room. Leaning on the railing, she breathed in the scent of petunias and geraniums, freshly mown lawn and the sea breeze. She shivered in the slight coolness riffling off the ocean's surface. The water had turned deep lavender. The last of the sun's rays glinted off the red-roofed, conical water tower that rose like an outsize wedding cake at one end of the white hotel. It was so beautiful here. Perfect.

It was too perfect. She hated to spoil the mood. Perhaps he wouldn't be happy with her. She remembered how it had felt when Elliot had removed her clothes, one by one. The shame of it—Sam loomed up behind her. She inhaled his masculine scent, felt sheltered by his strong body. He placed his hands on her shoulders and she trembled.

He turned her to face him, cupping her chin gently. The caress of his fingers against her skin elicited another frisson. He raised her chin up a fraction with the tips of his fingers, so that their eyes were level. "There's nothing to be afraid of," he said. His love for her was easy to read; it showed in the dark blue-green depths as clearly as if he'd spoken aloud. Then, almost reverently, he lowered his mouth to hers. His lips brushed against her own, and like the sea breeze, he was gentle. His kiss lingered, bringing her desire to wakefulness. He increased the pressure.

The pleasure that shot through her made her stagger. His mouth ignited in her an answering flame, burning hot. Sparks of desire tingled through her veins like falling stars. Suddenly all her fears fell away. She clasped her arms around his neck and clung to him, as if letting go one moment would destroy them both. He kissed her harder, sending explosions of sweet agony through her. Her lips parted and she felt his tongue probe her own, and as the world revolved around them she forgot everything but the straining for closeness that sealed the pact between them.

Sensations bombarded her: The firm, sure touch of his hands as they slid warmly over her skin. The scent of flowers. The fresh breath of the ocean. And his lips, his mouth, his tongue. She felt the languor spread through her body, and at the same time realized that a certain agonizing sweetness pervaded one part of her, sharpening to one exquisite point. At the same time, her body felt heavy, warm, aching. It was an ache that needed attention, and some part of her leaped toward completion, release, although she had never felt it before. So this was what she had missed!

His lips left hers, and she felt bereft. But an instant later his mouth brushed her neck, down to the hollow of her collarbone, and the pleasure that burrowed there nearly drove her wild. Even through the white lawn of her walking dress, the sensations were beyond bearing.

"Please." She gasped.

He understood. His sure fingers worked at the buttons of her bodice, even as his mouth claimed the delicate skin behind her ear.

Her own hands explored the hardness of his muscles through his coat, and she marveled at the broadness of his chest under her flattened palm. His heart beat strong and quickly beneath her hand, and she swallowed. This man held her own heart in his hands like a fragile bird. How she loved him!

The last button came undone. Her dress whispered against her skin for an instant, then slipped soundlessly to the carpeted floor.

Sam seemed to lose his breath for an instant. "Oh, my love, you are so beautiful." He pulled her to him, pressing her to the length of him. She felt his desire, outsized, overweening. She felt his heart pounding against hers, as if it were a fist at the door of her being.

The room was dusky now, the rose-colored light of the sunset long gone. Billie closed her eyes as Sam kissed her collarbone again, ran his tongue down, down to the lacy edges of her French coutil corset.

"My corset—"

"Let me undo it." His voice was breathless, hurried. She felt the laces give, and then his firm, strong fingers spanned her waist, describing sensual circles on her back beneath the bunched muslin material. Then, with a rustle of cloth, she felt him lift the chemise up over her head. The flesh on her arms prickled with anticipation, and her own fumbling fingers found and released the drawstring of her under-skirt. Both underskirt and drawers fell into the ever-widening pool of silks and fine white lawn.

Sam laughed softly. "You look like the angel on top of the Christmas tree."

The sea breeze wafted over her naked skin. But she didn't feel naked. She felt beautiful, beloved.

Sam pulled her to him again, kissing her harder. His palms cupped her breasts, and he centered his attentions on her hardening nipples. When his mouth closed on them Billie knew what true ecstacy was.

Suddenly it was too much for both of them. Nothing could keep them apart. Sam lifted her up and carried her to the bed. He shucked off his coat and reached for the buttons of his shirt.

"Let me," Billie said. "I want to do my wifely duty."

"Duty," he said, shrugging out of his shirt. "There's been all too much of that, and not enough of this. God, Billie, I can't wait another minute."

And then the barriers between them were gone, and they came together as if this had always been the natural conclusion from the first day they met at La Zanja.

Sweetness pervaded Billie as Sam fit himself against her hip, and poised above her. His lips sought hers as he pushed gently. Billie gasped with the pure joy of it. Desire flowered in her loins, sang like a bird in her soul.

Afterward, as they lay tangled together on the

bed, Billie ran a finger down his chest. "Ranger, your devotion to duty is extraordinary."

Sam chuckled. "Devotion to duty," the Arizona Ranger muttered against his wife's hair, "is a highly overrated virtue."

DESPERADO

SANDRA HILL

Major Helen Prescott has always played by the rules. That's why Rafe Santiago nicknamed her "Prissy" at the military academy years before. Rafe's teasing made her life miserable back then, and with his irresistible good looks, he is the man responsible for her one momentary lapse in self control. When a routine skydive goes awry, the two parachute straight into the 1850 California Gold Rush. Mistaken for a notorious bandit and his infamously sensuous mistress, they find themselves on the wrong side of the law. In a time and place where rules have no meaning, Helen finds Rafe's hard, bronzed body strangely comforting, and his piercing blue eyes leave her all too willing to share his bedroll. Suddenly, his teasing remarks make her feel all woman, and she is ready to throw caution to the wind if she can spend every night in the arms of her very own desperado.

_52182-2 $5.99 US/$6.99 CAN

Beautiful and spirited Kathleen Haley sets sail from England for the family estate in Savannah. On board ship, she meets the man who will forever haunt her heart, the dashing and domineering Captain Reed Taylor. On the long, perilous voyage, she resists his bold advances—until she wakes from unconsciousness after a storm and hears Reed's shocking confession. She then knows she must marry the rogue.

But their fiery conflict is far from over. Through society balls, raging duels and torrid nights, Kathleen seeks vengeance on Reed's brutal passions and his secret alliance with pirates. At last she is forced to attack the very man who has warmed her icy heart and burned his way into her very soul.

Bestselling Author of *Hand & Heart of a Soldier*

With a name that belies his true nature, Joshua Angell was
born for deception. So when sophisticated and proper Ava
Moreland first sees the sexy drifter in a desolate Missouri
jail, she knows he is the one to save her sister from a ruined
reputation and a fatherless child. But she will need Angell to
fool New York society into thinking he is the ideal
husband—and only Ava can teach him how. But what start
as simple lessons in etiquette and speech soon become
smoldering lessons in love. And as the beautiful socialite's
feelings for Angell deepen, so does her passion—and finally
she knows she will never be satisfied until she, and no other,
claims him as her very own...untamed angel.

___4274-6 $4.99 US/$5.99 CAN

Dorchester Publishing Co., Inc.
P.O. Box 6640
Wayne, PA 19087-8640

Please add $1.75 for shipping and handling for the first book and
$.50 for each book thereafter. NY, NYC, and PA residents,
please add appropriate sales tax. No cash, stamps, or C.O.D.s. All
orders shipped within 6 weeks via postal service book rate.
Canadian orders require $2.00 extra postage and must be paid in
U.S. dollars through a U.S. banking facility.

Name_____
Address_____
City_____State_____Zip_____
I have enclosed $_____ in payment for the checked book(s).
Payment <u>must</u> accompany all orders. ☐ Please send a free catalog.

TIMESWEPT TRAVELER

ELAINE FOX

With a thriving business and a stalled personal life, Shelby Manning never figures her life is any worse—or better—than the norm. Then a late-night stroll through a Civil War battlefield park leads her to a most intriguing stranger. Bloody, confused, and dressed in Union blue, he insists he has just come from the Battle of Fredericksburg—more than one hundred years in the past.

Maybe Shelby should dismiss Carter Lindsey as crazy—just another history reenactor taking his game a little too seriously. But there is something compelling in the pull of his eyes, something special in his tender touch. And before she knows it, Shelby finds herself swept into a passion like none she's ever known—and willing to defy time itself to keep Carter at her side.

_52074-5 $4.99 US/$6.99 CAN

THE LION'S BRIDE — CONNIE MASON

Winner of the *Romantic Times* Storyteller Of The Year Award!

Lord Lyon of Normandy has saved William the Conqueror from certain death on the battlefield, yet neither his strength nor his skill can defend him against the defiant beauty the king chooses for his wife.

Ariana of Cragmere has lost her lands and her virtue to the mighty warrior, but the willful beauty swears never to surrender her heart.

Saxon countess and Norman knight, Ariana and Lyon are born enemies. And in a land rent asunder by bloody wars and shifting loyalties, they are doomed to misery unless they can vanquish the hatred that divides them—and unite in glorious love.

_3884-6 $5.99 US/$7.99 CAN

KENTUCKY BRIDE

NORAH HESS

Winner of the *Romantic Times* Lifetime Achievement Award

Fleeing her abusive uncle, young D'lise Alexander trusts no man...until she is rescued by virile trapper Kane Devlin. His rugged strength and tender concern convince D'lise she will find a safe haven in his backwoods homestead. There, amid the simple pleasures of cornhuskings and barn raisings, she discovers that Kane has kindled a blaze of desire that burns even hotter than the flames in his rugged stone hearth. Beneath his soul-stirring kisses she is able to forget her fears, forget everything except her longing to become his sweet Kentucky bride.

_4046-8 $5.99 US/$6.99 CAN

NORAH HESS

Wildfire

Bestselling Author Of *Storm*

"A grand and beautiful love story....Never a dull moment! A masterpiece about the American spirit."
—*Affaire de Coeur*

The Yankees killed her sweetheart, imprisoned her brother, and drove her from her home, but beautiful, golden-haired Serena Bain faces the future boldly as the wagon trains roll out. Ahead lie countless dangers. But all the perils in the world won't change her bitter resentment of the darkly handsome Yankee wagon master, Josh Quade.

Soon, however, her heart betrays her will. Serena cannot resist her own mounting desire for the rough trapper from Michigan. His strong, rippling, buckskin-clad body sets her senses on fire. But pride and fate continue to tear them apart as the wagon trains roll west—until one night, in the soft, secret darkness of a bordello, Serena and Josh unleash their wildest passions and open their souls to the sweetest raptures of love.

__51988-7 $4.99 US/$5.99 CAN

Dorchester Publishing Co., Inc.
P.O. Box 6640
Wayne, PA 19087-8640